SEEDS OF RAGE

STAR TREK®

ERRAND OF FURY
BOOK 1
SEEDS OF RAGE

KEVIN RYAN

BASED UPON *STAR TREK*
CREATED BY
GENE RODDENBERRY

POCKET BOOKS
New York   London   Toronto   Sydney

An *Original* Publication of POCKET BOOKS

POCKET BOOKS, a division of Simon & Schuster, Inc.
1230 Avenue of the Americas, New York, NY 10020

This book is a work of fiction. Names, characters, places and incidents are products of the author's imagination or are used fictitiously. Any resemblance to actual events or locales or persons, living or dead, is entirely coincidental.

This book is published by Pocket Books, a division of Simon & Schuster, Inc., under exclusive license from Paramount Pictures.

ISBN: 978-1-4516-1345-2

First Pocket Books paperback edition April 2005

10 9 8 7 6 5 4 3 2 1

POCKET and colophon are registered trademarks of Simon & Schuster, Inc.

Cover design by Patrick Kang, cover illustration by Ben Perini

Manufactured in the United States of America

For information regarding special discounts for bulk purchases, please contact Simon & Schuster Special Sales at 1-800-456-6798 or business@simonandschuster.com

For my father, Michael Ryan

Acknowledgments

At Pocket Books, thanks to Associate Publisher Scott Shannon and editor Keith DeCandido for helping me to continue this adventure. And thanks to Elisa Kassin for her assistance, patience, and good humor.

At home, thanks to my daughter and first editor, Natasha, for her careful reading and thoughtful comments and to my wife, Paullina, for her support.

SEEDS OF RAGE

Prologue

**EARTH
2267**

ON THE WALK BACK to his apartment, Michael Fuller couldn't shake the feeling that something was wrong. Something bad had happened—he could feel it, and he trusted his instincts. They had been honed over decades on countless worlds, where he had seen the deaths of many friends, many crewmates, and even more enemies.

Too many friends. But not countless ones, because each loss was burned into his mind—and probably deeper than that. But Fuller was not a spiritual man and did not think much about deeper matters.

His first thought was of his son, who was on active duty aboard the *U.S.S. Enterprise.* Then he thought of his many friends still in Starfleet, at virtually all levels of the service. Any one of them might be in danger, or lost already. Whatever had happened, Fuller felt certain that he would find out soon. He knew from long experience that bad news never tarried long behind the feeling that announced it.

He quickened his pace.

There are two kinds of people: those who run away from trouble and those who run toward it—but there is only one kind of person in Starfleet Security. Fuller had originally heard that from his first security section chief, but he was certain that the axiom was as old as the service—probably even older.

Fuller was in his apartment minutes later. As soon as he entered the door, the feeling grew. He was practically running when he reached his desk and looked at the comm terminal there. A red light blinked on and off.

Suddenly, his throat was tight and he found it hard to breathe. As a feeling of certainty took hold of his mind, bile began to rise from his stomach to his throat. He had fought hundreds of battles on hundreds of different worlds, but he had never in his life felt such a strong urge to flee. He wanted to turn away, head for the door, and run. If he were on active duty, the feeling would have unnerved him, but it had been years since he had served. When he was still on active duty, he had feared failure far more than his own death.

Yet now he felt no shame at the growing desire to flee, only a dawning sureness.

Through force of will, he held his stance in front of the computer terminal, then he moved forward, making himself sit at the desk. Finally he performed the single most difficult act of his life: he flipped a switch on the console in front of him.

The screen immediately came to life, confirming that his instincts had indeed been correct. Fuller felt his ears burn and his stomach shrink to a solid dense ball. He found that he was trembling. He knew most of the message that followed by heart. He had seen too many similar ones, and he had recorded too many of them himself. Fuller also knew the man on the screen and recognized the steely, pained expression on his face.

"This is Captain James T. Kirk of the Starship Enterprise. *It has been my honor to serve with your son Samuel Fuller. Now, I am afraid that I have terrible news. I am sorry to tell you that your son was lost today on a mission on board the* Enterprise."

Fuller had been waiting for it, expecting it. He felt the force of Kirk's words like a full-power phaser blast that tore through him but didn't have the decency to kill him. His hands went to his stomach, as if he could somehow hold himself together. As if he could somehow hold his son to him. . . .

"I regret that I cannot return Sam's body for you to bury, and I'm afraid that I cannot give you any details about his death and his final sacrifice. The mission on which Sam gave his life is highly classified. I can tell you that he gave his life defending his shipmates, the Enterprise, *his Starfleet oath, and the United Federation of Planets, which we all serve. He saved many lives before he fell and did a great deal to ensure the survival of both Starfleet and the Federation. I hope that one day I will be able to make a full disclosure to you about Sam's courageous last moments. For now, all I can do is offer my condolences and return Sam's many commendations, citations, and medals to you."*

Then, for a moment, the veneer of steely calm on the captain's face rippled, threatening to falter. That moment nearly cost Fuller his own thin veil of control.

"I'm sorry, Michael. I owe you my own life and more debts than I can ever repay. I'm sorry that I could not return Sam to you." The captain held his gaze on Fuller's own. Though it was a recorded message, Fuller still felt the connection as Kirk's eyes met his.

Then the moment passed and Kirk said, *"It was an honor to serve with Sam. Kirk out."* The screen went blank.

Fuller felt as though he were standing on a precipice. In the past whenever he had been struck a blow, his instinct was to act, to take a step forward, to *do* something. Yet there was nothing he could do for his son now.

A flood of images filled Fuller's head. Sam as a baby. A toddler. A boy. And then a man. Some of the images were living memories. Too many of them were recorded images he had received while on duty. *While I was away.*

More failures to taunt him.

Fuller felt himself tottering on the edge. On one side was the duty and the action that had sustained him through losses in the past. On the other side was an abyss of grief, for Sam and for all of the others. Fuller had served long, and perhaps he deserved some release. He knew that it might be as simple as putting his head down and taking it in his hands. He would let it all come. Hell, it would come whether he let it or not.

It was a near thing, but Fuller held himself together. Held his ground.

A part of his brain that he didn't even know was working supplied: *Kirk was tired. That wasn't the only condolence message that he had to record.* Fuller had the feeling that it was the first message of the day, but from the look on Kirk's face it wasn't the last—not by a long shot. And there weren't many missions—classified or not—that could take such a large toll on a starship and its crew.

Before he even realized that he was doing it, Fuller found himself hitting buttons on the console, trying to trace the message's point of origin. The transmission was encrypted and theoretically untraceable, but that didn't bother Fuller. He was now absolutely certain that the message would have been Kirk's first of the day—their history together and Kirk's own nature guaranteed that. And the captain would have sent the message immediately after recording it. Well, Fuller's computer told him the time the message had been sent and when it arrived. It was simple math to determine the approximate distance it traveled, even allowing for the normal amount of rerouting and retransmitting necessary for long-distance subspace transmissions.

The message came from approximately forty-eight light-years away. It could have come from any direction, but Fuller knew exactly where it had come from: the Klingon-Federation border, not far from System 1324, where he knew his son had served during the incident there with the Orions. Suddenly, Fuller knew with grim certainty exactly what kind of mission had taken his son's life, and who had killed him.

Then, without even realizing it, Michael Fuller did the same thing he had always done on a mission when he lost someone close to him. He took his grief and pain and put it away into a strong box inside him so he could

5

do what he had to do. He had put many friends in that box. This time, he used gentler hands than he had in the past, but still, he sealed his son away. Fuller knew that the process would not be perfect and that Sam would not go as quietly as the others, but Fuller would be able to operate, to do what he had to.

And Fuller knew exactly what that was. He also knew with absolute certainty that this was one task, one mission that he would not fail to accomplish.

His first task was to tell Sam's mother, Alison. Because it would be so difficult, he decided he would do it as soon as possible. It would mean finding Alison and speaking to her for the first time in years.

Then he would make a series of calls. After that, he would almost certainly have to see a few people. There would be some convincing required. What Fuller intended would not be easy. In fact, it would be extremely difficult, almost impossible. Yet Fuller did not doubt for a moment that he would succeed. He had to.

His son deserved no less.

Chapter One

"NO RESPONSE from the ambassador," Fronde said, looking up from the viewscreen.

Ambassador Fox sighed, not bothering to hide his disappointment. He checked his chronometer. There was no mistake.

They were now almost two hours past due for their meeting. Getting the Klingon ambassador to meet with him directly had felt like a great victory after the runaround they had received from the Klingon High Council.

Fox had arranged for the meeting to take place on a station orbiting the Kraetian homeworld, a venue acceptable to both sides because Kraetia was a trading partner of both the Federation and the Klingon Empire but not aligned with either.

The whole time Fox was making the arrangements, he had felt a sense of hope for the first time in weeks, since his talks with the last Klingon ambassador had ended and the Klingon was recalled by his superiors. Fox knew that the key to preventing war between the Federation and the Klingon Empire lay in getting the Klingons talking. As long as talks continued, there was a chance of preventing open fighting.

Sometimes in diplomacy, all that was required was a delay to let passions cool. Of course, this crisis between the Federation and the Klingon Empire had been brewing—at least on the Klingon side—for twenty-five years, since the inconclusive Battle of Donatu V. Nevertheless, the immediate crisis and recent bloodshed were the reasons he was here. His job was to defuse the current situation. If he did that, time might take care of the rest.

"Perhaps the Klingons have a more elastic notion of timeliness than we have previously believed," Fronde said.

Fox wished that were true. He had endured some frustrating negotiations where he had dealt with races whose concept of time meant that a meeting scheduled months in advance might take place hours, days, or even weeks after Fox arrived. However, he felt certain that this was not the case with the Klingons. Martial cultures like theirs depended on precise coordination of military activities. That sensibility spilled over into every aspect of their culture, including diplomacy. On this point, both Starfleet's and the diplomatic corps's analysis were in agreement.

Reading Fox's expression, Fronde said, "Maybe it's just a quirk of the new ambassador."

"No, they're making us wait for a reason," Fox said.

Fronde nodded, immediately accepting the judgment even though Fox had offered no facts to back it up. "What are you going to do?" Fronde asked. His eyes looked at Fox with great respect and something else. Expectation. Fronde fully expected Fox to have a strategy for this contingency, a plan of some kind to get the Klingons talking. Fox wished he had the young man's confidence.

Fox had found Fronde when he was giving a lecture at Fronde's school about his settlement of a Tellarite-Andorian conflict. Fronde had asked insightful questions, and Fox had been impressed by his command of the subtleties of the situation. Now four years out of university, Fronde had shown remarkable promise and Fox felt lucky to have him as his chief of staff.

In the past, Fox had broken impasses in negotiations by working within the framework of the culture or cultures involved. Sometimes that meant wearing traditional dress—or no clothing at all. Other times he'd had to participate in obscure rituals, including one that involved becoming a sort of godfather to a young prince—a relationship he had maintained for more than a decade now.

Each time Fox had found a way to accomplish his objective, but he had never faced stakes this high before. And Fox had rarely seen such a lack of goodwill on the other side before. Yet there it was: Fronde's absolute confidence in him showing in the younger man's eyes.

To his surprise, Fox found that some of that confidence seemed to seep into his own consciousness. There were billions of lives at stake, and many worlds were depending on his team, but for the moment, Fox realized that he was moved by the simple belief of a promising young aide.

He made up his mind in an instant and said, "Hail the ambassador's office."

Fronde worked the console as Fox stood in front of the viewscreen, preparing himself for what he had to do. The course had been suggested by a Starfleet report, but Fox had resisted using it until now, partly because it went against all of his training and experience, and partly because he didn't think it would work.

Now it seemed to be all he had, and Fox's instincts told him that it might just work. In any case, at this point it could hardly hurt. After a few seconds, a Klingon face appeared on the viewscreen. It was Kreg, a diplomatic aide that Fox recognized from his previous talks with the Klingons.

"What do you want?" the Klingon asked gruffly.

Fox took the customary Klingon greeting in stride, but put an edge in his voice when he said, "I demand to speak with the ambassador immediately." Kreg looked at Fox for a moment and than laughed unpleasantly. "Are you afraid to relay my demand, or simply too stupid to perform such a simple task?" Fox added.

Fox could hear Fronde draw a sharp breath in surprise, as the Klingon looked at him in disbelief.

"I asked if you were afraid or stupid?" Fox said. Before the Klingon could reply, Fox used his ace in the hole and added, "I *challenge* you to find the ambassador and tell him of my demands."

A vein on the Klingon's neck was bulging, and for a moment he looked as though he might explode. *"You are taking a great risk, human."*

Fox ignored the comment and said, "Are you refusing my challenge?"

The Klingon hit a button in front of him, and the screen changed to the trefoil symbol of the Klingon Empire.

"Ambassador, that was . . . unusual," Fronde said, no doubt putting to words what the other three staff members in the room were thinking.

"Let's see if it worked," Fox said.

A few seconds later, the image on the viewscreen changed again and the Klingon ambassador appeared.

"My aide tells me that you insulted us," Ambassador Wolt said.

"No, I insulted *him*," Fox said forcefully. "For you, I have a challenge."

"A challenge?"

"I challenge you to live up to our previous agreement and meet with me face-to-face so that we may settle the differences between our people," Fox said.

Ambassador Wolt was silent for a moment, then said, *"Wait. I will contact you soon with my response."*

"No!" Fox said. "You will meet my challenge now if you have the courage."

There was an edge to the ambassador's voice when he replied, *"I accept your challenge and will meet with you in our arranged place immediately."* Then the screen went blank.

There was silence in the room. Fox turned to his staff and said, "It appears that the ambassador has accepted our invitation to begin talks."

Nervous laughter filled the room. *Well, they needed it,* Fox realized. The pressure on the diplomatic team was enormous. And soon enough they would be in the thick of tense negotiations with the Klingons.

"Before we go, I have something for each of you," Fox said. He opened the cargo container that had been left on his high-speed shuttle prior to their departure, a gift from a Starfleet xeno-studies analyst named West. At first, Fox thought the gift another example of Starfleet arrogance, a message from the analyst saying that Fox didn't know how to do his job.

Fox never dreamed that he'd actually be using the contents of the container, but he'd already done a number of things he'd never thought he would do on this mission, and he thought he might do even more before his job was finished.

"Mister Fronde, you first," Fox said, holding two items in his hands.

"Ambassador, do you intend to go into negotiations armed with swords and phasers?" Fronde said, disbelief on his face.

"As a matter of fact I do," Fox said. "The Klingons respect strength. Think of it as wearing another culture's traditional dress." The swords were antiques, more ceremonial than useful. They were United States Civil War–era sabers, and Fox couldn't be sure if the Starfleet analyst had intended them to convey a message to him. The other items weren't actually phasers, they were laser pistols, of the kind used by Starfleet twenty-five years ago when the service had fought the Klingons to a draw at the Battle of Donatu V.

Fox didn't have to wonder if there was a message attached to those energy weapons: it was clear, and it was intended for both Fox and the Klingons. *We're anything but weak and at least a match for the Klingon Empire.* Normally, Fox would worry about provoking the other side of a negotiation, but he'd already had to provoke the Klingons just to get them to talk. When he had first examined the laser pistols, he had been surprised and more than a little offended that they were functional and fully charged.

Now he found that fact comforting.

However, he could see that Fronde and the rest of the staff weren't pleased. Fox understood. There was an old saying: "A man who carries only a hammer sees every problem as a nail." Well, Fox liked to think he carried a universal translator instead of a hammer—or a weapon. But he realized that he just might have to carry a few other tools in his kit to make enough of an impression on the Klingons to use that translator.

He strapped on his own weapons. As he turned for the door, Fronde said, "Ambassador, good luck in there."

Fox nodded. "Good luck to all of us. I suspect we'll need it."

Fronde and the three other faces looked at Fox with frank admiration. Once again, he found that their confidence in him lifted his own spirits. He only hoped that the day would find him worthy of their respect.

He led his small group to the conference room provided by the Kraetians. At twenty meters across, it was the largest open space on the station. The utilitarian room had no windows, and cargo containers took up space along the walls. In the center of the room was a square table. Fox would have preferred a round one, but square was almost as good.

Barely a few seconds after they arrived, Fox heard

the doors open behind them. He turned to see Ambassador Wolt enter with four aides. Klingon diplomatic parties operated in groups of five because of some obscure custom related to small fighting groups in their distant past. For these talks, Fox had chosen four aides so the groups would be equal in number.

Klingon diplomats, unsurprisingly, wore weapons. Each Klingon had a large daggerlike blade at his side, as well as a pistol that Fox recognized as a disruptor. Two of the aides wore larger blades strung across their backs. These curved weapons, more than a meter in length, were *bat'leth*s, and Fox knew that they had special significance in Klingon culture. Fox recognized one of the aides carrying a *bat'leth* as Kreg, the Klingon he had insulted over the viewscreen only a few minutes ago. Kreg glowered at him, and Fox saw that he had not forgotten the insult.

The Klingons looked them over, and Fox saw the ambassador's eyes deliberately move to see the weapons Fox was wearing. They lingered on the laser pistol, and suddenly Fox was certain that Wolt understood its significance.

Restraining an urge to smile and extend his hand, Fox simply nodded to Ambassador Wolt, who grunted and motioned for his party to sit. Fox did the same, and both teams faced each other from opposite sides of the table. Looking at Wolt, Fox said, "Ambassador, I am pleased that you have accepted my challenge. I hope we can come to an honorable and mutually beneficial resolution to our differences." From the reports he had read, and his own studies, Fox knew that honor was an important concept to many Klingons.

Wolt gave him an unpleasant smile. "There is a simple way to settle our differences. You and your Federation could simply surrender now."

Fox gave the Klingon a grim smile of his own. "Impossible."

"We could always conquer you," Wolt said.

"Unlikely. The fact is that the Klingon Empire has never beaten a Federation force," Fox said, making a thinly veiled reference to Donatu V. He waited for a moment for that to sink in and saw the ambassador grow both uncomfortable and angry. Fox decided to press a little harder. "And of course, there was the recent incident on Starbase 42. Not what I would call a victory for the Klingon people, Ambassador."

"Those Klingons acted on their own. That attack was not sanctioned by the empire," Wolt said, his face darkening.

"Then we can agree that their failure does not reflect on the High Council," Fox said. "But they failed in their mission nonetheless and were repelled by Starfleet."

The ambassador looked ready to burst, and Fox knew he had to tread carefully. He needed to establish that the Federation was strong and was perfectly able to defend itself. However, if he pushed too hard, the talks might end here and now. Softening his tone, he said, "Of course, no one wants an all-out conflict."

The Klingon gave a short laugh. "Speak for yourself, Earther. We Klingons live for 'all-out conflict.'" Then he gave Fox a smile and said, "That is the primary difference between us. You have studied Klingons and believe that you know how we think. You taunt me with a challenge, with references to the past, but you live in fear of war. We do not."

Fox could feel the situation slipping away from him. He knew he had to do something quickly. "True, we do not embrace battle as you Klingons do, but we do not run from a fight. In fact, we tend to win our battles." Then, before the ambassador could reply, Fox pressed on. "And for now, I think both of our peoples have good reason to settle our differences without bloodshed. A victory for either side would be costly for all. Isn't it better to achieve our objectives, here, in this room? That is the challenge I put to all of us."

The Klingon actually thought about that for a moment before answering. "We have legitimate grievances against the Federation."

"And we have some of our own against the Klingon Empire. Perhaps we can put them to rest and begin to forge a new relationship today. 'Better a strong ally than a strong enemy.'" The last was a quote from Kahless the Unforgettable, an important figure in some segments of Klingon society. From the look on Wolt's face, Fox thought that he had struck a nerve.

The Klingon looked at him for a moment and said, "We must confer."

Fox nodded, and the Klingons got up and headed to the other side of the room. They immediately began an animated conversation.

"You do have his attention, sir," Fronde said.

"It is a promising start, but this is only the first step," Fox said. Fronde and the others nodded.

After less than a minute the Klingon party approached. Now both teams stood facing each other. Wolt gave Fox another unpleasant smile and said, "We may be able to talk, but first there is an important issue that must be settled immediately."

"What is that?" Fox said, suddenly wary.

"You have insulted my aide. Honor demands that the insult be answered," Wolt said.

"Answered?" Fox said.

"He challenges one of your aides to single combat," Wolt said.

"What?" Fox said, unable to hide his surprise.

"You have obviously studied Klingons. You know something about Klingon honor. Well, honor demands that such an insult be answered," the Klingon said.

"That is ridiculous," Fox said, aghast.

"You think us ridiculous? You would care to insult us again?" Wolt said. Fox saw that there was something going on here. He had thought he was subtly influencing the Klingons, using what he knew about them to get them to talk. Now he realized that Wolt was far from a fool and was playing a game of his own—a game that Fox did not yet understand.

Fox put an edge into his voice and said, "You know very well that I meant no insult. Just as you know that single combat is not how *we* settle differences." There it was. He had spent a career trying to understand other cultures, tying himself into knots to accommodate other world's customs. Well, it was time that the other side paid heed to Federation customs.

"Do you reject the challenge?" Wolt asked.

"Absolutely," Fox said.

"You come to me referring to past battles, proclaiming the Federation's willingness to fight, declaring yourselves equal to Klingons in might. Yet you will not answer a simple challenge?"

"We fight when we must, not over insults," Fox said.

"Then this meeting is over," the Klingon said, turning on his heel and heading for the door as his aides followed him. For a moment, Fox was too stunned to say anything. Hundreds of billions of lives were at stake. It couldn't end like this, falling apart over bruised feelings. Wracking his brain, Fox tried to think of something, anything to say to get the meeting back on track.

Before he could say a word, Fronde spoke. "I accept."

"What?" Fox said as the Klingons turned around.

"Kreg, I accept your challenge," Fronde said.

"You can't," Fox said.

"He already has," Wolt said, smiling.

"I won't allow it," Fox said.

"I speak for myself," Fronde said.

Fox realized that Fronde was right. The diplomatic corps was not Starfleet. Fox might have been Fronde's superior, but an order from him did not carry the weight it would in the service. The most Fox could do was reprimand or dismiss him.

And it may be the only way, a voice in the back of his mind said. He knew it was true. The Federation and the Klingon Empire were teetering on the brink. War was weeks away at most. If these talks failed, there would be no other talks.

Still, Fox turned to his aide and said, "Randall, you don't have to do this."

Fronde just smiled. Both men knew that there were no other real options. Nevertheless, Fox found himself desperately trying to come up with another solution.

"What are the rules?" Fronde asked the Klingon ambassador.

"Rules? You fight, with blades, until one of you dies," Wolt answered.

"No," Fox said.

"It is our way," the Klingon said.

"Well, it is *not* our way. These negotiations must be a two-way street," Fox said. The Klingon may not have known the idiom, but he understood it well enough. Fox didn't wait for his reply, "The fight ends when one party surrenders."

Ambassador Wolt grunted but nodded his head. Then the Klingon looked over Fronde's slim form and smiled again. "You may use your human blade, or we can provide you with a more honorable Klingon weapon," he added, pointing to one of the heavy *bat'leth* blades.

Fronde's hand went to the saber at his side and said, "Our weapons carry their own history and their own honor." Fronde's voice was surprisingly firm, but Fox could see his hand shaking slightly as it rested on the hilt of his sword. The four-hundred-year-old saber might have had an honorable history, but it looked flimsy compared to the heavy Klingon weapons.

Leaning down, Fox whispered, "Consider the Klingon weapon."

Fronde shook his head. "Too heavy. And the Klingons have trained on those weapons. I can move more quickly with this." Fox shot Fronde a look, and Fronde gave him a thin smile. "I didn't accept lightly. I was fencing team captain two years in a row at university."

Fox felt a pang of relief. Perhaps there was a chance.

Fronde might get injured, but Fox would stop the fight before it got out of hand.

"Now," Wolt said. Fronde nodded, and both groups made their way to the open space between the conference table and the cargo containers on one wall. Fox had built his career on his ability to keep his cool in tense situations, but he found himself sweating freely. It had all happened too fast.

Negotiations moved slowly. It was the nature of the process, which was often a delicate dance. Just setting up this meeting took weeks of work in the aftermath of the incident at Starbase 42. Now, the future of the negotiations might be decided in minutes.

Fronde looked cool himself, but Fox could see the sweat on his brow. His other three aides were looking at him, nearly in shock. Violence was the thing they worked their entire professional careers to avoid. They had studied for years to learn how to prevent it, and now they were watching it become part of the diplomatic process.

For a moment, Fox wondered if diplomacy as they all understood it was even possible with the Klingons. Perhaps the Starfleet reports were correct. Perhaps the Klingons were culturally unsuited to settling differences through discussion.

Fox pushed the thought aside. He had seen diplomacy work too many times, with too many different races. This *had* to work. Too many beings were depending on them.

Kreg hefted the blade off his back and gave it a swing. It was obviously very heavy and very deadly.

Fronde replied with a smile of his own, unsheathed

his sword, and slashed it up and down in a series of quick movements that looked impressive to Fox . . . and apparently to the Klingon, as well, who appeared genuinely surprised. For a moment, Fox once again entertained the hope that perhaps this might turn out all right. Perhaps this would end up as nothing more than a ceremonial conflict. All Fronde had to do was fight well enough to earn the Klingon's respect.

"Begin," Wolt said.

The Klingon swung his weapon a few times, watching Fronde's reaction carefully. Fronde kept his sword in front of him, but he did not move. Then, without warning, the Klingon charged full bore at the man, shouting a battle cry as he moved.

Fox started in surprise and was pleased to see that Fronde had reacted quickly, leaping to one side as the Klingon tore past him. Kreg made a sideways pass with his weapon, but it didn't even come close. Somehow, Fronde managed to swing his saber down and hit the Klingon on the back with a flat end, in more of a smack than a blow. Hope rose up in Fox and he entertained a new idea: How would he approach the talks if Fronde actually won this contest?

There was little time to consider that possibility because the Klingon had turned and was now facing Fronde again, wearing a scowl on his face. "You will die today, Earther."

"Not if that's the best you can do," Fronde said, his voice even. Fox was proud of his aide. He was facing this situation with considerable courage and had obviously learned a thing or two himself from the Starfleet xeno-studies report on Klingons.

21

The Klingon began circling, and Fronde matched his movements, a look of total concentration on his face. Kreg made a series of slow sweeps with his *bat'leth*, movements that even Fox recognized as designed to test Fronde's reflexes. Fronde parried, and there was a clang when the two weapons met. Each time it happened, Fox jumped, thinking it might be the start of the Klingon's next attack.

Finally, the Klingon swung his blade sharply, coming closer than he had done previously. This time, Fronde reacted with astonishing speed. He leaned out of the way, and instead of parrying with his saber, he waited until the *bat'leth* passed him and brought his sword down in a counterattack. Watching in wonder, Fox saw Fronde's blade make contact with the Klingon's right forearm.

The only one more surprised than Fox was Fronde himself, who stopped moving and looked on in wonder as a dark stain appeared on the sleeve of the Klingon's clothing. That hesitation, however, nearly cost Fronde his life because the Klingon didn't show any surprise. He showed rage.

Kreg was a blur of movement as he charged Fronde, swinging his *bat'leth* back and forth. Fronde parried as he backpedaled, and Fox saw that Fronde was quickly running out of space behind him.

Fox nearly cried out a warning, but a quick shift of Fronde's head told him that he saw the danger. When he was nearly touching the cargo containers, he parried one last time and leaped to one side, jumping just outside the arc of the Klingon blade. The momentum of the weapon pulled Kreg to one side, even as his head followed Fronde's movements.

For a moment, Fox saw that with the blade in front of him, the Klingon was vulnerable on the side closest to Fronde. Apparently, Fronde saw it too and lifted his saber. However, before he could strike a blow, the Klingon lifted one foot and brought it down sharply on Fronde's ankle.

Crying out, Fronde pulled back and the Klingon was able to get his blade in front of him again. Immediately, Fox could see that his aide had been injured and could barely step on his left ankle. Before, Fox had been hopeful when he saw that Fronde had perhaps more skill with his weapon than the Klingon had with his own. But this wasn't just a battle of skill. The Klingon had brute strength on his side as well as a natural aggressiveness—and now, an injury to his opponent.

Kreg charged again, this time coming in on Fronde's left side. Fronde tried to move out of the way, but his injury slowed his movement, and Fox could see that he would not be able to dodge the arcing blade this time. Apparently, Fronde saw the same thing because at the last moment, he ceased moving and lifted his saber to meet the *bat'leth* straight on.

There was a loud clang, and Fox watched as the *bat'leth* struck the sword directly and broke it in two. Fronde had slowed the Klingon weapon but had not stopped it, and Fox watched in horror as one point of the weapon dug into Fronde's right shoulder. His aide's hand immediately let go of the broken saber and he stumbled back, somehow managing to stay on his feet.

As Fronde brought his hand up to his shoulder, Fox saw that the wound was deep and would need immediate medical attention. "Stop," Fox shouted as he stepped forward. Kreg stopped, and so did all other movement in the room. "We concede," he said.

"Earther," Ambassador Wolt said to Fronde. "Do you *surrender?*"

Fronde tried to catch his breath as blood seeped out from beneath the hand that was holding his wounded shoulder. Before Fronde could speak, there was a blur of movement as Kreg lunged at him, pushing forward with his *bat'leth,* the point of which made direct contact with the center of Fronde's chest and buried itself inside.

Even as he watched it happen, Fox's mind rejected what he was seeing as impossible. The Klingon kept moving forward, driving the blade even deeper. Then Kreg stopped his advance and *lifted* Fronde in the air with the *bat'leth.*

As Fox shouted, "No!" and lunged for the Klingon, he saw Kreg give the blade a sharp twist and then pull it from Fronde's chest. Fronde immediately fell to the floor and Fox dove to his side. His aide choked for a moment, his eyes bulging in surprise, and then he was still.

Automatically, Fox felt Fronde's neck for a pulse, even as his eyes saw that the large open wound in his chest meant that his heart would not only be damaged, it would have been torn apart.

"Call for help!" he said.

"The Earther is beyond help," Wolt said. It was true; if this injury had been sustained inside a state-of-the-art emergency medical suite, Fronde might have had a chance—though not a good one. Here, it was hopeless.

Something began to well in Fox's chest. To his surprise, it wasn't grief, it was rage. Without thinking, he got up, took a step toward Kreg and pushed the Klingon back with both hands.

"Why?" he shouted.

"The fight was until one of the combatants was either dead or had surrendered," Wolt said.

"He was injured, and he was about to surrender," Fox said, glaring at Wolt.

"The Earther was too slow then," Kreg said, a grin on his face. Never in his life had Fox wanted to strike another being so much.

Though it took a substantial physical effort, Fox forced down the impulse and said, "Is this Klingon fairness—Klingon honor?" he said to Ambassador Wolt.

"Fairness, like history, is decided by the victor. Today, Kreg is the victor," Wolt replied.

"I have given your aide a gift, an honorable death," Kreg said.

Then Wolt turned and headed for the door. He raised a hand and said, "Kill the rest of them."

As the Klingons reached for their weapons, Fox found himself leaping at the Klingon ambassador. With one hand he reached out and grabbed Wolt by the shoulder, spinning him around. Then Fox shoved the Klingon backward and drew his laser pistol, pointing it directly at the Klingon's head from a distance of two feet.

There was surprise on the Klingon's face.

"Make a move against any of us and he dies," Fox called out.

"You would not dare," Kreg said from behind him.

Fox pointed the pistol a few feet to the right and fired once. The beam slammed into the wall and sent up sparks, more than a few of which hit Wolt in the face. "Call them off," he said.

"Halt," the ambassador said, looking deeply into Fox's eyes. Then Wolt laughed roughly. "I think we may be able to do business, Earther."

"What?" Fox said, shaking his head.

"I think it is time to begin our negotiations," Wolt said. Fox didn't bother trying to hide the confusion on his face. "You Earthers have surprised me today. You have shown that there are things for which you are willing to die—and to kill."

"To kill . . ." Fox repeated, looking at the laser pistol in his hand.

"I saw it in your eyes, your desire to kill me. You have convinced me of your seriousness of purpose," Wolt said.

Slowly, Fox lowered his laser and turned to his people. They were frightened, grieved, and angry—like Fox himself. But there it was again, the belief in him. He saw that look in their eyes. Fronde had had the same look, until Fox had allowed him to be murdered.

Yet that belief reminded him of why they were there. Fronde had died, but perhaps Fox could ensure that he had died for something. "Very well, we can begin tomorrow—"

"No, we begin now or we can all go home," Wolt said. "We Klingons have a saying: 'Negotiations are best begun when the blood of the fallen is still warm.' "

Fox looked at his people, the ones who looked back at him and the one who lay on the floor in his own blood. Then he made the most difficult decision of his career, of his entire life.

"Take your seats," he said. Walking back to the negotiating table, he waited for the others to find their places, then he sat.

"I am authorized to come to terms in all of our outstanding areas of contention . . ." A feeling of unreality washed over Fox as Wolt spoke. Looking down at his bloodied hands, he barely heard the Klingon ambassador's words. ". . . is that acceptable, Earther?"

"Call me Earther one more time and you will die today," Fox found himself saying. He remembered from the Starfleet reports that *Earther* was considered an insult.

Wolt nodded and said, "Very well, Ambassador Fox."

Through sheer force of will, Fox made himself listen, pushing aside his grief and his anger. A good and brave young man had died today. But if Fox did his job, Fronde would be the last to die in this conflict.

"I am willing to discuss trade, but don't waste my time trying to renegotiate borders that have stood for one hundred years," Fox said, putting steel into his voice.

Chapter Two

SECTION CHIEF LESLIE PARRISH waited until the end of her shift to visit sickbay. She had not been herself for days, but she didn't want her people to know that. A security section chief was like a parent to his or her squad. And the people in the section needed that parent to be infallible.

And Parrish knew that was exactly what she needed to be, because if she made mistakes, people died. "See you in the dining room, Lieutenant?" one of her squad asked.

"I'll be along later," Parrish said. Then she did what she had been putting off for days: she headed for sickbay. She felt unsettled as she approached the doors. Unlike many security people, she didn't have a particular

28

aversion to sickbay. For some, she knew, the feeling bordered on superstition.

For her, it was more personal and more specific. The last time she was here, the captain had told her that her squad mate Jon Anderson was dead. Of course, squad mate was both a completely accurate and a grossly inadequate term for what he had been to her, but so were all of the terms that came to mind. She felt a chill as the sickbay doors opened and she stepped inside. For a moment, she felt a desire to turn around and leave, but she stayed her course. If she was actually sick, she could endanger her squad, and that was unacceptable.

The desire passed as Nurse Chapel approached her with a smile. "Lieutenant?"

Parrish was glad to see that sickbay seemed to be empty except for the nurse, though she heard noise coming from the direction of the doctor's office that told her there was at least one other person there.

"I've been a little under the weather," Parrish explained. At that moment, Dr. McCoy appeared and Parrish was relieved. The doctor had treated the injuries she had sustained battling the Klingons on Starbase 42, and she felt most comfortable with him.

"How are you, Lieutenant?" McCoy asked with polite concern and a welcoming smile on his face.

He is good at what he does, Parrish thought. *Very good.* She found herself returning the smile and relaxing by degrees. She also noticed that Nurse Chapel had disappeared as the doctor led her to an examination table.

"My stomach's been bothering me, and my energy has been down. I'm afraid that I may have picked up

29

something," she said as she climbed onto the examination table and lay down. Lying down while the doctor hovered over her made Parrish feel vulnerable, but the doctor quelled that feeling with another smile.

Then he raised his scanner and said, "Well, let's just see how accurate your diagnosis is, Lieutenant." He studied the medical readout on the wall above her head as the hand scanner trilled in his hand. For a moment, his face showed only concentration, then there was a slight twitch of his eyebrow that Parrish immediately read as surprise.

"Doctor?" she asked.

The kindly concern was gone. Suddenly he was unreadable, his face a blank except for a slight squinting of one eye, then another twitch. Something was going on. Something unusual.

"What is it?" she asked.

He took a step back and gestured for her to sit up.

"What's wrong?" she asked, keeping her own voice neutral, even as she felt her heart rate increase.

"Nothing," he said, shaking his head unconvincingly.

"That's not true," she said, keeping her eyes on his.

McCoy held her gaze, hesitated for only a moment, and said, "You're pregnant, Lieutenant." His voice was flat, except for a tone of . . . she wasn't sure what.

"What?" was all she could say.

"You're pregnant, Lieutenant Parrish," he said, his voice maddeningly calm as he delivered the single most surprising piece of news she had ever received.

"That's impossible. I took the standard Starfleet precautions," she said.

"Well, nothing is one hundred percent effective,"

McCoy said. But there was something in his eyes when he said it. He wasn't exactly lying, but there was something he wasn't telling her. When he spoke next he was, for him, surprisingly hesitant. "You were seeing Jon Anderson before he died."

"The baby is his," she said immediately, not even giving thought to the fact that she was under no obligation to reveal that information. She had nothing to hide, certainly not where Jon was concerned. Yet that information registered on the doctor's face. The fact that Jon was the father was very significant to McCoy.

"This is a lot to take in, Lieutenant," the doctor said, again hesitant. "You might want some time to consider . . ."

Parrish didn't even hear the rest of McCoy's sentence. She knew what pregnancy meant for someone in her position. If she had the baby, then her career as a Starfleet security officer on active duty was over. There were no children on starships, and Parrish doubted there ever would be. And serving on a starship had been her life's dream. There were only a few thousand people in the whole Federation who had achieved that honor.

So that was the choice, her career and her life's ambition, or her and Jon's child? "Doctor, I . . ." she began.

"You don't have to decide anything now," McCoy said. As he talked, there was a seriousness in his expression that nagged at Parrish. There was something he was not telling her and it had something to do with the baby or maybe with Jon.

"Leslie," McCoy said, "I'd like to share this with the captain. I'm sure he would like to talk to you."

31

She nodded. "Of course." It might be the only way she would find out what was really going on here.

"Wait here for a moment." Then he called out to the other room. "Nurse, would you see if there is anything that Lieutenant Parrish needs."

McCoy disappeared into his office as Nurse Chapel appeared. Parrish said she didn't need anything, so Chapel just waited with her. Parrish felt blood rise to her face and her heart speed up. Then, a remarkably short time later, the doctor appeared again.

"The captain would like to talk to us both in the briefing room immediately," he said. Parrish nodded and jumped off the table. Then he added as they headed for the door, "He would like Mister Spock to join us, if that's all right with you."

Parrish noted that his tone of kindly concern was back. It cemented the idea that something was going on here. It was near the end of the shift, dinnertime, and yet both the captain and the first officer were dropping everything to talk to her. "Fine. Will we all be able to talk frankly about what this is really all about?" Parrish asked.

"Yes," McCoy said, his face betraying no surprise that she had figured out that much more was at work than the relatively simple matter of an officer becoming pregnant. They walked the rest of the way and rode the turbolift in silence. Less than one minute later they approached the briefing room. The doors opened, and Parrish was not surprised to see Captain Kirk and Mister Spock already seated at the table. The captain's face was unreadable, as was—of course—the Vulcan's.

"Lieutenant, Doctor," Kirk said. "Have a seat."

Parrish sat across from both men as the doctor sat next to her. The captain studied her for a moment. So did Spock. She could see McCoy lean forward, and for a moment she had the feeling that he was trying to protect her.

Though Parrish had seen the captain a number of times in the last few weeks, they had not exchanged more than a few words. He had asked how she was several times, and she had given him about half a dozen reports. The last time they had spoken face-to-face for any length of time had been in sickbay when she was recovering from the Battle of Starbase 42.

At that time, he had come to confirm what she had already guessed. That her section chief, Sam Fuller, and Jon had been among those lost in the fighting on the starbase. Kirk had known about Parrish and Jon's relationship and had offered her Jon's communicator, tricorder, and phaser. She had accepted them, and he had returned later to bring them to sickbay personally. It had been a small gesture, but it was all he had been able to do, since Jon's personal effects and citations would naturally go to his family.

Though Parrish was glad to have Jon's field equipment, she knew even then that she didn't need them to remember Jon. She found herself wondering if somehow she had known that she was literally carrying part of Jon.

"Doctor McCoy has informed me of your situation," Kirk said.

"My pregnancy?" she said immediately. She wanted this out in the open as quickly as possible.

Kirk nodded. Then he looked uncharacteristically un-

33

certain for a moment, as if he did not know quite how to proceed or, more likely, how much to reveal to her.

"Permission to speak freely, sir?" she asked.

"Yes, Lieutenant," he said.

"Captain, I realize there is something going on here other than a commander's concern about a pregnancy. It's also clear to me that this has something to do with Jon, and it is—for some reason that I don't understand—a sensitive security matter. I would like to get it out in the open immediately."

The captain's face betrayed a mild surprise, but she could see that he was pleased as well. He glanced quickly at Spock, who raised an eyebrow, then the captain turned back to her. She could see him coming to a decision in front of her. When he spoke, he did it without hesitation. "Lieutenant, you are correct on all counts. Though the doctor tells me that there is every indication that your child is healthy, your pregnancy is more complicated than usual—significantly more complicated. To tell you what I am about to, I am going to have to grant you level-one security clearance effective immediately. I assume you remember your Starfleet regulations and know what that means?"

Parrish nodded. "Yes, sir."

"Lieutenant Parrish, I am afraid that Lieutenant Jon Anderson, the father of your child, was a Klingon agent who was surgically altered to resemble a human. He was sent on board the *Enterprise* as part of a Klingon plot to install agents at various levels of Starfleet service."

No, her mind screamed, though Parrish willed herself silent. It was impossible. She waited for a moment and collected herself before she spoke.

"Sir, there *must* be some mistake. I've spoken to his family since he died, to his mother . . ." Even as she spoke, Parrish felt a dawning realization within her. What Kirk had just said was impossible, yet it explained some things about Jon.

"Doctor McCoy confirmed that Lieutenant Anderson was a biological Klingon. There is no mistake," Kirk said. "The real Anderson was kidnapped—presumably by Klingon agents—sometime before the Anderson we knew was posted to the *Enterprise*."

"But, sir, I served on Jon's squad, he never . . ." She didn't finish the sentence. How could she explain that she had fought with Jon, and watched him fight like no one she had ever seen. More than one member of this crew, as well as scores of Federation civilians, owed their lives to him. And while there were depths to him that she had never been able to penetrate, she had never had any doubts about his loyalty. She had known him as well as she had known any man. Whatever he was, he had never betrayed his Starfleet oath.

"I know this is hard to take," Kirk said.

She shook her head. "The Jon I knew was no traitor."

"Technically, that is true. He was a Klingon," Spock said.

"These are the facts as we know them, Lieutenant," Kirk said. "However, I can also say without a doubt that our Jon never gave less than his all for his shipmates. He was a decorated member of this crew who honored his oath. I don't know what he was thinking during his time here, but I suspect that he may have had a change of heart."

Change of heart? She wondered. *No, not Jon.* Even if

he had switched sides somehow at the end, it wasn't because he had changed, it was because he hadn't—because he was what he was and remained that to the end. But that was something she couldn't explain to these men, not even to McCoy, whose concern for her she could feel coming from him in waves.

"He saved my life on Starbase 42, and not just mine," was all she said in the end. He had fought Klingons then. *Fellow Klingons,* her mind supplied.

Kirk nodded. "Except for the secret of his biology, he was never less than an exemplary member of this crew."

Those words hung in the air for a moment, and Parrish realized that Kirk understood things about Jon that she could never have explained. Insight that bordered on sorcery, she realized. Well, he *was* a starship captain.

"Take some time to think about what you want to do," Kirk said. "No one believes that you or anyone else who had close contact with Jon knew anything about his identity or his mission for the Klingon Empire. You are a valued member of this crew whatever you decide."

Then McCoy spoke, "This is a lot to take in. It may change things for you."

May change things . . . she thought. It felt like the ship was crumbling around her. *Jon, a Klingon?* It was impossible. Yet, it was also true. And it didn't change *some* things, it changed *everything*.

Except the truth of what she and Jon had had, and the truth of who Jon was, whatever his biology.

"I encourage you to discuss your situation with Doctor McCoy and to take some time to think about what you want to do. However, until this matter is resolved, you are hereby removed from active duty."

"Sir?" Parrish said, unable to hide her surprise.

"You cannot remain on active duty, given the circumstances," Kirk said.

"Captain, I'm pregnant, not injured or ill," Parrish said.

"And as a security officer, you are blazing new ground here. According to records, there are no examples of a pregnancy occurring with a security officer on board a starship," Kirk said.

"I think that the combination of Klingon and human biology may have led to the failure of the normal birth control methods," McCoy added.

Parrish nodded. She knew that there had been very rare cases of pregnancies on starships, but she had no doubt that she was the first starship security officer to have it happen to her. That was partly because of the relatively low concentration of women in her field.

"Captain, I can still make a contribution," she said.

"I have no doubt that's true, and the fact is that your experience in the recent Klingon incidents makes you invaluable," Kirk said.

"Then I don't see why I can't remain on active duty for at least another few—" Parrish began.

"Absolutely not," Kirk said. Then before she could protest, he added, "I cannot send a pregnant woman into a combat situation. I will allow you to remain on limited duty until we reach Starbase 56. You can train your new squad, but nothing more. And even that duty will be subject to Doctor McCoy's ongoing review." Kirk's tone made it clear that the discussion was over. "But you still have a decision to make and some time to make it."

37

The enormity of her situation hit her. She had wanted a career in Starfleet her whole life. And the fact was that the service needed her now more than ever. But then there was Jon . . .

His baby . . .

Their baby . . .

"Doctor, what is the history here? Am I the first human woman to conceive a Klingon-human child?" Parrish asked.

"Probably not," McCoy said. "I haven't been able to find any case histories yet, but I'm still looking. The fact is that though everything looks fine now, I don't know quite what we can expect if you go forward."

Parrish nodded. Over the roar in her ears, she found herself standing and thanking the captain for his candor. She agreed to see the doctor tomorrow before she reported to duty, and then she was in the corridor, heading for her quarters.

Two weeks later, Kirk and Spock were walking the corridors of the *Enterprise,* heading for the briefing room. Lieutenant Uhura had just informed them of a priority-one message from Starfleet Command. There was only one thought going through Kirk's head, the same one he was sure was going through the head of everyone on the bridge.

Is this the call? Is this the one? Is this the moment when everything changes? When the war begins?

The only positive note was that the message was possible at all. Just weeks ago, Starfleet security had been so compromised that high-priority messages and orders had had to be delivered in person. Klingon agents had infiltrated Starfleet at virtually all levels from Admiral Justman's offices to the decks of the *Enterprise*.

Fortunately, Justman's Klingon assassin had failed in her mission. Admiral Justman had survived the attempt on his life to lead the defense of Starbase 42. The admiral had given his life in that fight, and in so doing had protected the valuable dilithium deposits on the planet below the starbase.

Had the Klingons overtaken the starbase and the planet, the Federation and the Klingon Empire would probably already be at war, and the Klingons would have had a huge tactical advantage. The time Justman had bought them with his life may well have saved the Federation. It had certainly given them the time they desperately needed to prepare, to mount the necessary defense against the . . .

Inevitable. Kirk didn't like to think that way, but as a commander, he had to be a pragmatist. He did not see any diplomatic solution for the Federation. The Klingons would attack; it was simply a matter of when. That outcome had been assured twenty-five years before at the Battle of Donatu V, where Bob Justman—then only a lieutenant—and a small Starfleet force had fought a larger number of Klingon ships to a draw. For the Klingons, the tie was worse than a defeat. It was a stain on their pride that had to be expunged, had to be avenged.

There hadn't been an all-out interstellar war in over a century—since the Romulan conflict—and there had not been any since the formation of the Federation. Kirk's own great-grandmother had talked about the days before the Federation, but most of the younger crew had never even heard first-person stories of that time. For them, the Federation had always been there and always would be.

Yet, Kirk knew that the Federation was very young, as political bodies went. And he knew that there was a real possibility it would not survive the coming battle. Their chances were better than they had been even a few weeks before, but Kirk knew the possibility of defeat was real. So did the planners at Starfleet. This would likely be a fight to the death for the Federation. And there would be no truce this time, no end to the fighting until one side or the other scored a decisive victory.

They reached the briefing room and took their seats. Spock used the computer console to bring up the communication on the large screen at one end of the table. Almost immediately, the screen filled with the image of Admiral Solow.

So it is serious, Kirk thought.

"Captain Kirk, Commander Spock," Solow said, his voice solemn, his face serious and very alert. The admiral's thinning hair had been white since Kirk had met him. Despite being three decades older than Kirk himself, Solow had always been fit and energetic. He still was, Kirk had no doubt, but there were lines on his face that Kirk didn't remember from the last time they had spoken just weeks ago. And while his eyes were alert, almost electric, they looked . . . what? Haunted was the word that came to mind.

Most of it had to be the looming war with the Klingons. Most, Kirk guessed, but not all. The friendship between Solow and Justman had been legendary, and Kirk also knew that Solow had depended on Justman a great deal. His loss must be particularly hard now.

"This is not the call, Captain. Diplomatic efforts are still ongoing," Solow said, obviously reading Kirk's own expression accurately. *"However, there are some serious precautions that we must begin taking. I am transmitting a data packet of new security protocols as well as recent intelligence reports. I'm asking all starship commanders to review the material and provide feedback."*

"Of course," Kirk said, nodding. He felt an immediate sense of relief. If Starfleet Command was still refining plans, then there was still a chance that the worst would not happen.

"In the data packet you will also find a systems upgrade report. These are the refits you can expect at Starbase 56, primarily weapons and shield modifications. As you know, you will also be taking on some new crew."

Kirk nodded. They had suffered some losses lately, most recently on Janus IV. They had just held the memorial service two days ago, and Kirk still felt raw.

Then the admiral did something that Kirk had never seen before. He hesitated. For a moment, Solow seemed to be searching for words. *"I made a decision and I wanted to tell you in advance, because I don't want you to be surprised—"*

Then an aide called to the admiral from offscreen.

"I'm sorry, Captain, something has come up. Solow out." The screen went dark.

Kirk turned to Spock, who returned the look with a raised eyebrow.

"How long until we reach Starbase 56?" Kirk said.

"Three hours, forty-seven minutes," the Vulcan replied.

"Then I guess I can prepare to be surprised in just under four hours."

"Apparently."

"In the meantime, please review the refit specifications with Mister Scott and brief me before we arrive."

"Yes, sir," Spock said as he and Kirk got up.

As they entered the corridor, Kirk realized that while Solow hadn't delivered the worst possible news, his news had not been good. Weapons and defensive upgrades themselves were not a declaration of war. On the other hand, he knew from military history that wars almost never occurred overnight. They built slowly, advanced by degrees and small steps until the first real explosion came and there was no looking back.

And today they had taken another step closer to the abyss.

Chapter Three

EARTH
2267

"ADMIRAL SOLOW, there's been a development," Lieutenant West said. The admiral's eyes were on him immediately. West was still getting used to working for the admiral. He still felt unnerved by the man's attention. There was something intimidating about being on the receiving end of the man's intense stare.

"Sir, it's Ambassador Fox," West said.

"A message?" the admiral asked.

"Yes, sir, but it's from Paris."

"That can't be. He's right in the middle of . . ."

"Well, he's returned for an emergency briefing. His team is waiting for you in Paris," West said. The admiral was already walking through the door and into the corridor. West had to hurry to keep up with him.

"And, sir," West said, "a meeting is set for the president's office."

"Fine," Solow said.

West had been surprised to hear that Ambassador Fox was on Earth, but he was nonplussed to hear that in a few minutes Solow would be meeting with the president himself.

The admiral's personal transporter was only a few paces away. "Sir, who on the staff would you like to attend? I can have them meet you."

"Just you, Lieutenant," Solow said.

"Sir?"

"Is there anyone with a clearer understanding of our current situation?" Solow asked as they entered the small transporter room, where an attendant was waiting.

West gave it a moment's thought. There were a lot of very intelligent, very capable people on the admiral's staff. Solow had had his pick of the best minds in the fleet and had made use of them.

"No, sir, not with respect to the current situation," West said honestly. "It's just that I'm still the most junior member of your staff."

"You'll probably piss some people off today. Does that bother you?"

"Sir?"

"Did you join Starfleet to make friends, Lieutenant, or to do a job?"

"To do a job, sir."

"Excellent. You'll get a chance to earn your braids today then," Solow said, stepping on one of the pads for the two-person transporter. West took his place on the other pad.

"Do you think Admiral Nogura will be joining us?" West asked.

"No," Solow said. "We can't be in the same place during a security alert."

Of course, West thought. Starfleet could survive the loss of both men, but there is no doubt that the fleet would be seriously impaired, and that was something they could not afford with all-out war looming. West found it interesting that Solow and the president *could* risk being in the same place at the same time. He wondered what that meant.

He didn't have long to think, however, because Solow nodded to the transporter operator and said, "Energize."

West felt the transporter beam take him. He'd only traveled by transporter a few times, and the last time he had been unconscious after an attack by a Klingon assassin.

Thus, under any circumstances, transporter travel would be a novelty for him. However, a transporter trip from Starfleet Command directly to the Palais de la Concorde was almost too much to believe.

A moment later, he found himself looking at another transporter operator who was wearing civilian clothes. Gone were the gray walls of Starfleet Command. Instead, West could see wood paneling and antique furniture.

A well-dressed Andorian that West recognized as the president's chief of staff stepped forward and extended his hand to Solow, who shook it. "Admiral, thank you for coming so quickly."

"Of course. This is my aide, Lieutenant West," Solow said.

"A pleasure, Lieutenant. I am Vilashrel th'Rithsiria, President Wescott's chief of staff, but please, call me Shrel. Now, if you don't mind, the president is waiting." He pointed to the elevator nearby.

West, Solow, and Shrel stepped inside and the doors closed. A moment later, the doors opened and West was looking out at the president's office. The room was a half-circle, with windows offering a nearly one-hundred-eighty-degree view of Paris.

And West had thought the view of San Francisco and the Golden Gate Bridge from Starfleet Command was impressive. . . .

He had been to Paris briefly before, so he immediately recognized many of the landmarks. The Tour Eiffel, he knew, dated back to the nineteenth century. And Notre Dame Cathedral to the twelfth, making it one of the oldest buildings still in use on Earth.

Much of the past remained alive in Paris, with architecture from every period of Earth's history since the Middle Ages as well as some of the most modern facilities on Earth—like the Palais de la Concorde, the home of the offices of both the president and the Federation Council, which, at fifteen stories high, towered over most of the city, seeming to preside over the past, present, and future all at once.

Once one of Earth's premier international cities, Paris was now an intergalactic city. The proof of that was the spaceport that West could see in the distance, one of the busiest on Earth.

Federation President Wescott was arguably the most powerful person in the known galaxy, and he was seated at a round conference table less than twenty feet from the spot where West was standing. The conference table was near the northern outer edge of the room. The center of the room was dominated by the president's large, circular mahogany desk. The message was clear: this office was the center of the Federation and the desk was the center of its government.

Though West had seen countless images of the room and understood intellectually that it had been designed to impress visitors, he was still surprised at how effective it was at doing just that. For a moment, he stopped breathing and realized that he was gawking like a first-year cadet.

Shaking off his bemusement, West focused on the president. Next to Wescott were one Vulcan and two human aides, who were immediately joined by Shrel. Also sitting at the table were Ambassador Fox and three of his aides, whom West recognized. One aide, Fronde, was missing, West realized. It struck him as odd; he had never seen Fox in a meeting without the man.

Two important men and two groups with them. And into the room of nine people, Admiral Solow and Lieutenant West walked. West should have felt outnumbered, but he didn't. The admiral was right, just the two of them were necessary. But West still wondered why Solow had not included more of his staff to even out the numbers. Even if the meeting was a waste of time for a few people, it would have been a small one.

West looked at Solow's face and saw that it was unreadable, which was no surprise. But he was sure that Solow was sending both Wescott and Fox a message about the difference between how Starfleet operated and how they did. West realized that the meeting, and the

47

subtle shifting of power and influence that would go on there, had begun before they entered the room.

West found it interesting that though Wescott was human, two of his senior staff were not: one was a Vulcan, another an Andorian. *Very interesting choices,* he thought. West was suddenly sure that the presence of representatives from those two historically antagonistic races on the president's staff was no accident. No doubt the choice had been made according to some calculus that West was only beginning to understand.

As soon as they entered, Wescott and the others stood up. An imposing figure, the president was more than two meters tall. He towered over his staff and was easily the tallest person in the room. His hair was a light brown, with gray starting at the temples. He looked very fit and alert, and West was surprised by how young the man looked. At forty-six, Wescott was the youngest president in the Federation's history.

The president's gaze immediately focused on Solow, and he smiled broadly. "Admiral," the president said, extending his hand as West and Solow approached.

"Mister President," the admiral said as he shook the president's hand.

"Good to see you, Herbert. I wish it were under better circumstances," Wescott said.

"I do as well." Then Solow nodded toward West and said, "This is my aide, Lieutenant Patrick—"

"West," the president finished for him as he turned his gaze to West. "I never met your father, Lieutenant, but I suspect I owe him my current job."

"Sir?" West said.

"The entire Federation owes him and Captain Garth for what they did at Axanar."

Then West understood. A loss at the Battle of Axanar could have meant the end of the Federation. Instead, the Federation won the battle and survived one of the greatest threats to its existence since its formation.

"Please send your father my regards, and my thanks," Wescott added.

"I will do that, sir."

"I see that you've made quite a name for yourself in your short time at Command. I have made your reports on the Klingon situation required reading for everyone on my staff. And the ambassador has been telling me how useful your insights have been in his negotiations."

The combination of the president's attention and his words of praise made West feel lightheaded for a moment. Not only had he just met the president, that man had just told him that he was not only aware of but impressed by West's work. To his chagrin, West felt his face begin to flush.

"I may have to steal you away from the admiral. You'd make a fine addition to the Federation Council's xeno-studies department." The man held West's eyes for a moment longer, and the lieutenant saw that this might be a genuine offer.

Then Wescott said, "I think we would all have a great deal to talk about even without the current situation, but we have some urgent business, so let's begin." The president sat down, and only then did everyone else take their seats at the round table. "Ambassador Fox can brief you on the breakthrough he has achieved in negotiations with the Klingon delegation."

Breakthrough? West thought. The president seemed pleased, and West knew he should have been elated himself. Instead, he found that he was on his guard.

"Thank you, Mister President," Fox said. "I just finished another session with Ambassador Wolt."

"The ambassador himself?" West said, unable to contain his surprise.

"Yes," Fox said, with some pride. West understood. The fact that the session had happened at all, West knew, was an accomplishment. The previous Klingon ambassador had more than once refused to meet directly with Ambassador Fox. Instead, he had sent subordinates to conduct meetings that could only be termed wastes of time. In fact, West suspected they were deliberate stalling tactics staged by the Klingons to give the empire more time to prepare for war.

"Yes, we had substantial talks and discussed all major issues currently confronting us. They have agreed to begin standing down their military mobilization, while we have agreed to immediate talks about trade routes through some of the disputed territories," Fox said.

"You seem surprised, Lieutenant West," the president said.

"I am, sir. It seems too easy," West said.

Fox immediately leaned forward. His face was red, and West could see the telltale signs of still-healing cuts and bruises on his forehead. "I assure you, Lieutenant, these negotiations were *anything* but easy. The Klingons made many important concessions, and one of my staff, Randall Fronde, was killed during the talks."

"Killed?" Solow said.

That's why Fronde isn't here, West thought sadly.

Fox nodded. "He chose to accept a Klingon challenge. His courage and sacrifice impressed Wolt enough to begin serious talks. He gave his life for these negotiations."

West saw the pain written on Fox's face, a grief that West understood after his own experience on Starbase 42. Though West had often found himself disagreeing with Fox, he had never doubted the man's sincerity, and he didn't doubt it now. However, that didn't change the fact that he was sure that Fox was wrong—at the moment, dangerously so.

"I am truly sorry for your loss, Ambassador, and we all appreciate Mister Fronde's sacrifice," West said finally. He took a breath and added, "However, as you know, dozens of Starfleet officers have given their lives defending against Klingon aggression in the last few months. Admiral Justman gave his own life on Starbase 42 so we would have the luxury of a few more weeks to prepare for a war that has been inevitable since Donatu V."

Wescott leaned forward and said, "And we appreciate *that* sacrifice. It was a sacrifice that showed the Klingons that the Federation is a formidable foe. I suspect the incident on Starbase 42 is one of the primary reasons they agreed to serious negotiations. We gave them good reason to reconsider their plans. After all, no one truly wants war."

"With all due respect, sir, the Klingons do," West said. "Conflict and conquest are ingrained into their culture. We see ourselves as peaceful people who occasionally have to resort to force to defend ourselves. They see themselves as a conquering, aggressive people who occasionally have to resort to peace."

51

"As I said, I have read your reports on Klingon culture," Wescott said. "But it would be arrogant of us to think that we are the only beings in the galaxy capable of change."

West felt his face flush for the second time that day. "Sir, it's not arrogance to learn the lessons of history. We have to make predictions based on available facts. And there is overwhelming precedent here. An Earth historian of the twentieth century once said, 'Wars only end when the conditions that started them have ended.' Humans didn't learn this after World War I led directly into World War II. They didn't learn it when the Korean War—"

The president raised his hand, and West immediately stopped speaking. "We do have reason to be suspicious, given the fact that the Klingons have not always been trustworthy in the past."

"Not trustworthy? They infiltrated Starfleet at every level with surgically altered agents while they tested our capabilities and engaged us in pointless negotiations," West said, realizing only when he had finished that his tone was much too strong for a newly minted lieutenant to use with the president. Yes, it was too strong, but West found that he didn't regret it. The stakes here were too high to mince words.

"Why is it that Starfleet is ready to accept that war will have risks, but not that peace might also have risks?" Fox said.

Wescott raised both hands and said, "Gentlemen, if we can't agree on a course of action, how can we come to an agreement with the Klingons?"

We can't, West thought, but this time held his tongue.

"The Klingons did have a condition before they ratified current agreements and continued peace talks," Wescott said. "Ambassador?"

Fox nodded and said, "The Klingons want to annex System 7348."

West couldn't begin to hide his shock. He even felt Solow give a start next to him.

"You can't be considering—" Solow started.

"Our immediate answer was no," Fox said. "However, I conferred with the president, who conferred with the Federation Council, and we agreed that we could allow a small Klingon delegation to meet with the people on the planet. Ultimately, they will decide for themselves whether or not they want to enter into any larger political bodies."

"You must see this for what it is," West said, "a crude attempt to get a foothold in Federation space. Besides the dilithium on the third planet, that system would be an excellent staging area for an invasion."

"True," Fox said, "but we're talking about a long process here. The Klingon delegation would only be a first step. The immediate Federation-Klingon crisis will be over long before the process is finished."

"Ambassador, this crisis has been twenty-five years in the making. No process will be long enough here." West was fighting to keep the exasperation from his voice.

"To be fair, the people in that system are biological Klingons," Fox said.

West shook his head. "Biological Klingons that would have been killed if Starfleet had not shut down the illegal Orion mining operation that was funded and supported

53

by the Klingons." Fox tried to interject, but West kept going. "Who then tried to destroy the entire world to eliminate any evidence of what they had been doing."

"The Klingons continue to deny any involvement in that operation," Fox said. To his credit, he didn't look as if he believed it.

"I'm sure they do, but no one in this room doubts it," Solow said.

Fox nodded and said, "Ambassador Wolt alluded to dissent within the Klingon High Council. One of the factions there might have been responsible for the mining operation in System 7348."

"Do you believe that? That the mining operation and orders to destroy the planet full of Klingons did not come from the entire High Council?" Solow asked.

Fox thought for a moment before he answered. "I do think it is a possibility that the entire High Council was not involved."

"How strong a possibility?" West asked.

"Strong enough that I think it is worth exploring this recent proposal by the Klingons. The fact is that we know almost nothing about the workings of the Klingon government. And this is without a doubt our only remaining path to peace," Fox said.

West considered Fox for a moment. He was sure the ambassador believed what he was saying. Fox believed it because he wanted to, because he needed to, and because he had spent his whole life waging peace. However, West knew the man just didn't understand how different the enemy was from himself.

And in this case, being wrong could mean the end of the Federation, the end of everything they knew. Survivors would live under harsh Klingon rule. West had learned enough about the Klingons to wonder whether the survivors of the war would be the lucky ones.

Wescott spoke next. His tone told West that his decision was final and had probably been made in advance of the meeting. "I have given this considerable thought. Until this development, we thought that war was inevitable. If there is even a chance that we may peacefully resolve the current crisis, then we have to take it. The citizens of the Federation would demand that much of us. We will allow a Klingon delegation to meet with the population of the third planet of System 7348." Before West could protest, the president added, "A Federation delegation will be there at the same time to also meet with the people of the system and to monitor the situation."

Solow leaned forward and said, "I presume that while this process is ongoing we will continue with the planned starship and planetary defense upgrades."

"We know the Klingons will be more likely to talk if they believe we are dealing from strength," West added.

Wescott nodded and said, "Of course."

"In the same vein," Solow said, "there is one more request that I would like to make. I would like the Federation delegation to be the *Enterprise*."

Fox betrayed some surprise at that. Wescott raised an eyebrow and asked, "Why them?"

"Captain Kirk and his crew saved the planet, they have the respect of the local people, and a *Constitution*-class starship would be a show of strength to the Klingons and stand as a warning if they are planning anything duplicitous or aggressive."

Kevin Ryan

Wescott had listened carefully and looked at Fox when Solow was done. To his credit the ambassador nodded and said, "That would be prudent."

The president smiled warmly and said, "This is a good sign, gentlemen. If we can agree on a course of action, then there may yet be hope."

West sat amazed at what had just happened. He and Solow had walked into an ambush. Fox and the president had discussed the situation in advance and made the decision to go ahead with the proposal before West and Solow had stepped into the room. The admiral had been silent for most of the meeting. Then, at the end, he had outmaneuvered Fox and arranged to have a starship monitor a situation that West knew would almost certainly not end well. That starship, West knew, might be the only thing that stood between the Federation and a disaster of the sort that they had never seen before.

At the close of the meeting there were brief pleasantries, which seemed somewhat forced. Suddenly, West was sure that there would be no job offer from the president's office any time soon.

Then, less than a half hour after West got the first message from the president's office, he and Solow were headed back to the transporter. "We'll immediately need to redo our deployment and tactical response reports to include the possibility of an invasion with a primary launching point from System 7348. We'll also need to review our Klingon resource assessments to include dilithium from the planet."

West nodded, then as they entered the small transporter room, he said, "Sir, what you did in there . . . that could have been a disaster."

The admiral waved his hand. "It still may be. Sometimes the best you can hope for is to have a positive influence."

"But the president was ready to just . . ." West began.

"He's a good man, but he has to worry about things we never have to think about. And he is, after all, a politician. Whether it's election day, the day before, the day after, or any day in between, they are always running for office."

West nodded, "But the stakes here are . . . everything."

Solow nodded, "Don't be too hard on him. It's a politician's nature. You might as well get upset with humanoids for breathing oxygen. It's our job to give him the leeway to make mistakes and pick up the pieces when he does. And don't sell President Wescott short. He crafted a compromise that kept all options open and still gave us reasonable security under the circumstances."

Chapter Four

As DOCTOR McCOY concluded his examination, Parrish asked, "Can I get up now?"

The doctor nodded, and Parrish got off the bed and to her feet. She realized that she was very uncomfortable being in sickbay at all, and even more so when she was lying on her back. The psychology was fairly easy to work out: she had been lying in one of these beds when the captain had given her the news about Jon's death on Starbase 42.

Jon's death . . . It had been hard for her to accept. To her surprise she had found it easier to accept that he was a Klingon. His death had not made sense because she had thought him a better person than the Klingons they had fought on the starbase. It had seemed unfair, cosmically so, that the brutal Klingons could have ended his life.

Yet he had been a Klingon himself. Since the captain had told her Jon's secret, she had learned as much as she could about Klingons. Of course, she had studied their military history and was aware of the martial nature of their empire, but she had not learned much about their culture or their history apart from warfare.

The Starfleet database had a fair amount of information, but surprisingly little of it was useful. And none of it could explain how Jon could have been the man he was, the man she knew him to be, and still be a Klingon.

Surprisingly, the revelation changed nothing in her mind about Jon. However, she had to admit that there had to be more to the Klingons than the Starfleet database—or the *Enterprise*'s recent experience—could show her.

She might never understand. Jon's secrets had died with him. And yet, not all of him had died. He had left something of himself in her heart, her mind . . . and her body. But even if she had this baby—assuming it was medically possible—she still might not understand.

"Have you thought about what you want to do?" Doctor McCoy asked. He studied her for a moment as she tried to figure out what to say. Then he smiled and said, "Let me put it another way. Have you thought about anything else?"

Parrish found herself smiling.

"Let's continue this in my office," McCoy said, and Parrish followed him. She felt relieved to leave the examination area and sat down in front of Doctor McCoy's desk as he took his own seat.

"I would like to know more . . . about whether or not

this is even possible, whether I can have this baby," she said finally.

McCoy nodded. "I'm sorry I haven't been more help there. I hope that the starbase will have more information. However, even if we find out more while we're here, you probably won't have much time to make your decision."

"I won't need much time," Parrish said, with much more confidence than she felt.

Just then, there was a beep, and Nurse Chapel's voice came over the intercom, *"Doctor, the captain is outside. He would like to speak with you and Lieutenant Parrish."*

McCoy's face showed mild surprise, but his voice was casual as he replied, "Send him in."

Almost immediately, the captain stepped through the door and Parrish was on her feet.

"At ease, Lieutenant," Kirk said to her. Then he looked at the doctor and said, "I'm sorry to interrupt, but I have news that affects Lieutenant Parrish."

"What is it, Captain?" McCoy asked.

"I have just been informed that all civilian and nonessential transport to the starbase has been suspended," Kirk said.

McCoy's surprise wasn't mild this time. "Are things that bad?"

"Not necessarily. Because of the starbase's importance to the starship refit program, security is very tight," Kirk said.

"What does that have to do with the lieutenant?" McCoy asked.

"It means that if I choose to go home, I won't be able

to get a transport from the starbase . . . well, indefinitely," Parrish said.

"At least for the duration of the current crisis," Kirk said.

Parrish had begun to consider having the baby at home, with her family. She couldn't imagine doing it on a starbase surrounded by strangers.

Kirk continued, "I wouldn't leave you on the starbase. In the long run, it would be no safer than the *Enterprise*. You could remain on board for a short time as we try to arrange a rendezvous with a civilian transport or another Starfleet vessel."

That changed things, but Parrish realized that one thought was pushing the others aside. "Does this mean that I can remain on limited duty?" Parrish asked.

"I will accept Doctor McCoy's recommendation on your status," Kirk said.

"Doctor?" Parrish asked.

"I will want to monitor you closely, but you can continue at your current level," McCoy said.

Parrish felt relief.

"Mister Giotto has said that he would like to have you oversee the initial training for a new squad that we'll be picking up on the starbase," Kirk said.

"I would like to continue to contribute as much as I can, Captain," Parrish said.

"Excellent," Kirk said. Then he looked at McCoy. "Bones, can you join me on the bridge?"

McCoy nodded and said, "Lieutenant, I will let you know as soon as I find anything."

"Thank you, Doctor," Parrish said. She watched the captain and the doctor leave, then, a moment later, she

Kevin Ryan

followed them out the door. All thoughts of her pregnancy had been pushed aside. If she was going to be training a new squad, she had quite a bit of preparation to do.

Kirk entered the briefing room at a quick pace, McCoy struggling to keep up with him and muttering about where the fire might be. Kirk ignored him and kept walking. The incident with the Romulan bird-of-prey was still fresh in his mind and the minds of the crew. Interstellar war would be several levels of magnitude worse.

The briefing-room door opened at their approach. Inside, Mister Spock and Chief Engineer Scott were huddled over the small triangular viewer in the center of the table, looking at readouts. Both men looked up as Kirk and McCoy walked in.

"Captain," Spock said with a nod.

"Sir," Scotty said. Immediately, Kirk could see that his chief engineer was unhappy about something. And he had a strong suspicion what that something might be.

"Gentlemen," he said as he took his seat. "Report."

Spock began. "Upgrades are scheduled for phasers, tactical sensors, and defensive shields. We will also be receiving a new supply of more powerful photon torpedo warheads. They achieve a twenty-two percent greater immediate particle annihilation, with a corresponding increase in power."

Kirk could see a shadow on his chief engineer's face. "What's the problem, Scotty?"

"The upgrades are all good pieces of engineering, but I'm uncomfortable with some of the trade-offs," Scott said. Then, before Kirk could ask, he continued. "Phasers and shields will be more effective against, for instance, Klingon shields and disruptors, but less flexible and less effective against a broad range of threats. Same with the sensors. Tactical sensors get a fairly big boost, but we lose power in nontactical applications."

"Including astronomical study and research," Spock added.

Kirk absorbed this for a moment. After a brief silence, McCoy was the first to speak and when he did, it was an observation, not a protest. "They're turning us into a warship."

Technically, of course, the *Enterprise* was part of Starfleet's defensive force. And this ship and crew had seen their share of conflict, from the Romulans to the Gorn. However, as a practical matter, most of the ship's duties were scientific and related to exploration. *Constitution*-class vessels were true multipurpose ships. Now, it seemed they were going to be retooled for a very specific purpose: fighting Klingons.

"Not just a warship, but a warship optimized for battle with a single enemy," Scotty said.

"The situation is regrettable but necessary, given the current crisis with the Klingon Empire," Spock said.

"And, we can only hope, temporary," Kirk said.

"Temporary if we win," McCoy said.

"What?" Kirk asked.

"I said the changes will only be temporary if we win," McCoy said.

"Yes, and irrelevant if we lose," Kirk said. The *Enterprise* might survive a Federation victory, but the ship and crew would never survive a defeat. Even if Kirk were inclined to surrender when overwhelmed, the Klingons didn't take prisoners.

"Jim, is there any hope of a diplomatic solution?" McCoy asked.

"There's always hope, Bones, but you've seen Admiral Solow's reports . . ."

"Then we'll have to hope for a miracle," McCoy said.

"Gentlemen, we can hope, but I suspect that if we're going to have a miracle here, we're going to have to make it ourselves."

Michael Fuller saw the figure from behind. Brown hair, tall, dressed in a red Starfleet ship's services uniform. Fuller's throat caught, and he felt a rush of emotions. It was all a mistake. Sam was alive and walking the halls of the starbase. There was a moment of relief, then outright joy as Fuller saw his son.

He quickened his pace as his eyes tracked the tall young man. Even after Fuller's rational mind had reasserted itself, he decided to watch the figure until he turned around.

The young Starfleet officer did turn around a few seconds later, and Fuller saw that it was not his son. That moment of confirmation was perhaps worse than any he had had in weeks. In that second, he again knew a rush of grief, a reminder that his son was gone. In that moment, his son died again in his mind. The pain was surprisingly fresh, reminding Michael Fuller of the moment when he realized why Jim Kirk had sent him a message.

From long practice, Fuller took control of himself, willing the grief to recede. Once again locking away his son's death in a box in his mind, Fuller headed back to his quarters on the starbase. The starbase was full of young men in uniforms. Many of those young men would be about Sam's age and size, and they would be wearing the red tunics of ship's services, of security.

How many more times would he see Sam? And how many more times would his son die again in his mind and heart?

Fuller wondered if things would be easier if he had been able to bury his son. Neither the official Starfleet notification nor Kirk's personal message had included any details, but Fuller had deduced that his son had been disintegrated and there had been no remains to send home.

At that thought, Fuller felt his stomach lurch and his throat close up. It took another act of will to pull himself together, but he did it. He decided not to eat dinner after all that day.

For the next two days, Fuller barely left his quarters, and then only at odd times, when there was less chance of seeing people in uniform, less chance of seeing his son again in a crowd. Nevertheless, Fuller "saw" Sam four more times in the two days. Each time, the view startled him. And each time he experienced the same cycle of relief followed by the cold rush of reality. Each time he had felt his son die again.

But the cycle was shorter by the fourth time. And by the third day, Fuller was ready to lift his near exile from other people. Partly because he saw that it hadn't worked. Many of the young people on the starbase were new officers and enlisted personnel awaiting assignment and had been in their uniforms since the moment the base quartermaster had issued them. They never took their uniforms off, even during their off-duty hours. Fuller remembered his own feelings at that age—he doubted he wore civilian clothes once in his first year in the service.

However, since his reinstatement, he had not put on his own uniform. Until now he simply hadn't been ready because he was still seeing his dead son in every crowd.

On the fourth day, he made a point of seeking out large groups. He saw his son more times than he could count, but being among people was necessary. Everything depended on his being able to perform his duties flawlessly. By the sixth day, he could function normally and he did, though he kept mostly to himself. It was two weeks after that that the inevitable happened.

"Sections one through four to the assembly area in ten minutes," the voice on the intercom said.

Ten minutes would be plenty of time, Michael Fuller knew. The few things he would be bringing with him were already packed in his small canvas bag. In fact, his personal effects had fallen well below the already low mass limits for junior officers.

There was only one thing that remained. There was one task that he had put off—and putting things off was something he never did. In fact, he had always made it a point to perform his most difficult or least pleasant tasks first in any situation. His one remaining task was neither difficult nor unpleasant, but a part of him had resisted doing it nevertheless.

Fuller put on his uniform. He well remembered his excitement when he had put on his first Starfleet uniform three decades ago—before Sam was born. He had felt excitement, pride, and a touch of fear. Now, he remembered that moment as if it had been yesterday.

A part of aging, at least for him, was the sensation that time sped up as you moved through it. Yet, he felt closer to his past than he ever had before. Enlisting in Starfleet, becoming a father, serving with the finest men and women in the fleet on six different vessels.

Losing his son.

Each experience, no matter how far in the past, seemed close by—*felt* close by—as if it were just a day away and not a year or a decade. But for a moment, everything else disappeared as he pulled the red tunic over his head. He ceased to be a fifty-two-year-old ensign, and once again because a twenty-two-year-old crewman putting on his first Starfleet uniform.

Suddenly, he wasn't *remembering* what he had felt all those years ago, he was *feeling* it.

He was surprised by the intensity of the emotion. The moment passed quickly, but left behind a lingering feeling of . . . what? Excitement? Pride? Exhilaration? Fuller didn't question the feeling any further. He simply enjoyed it. He knew it would help him fit in, and fitting in was essential now.

With nearly five minutes to spare, Fuller stepped out of his quarters with his canvas bag strapped over his shoulder. Few people took notice of him; he was just another person in uniform.

His destination was on the same level as the temporary officers' quarters. After a short walk he was there with minutes to spare. The assembly area was a large room with exactly twenty-three other people. Fuller didn't have to count to know how many others were there. He knew there were four sections of six people each. He had no doubt that he was the last person to arrive, and he guessed that the others had been there within a minute of the announcement. Their eager, excited faces told him that much.

The fact that Starfleet was on war footing didn't diminish their excitement. In fact, the reason that many of them were there was that Starfleet was increasing the number of security personnel on starships due to the Klingon crisis. For now, they were too happy about getting posted to a starship to wonder about the emergency that had gotten them there, or what the crisis might mean for them in the very near future.

Michael Fuller forgave them their naïveté. After all, they were young and had never seen real danger or fighting, certainly not with Klingons. The fact was that few people in Starfleet had seen conflict with Klingons. Most of those who had were dead, and most of the remaining were retired.

However, Fuller was neither dead nor retired, and he had plenty of experience against the Klingons. In his time, he had seen too much to share his young peers' almost childlike excitement, though he found it almost touching. It made him remember the day Sam received his commission.

Fuller had spent much of his son's childhood and youth away from Earth, but he had been able to attend Sam's Starfleet Academy graduation. He had surprised his son by showing up a day before the ceremony. Fuller remembered the look of surprise and pure pleasure on Sam's face when his father arrived. The fact that Fuller

68

knew he didn't deserve his son's admiration had not diminished his own pleasure one bit.

That night he had taken Sam for a drink at a local Starfleet bar. Sam had said no to a number of offers from his friends to celebrate with them, and the two of them had sat for most of the night talking over their drinks. It was the kind of father-son moment that had been all too rare in their lives. Of course, Fuller had always thought there would be time, that they would catch up on his next leave, or—after he retired—Sam's next leave.

Now there were no more leaves. No more talks. No more quiet drinks. There wouldn't even be the occasional subspace communication from Sam to share news or ask advice.

There was no more time.

Fuller felt a hatch opening in his mind and shut it down with force. He immediately turned his attention to the others in the room with him. He realized that several of the young recruits were looking at him.

Michael Fuller was too old to worry about the stares. Still, he couldn't help but notice them. He also understood them.

"Section four to the transporter room," a voice said on the intercom. Immediately, five of the people around him came to attention. A moment later, Fuller left the assembly area with five other people who were now so excited that they barely noticed him. A few moments later he stepped into the transporter room, where a lieutenant from the base nodded to them.

"Congratulations to all of you, and good luck on the *Enterprise,*" the officer said. Then she turned to the transporter room operator and said, "Energize."

Fuller heard the familiar hum as the system powered up. The next few minutes wouldn't be easy, but they were extremely important. In the past, he had measured new difficulties against what he had seen at the Battle of Donatu V. In that fight, he had seen things that he wished he could forget, and had done things he didn't think he could do. Now, however, he knew that the decades-ago battle was no longer the yardstick he would use to measure difficult events in his life—that dubious distinction would now go to the effort it took for him to sit down and listen to the message from his son's captain.

After that, he knew he could face anything that would come, from Klingons to the meeting that was still ahead of him.

No, the next few minutes wouldn't be easy, but Fuller knew that he would not fail.

"Captain, the first team is awaiting transport now," Uhura's voice said through the intercom.

Kirk hit the button on the desk of the security office and said, "Thank you, Lieutenant."

Chief of Security Giotto was already on his feet. Kirk nodded to him, and the two men headed for the door. After a turbolift trip and a short walk, they were outside the transporter room door. The two men had repeated this ritual so many times in the past that no discussion was required. They merely waited outside the door for the right time.

From the corridor, Kirk heard the hum of the transporter and he imagined the young faces now standing on the pad, looking around them in wonder. Then, on cue, their section chief greeted them.

"Hello, I'm Lieutenant Leslie Parrish, your section chief or squad leader," Kirk heard dimly through the door. Then Parrish continued her standard greeting, which included a few words about the ship and her captain.

Then came a joke Kirk had first heard a variation of when he served on the *U.S.S. Republic,* though he suspected it long predated his time there. Kirk marveled that there once was a time when he actually thought the joke was funny.

"How many old security guards does it take to fire a phaser?" Parrish asked.

The response came unusually fast, in a voice that was firm, clear . . . *and familiar.* "There are no old security guards," the voice said. Then, instead of the customary laughter, there was a silence that even through the transporter room door seemed uncomfortable to Kirk.

He glanced at Giotto, who managed a shrug with only his eyes. When Parrish spoke again, her voice was normal. Consistent with Starfleet regulations, she offered the recruits the opportunity to resign, step back onto the transporter pad, and go home with no penalty. Particularly in this political climate, it would have been a wise move, but no one took her up on the offer. In Kirk's career, he had never seen anyone resign before being sworn in.

Then came the Starfleet oath that Parrish said and her new squad repeated, "I solemnly swear to uphold the regulations of Starfleet Command as well as the laws of the United Federation of Planets, to become an ambassador of peace and goodwill, to represent the highest ideals of peace and brotherhood, to protect and serve the Federation and its member worlds, to serve the interests of peace, to respect the Prime Directive, and to offer aid to any and all beings that request it."

"Congratulations, and welcome aboard," Parrish said.

That was their cue. Kirk entered the transporter room with Giotto right behind him. His eyes immediately sought out the owner of the voice that had sounded familiar. He wasn't hard to find. A fifty-two-year-old man in a room full of twenty-two-year-olds was easy to spot.

At the moment his eyes met Michael Fuller's, Kirk thought that seeing a Rigelian in his transporter room wouldn't have surprised him more. Yet, there Fuller was, standing with five freshly minted ensigns. The fact that it was impossible was clearly secondary to the fact that it was true.

Kirk had a duty to perform, so he didn't linger on the officer and scanned the group with his eyes.

Parrish said, "Recruits, I present Captain James T. Kirk and our chief of security, Lieutenant Commander Giotto."

"At ease, Lieutenant," Kirk said to Parrish. "Scared any of them off yet?" He added, with some humor in his voice.

"Not yet, sir, but it's still early," she deadpanned.

"That it is, Lieutenant." Kirk turned to the group. "Welcome to the *Enterprise*. I look forward to getting to know each of you in turn. For now, we'll trust you to Lieutenant Parrish's capable hands."

Then Kirk turned and exited the room, with Giotto behind him. Once they were in the hallway and a few paces from the door, Giotto said, "Captain, about Chief Fuller, the new crew manifests were incomplete because of some of the late additions. I'll find out how this happened."

"No need, Mister Giotto. I know exactly where to go for that information. Please inform Parrish that when she's finished with her squad she should tell Chief Fuller to expect to hear from me."

"Yes, sir," Giotto said.

Kirk stopped at the nearest corridor intercom and hit the button. "Kirk to Uhura," he said.

"Uhura here," she responded immediately.

"Get me Admiral Solow and patch him through to my quarters."

"Yes, sir."

"Kirk out." He headed for the turbolift and thence to his quarters. A light on his desk told him that he had an active communication waiting for him. Sitting at the desk, he flipped on the monitor and was surprised to see Admiral Solow's face on the screen. The admiral had responded immediately to Uhura's message and was actually *waiting* for Kirk. That spoke volumes.

"Admiral," Kirk said.

"Captain Kirk, I presume that you have seen Michael Fuller," Solow said.

"Yes, sir. I just greeted Mister Fuller with a new squad of recruits."

"And you're wondering if I've compromised the security of your ship and crew by saddling you with a grief-stricken father out for revenge against Klingons." Solow's tone made it a statement, not a question.

"Yes, sir." Kirk was glad he wouldn't have to beat around the bush.

"I think we both know him better than that."

That much was true, Kirk knew. "He has just lost his son."

"And Michael Fuller has enjoyed a long and distinguished career in Starfleet security. He has earned our trust and our gratitude."

Also true, Kirk conceded. Many throughout the ranks owed Fuller their lives. Solow did. And so did Kirk himself.

"I had the same doubts about his request to re-enlist. Then I read his psych report, which said he was more than fit for duty. Then I read the results of his physical and skills test certification, which were quite remarkable. And finally, I talked to Fuller. I suggest you do the same. As captain, you have final say on your crew assignments. And at the moment, you and I have something more pressing to discuss, the Enterprise's next assignment. This, Captain Kirk, comes directly from President Wescott's office."

Fuller slowed down and let the rest of the squad walk ahead of him. For the moment, the Enterprise was more interesting to the other new recruits than he was. Fuller understood that well. This was their first ship, and it was a starship, and it was the Enterprise. They would spend as long as they could exploring, many of them not even stopping to put their gear in their quarters.

It was then that he realized he was being followed. One of the squad had hung back even further than he did and was now pacing him by about six steps. Fuller's first thought was disgust: his reactions were way off. He should have been aware of his company immediately.

He had no doubt that the person was not a threat, but

security service had almost no margin of error. If future events played out as he suspected they would, his skills and instincts would have to be back up to one hundred percent very quickly, no matter how he was feeling. If he wasn't up to snuff, he would have very little time to worry about it—he knew from experience that Klingons were very unforgiving of mistakes.

He dismissed the new recruit behind him as someone who was just curious about the person old enough to be the father of everyone else in the squad. Fuller headed for his quarters. He was mildly surprised when the ensign behind him followed him right into the turbolift. Fuller shot the young man a quick appraising glance and saw that he was one of the new recruits—impossibly young, but weren't they all? This one had pale skin, dark hair and dark eyes. A quick mental tally told him that the young man was also a touch smaller than the other men in squad. Fuller found that he was relieved that the recruit looked nothing like Sam.

The ensign looked away quickly, but when Fuller's eyes concentrated on the turbolift door, his peripheral vision told him that the young man's eyes were studying him. Then the doors opened and Fuller headed to his quarters. The layout of the *Enterprise* was fairly standard for a *Constitution*-class vessel, and Fuller had made it a point to memorize any changes that had been made to the design. As a result, he found his quarters quickly.

His shadow followed him almost to the door, and Fuller decided it was time to put a stop to whatever was going on. Before he entered the room, he spun around and said, "Can I help you?"

The ensign looked startled, then mildly stricken. "Um, well . . ."

"Where are you headed?" Fuller asked.

"To my quarters . . . *These* are my quarters," the ensign said.

Of course, this is my roommate, Fuller realized, then felt himself relax. He smiled politely. "Sorry, I thought you were following me."

"Well, I was, sort of . . . I mean, you are . . . are you Michael Fuller?"

The young man had surprised him again. How had he known?

"Yes," he answered. "Who are you?" Fuller extended his hand.

"Ensign David Parmet, sir," he said, shaking Fuller's hand enthusiastically. "Good to meet you, sir, though I can't really believe this."

"Believe what, son? And please, don't call me 'sir.' "

"That you're here. I thought you retired. And, well, you are one of the greatest . . . and you're just one of the recruits? Frankly, that doesn't make any sense. I mean, sir, respectfully . . ." For a moment, thankfully, Parmet seemed to be at a loss for words.

"Hold on, now. It looks like we're going to be roommates, and I'll be happy to answer any of your questions, but I need you to do one thing for me, first."

"Anything, I mean, of course."

"I need you to let go of my hand."

"What?"

"My hand," Fuller repeated.

Parmet looked down and saw that he was still holding Fuller's hand in a firm grip. A look of surprise and then embarrassment crossed his face, and he released his hold on Fuller.

"Now, why don't we step inside and . . . get to know one another," Fuller said. Parmet nodded eagerly, and Fuller stepped into the quarters, which were dominated by two small beds. When he had first served on board ship, he had had trouble with the size of the Starfleet-issue beds, but years later, as a civilian, he found he could not sleep well on anything much bigger. There was also a dresser and a small desk for each of the two men. The accommodations had seemed luxurious to him as a young man, especially after serving on the *Icarus*-class ships, like the *Endeavour.*

Fuller waved at the two beds and said, "Do you have a preference?"

Parmet shook his head and said, "Sir, I couldn't, you choose."

Fuller knew that this could take all day, so he put his bag down on the bed closest to the door.

"Sir, I have a lot of questions for you," Parmet said.

"Why don't we take a moment and unpack first?" Fuller took out his civilian clothes and placed them in the dresser. He took a few data solids and put them in the top drawer. Taking out the only personal possessions he had brought, he put them on top of the dresser. They were two photos of Sam. One had been taken on his tenth birthday during one of the few birthday parties that Fuller had been able to attend. The other photo showed Sam in his first Starfleet uniform on the day he had received his commission.

When Fuller turned to his roommate, he saw Parmet standing by his own dresser and looking at him expectantly. Fuller saw that Parmet's bag was empty and the small shelf above his bed full of books. A quick mental calculation told Fuller that Parmet's books must have come very close to the mass limit allowed new officers.

Fuller sat down on his bed, but Parmet remained standing, nearly at attention. "Why don't you have a seat," Fuller offered.

Parmet complied immediately as if he'd been given an order. "Yes, sir."

"I'll say it again, Ensign, don't call me sir. You can call me Michael if you like, or just Fuller."

"Yes, sir," Parmet said, then he immediately corrected himself. "Yes, Mister Fuller."

Fuller sighed inside but let it go.

"That's what I don't understand: why would you come out of retirement as a regular security guard? You could easily be a section leader or better after the career you had."

"Starfleet regulations are very clear on the status of reenlistment after a certain period," Fuller explained, even though Solow had, in fact, offered him the very thing Parmet expected.

"But you, you . . ."

"The same regulations must apply to everyone, or they mean nothing."

Parmet nodded as if he were memorizing a lesson.

"Now I have a question for you. How do you know who I am, or anything about my career?" Fuller asked.

Parmet wore a confused expression on his face and said, "You're *Michael Fuller*. You were at the Battle of Donatu V aboard the *U.S.S. Endeavour* and the rescue operation on Lynwood IV. The tactics you used against the Klingon boarders on the *Endeavour* and your attack on an enemy holding hostages in a fortified position in the Lynwood system are still taught at the Academy. And that's just for starters. There's your work in the Rigelian incident of—"

Parmet looked ready to go on at some length. Fuller silenced him with a raised hand. "Okay, but no names of individual security officers appear in the Academy curriculum in those cases."

"True, but I did some additional research. I read all of the logs and firsthand reports," Parmet said.

That gave Fuller a chill. He had been approached only once before by a young officer who had studied his past missions in that detail and had done the additional research to find out the names of the lower-ranking officers involved. That young man was the captain of a starship now. *This* starship.

"Well, whatever you've read about me, you need to remember that there were a lot of other officers in all of the missions you studied," Fuller said.

"Of course, but you were . . . I mean, you *are* a hero."

That word took Fuller by surprise. For a moment Parmet was silent, the look of earnestness on his face giving Fuller a pang.

"No, I'm not. No matter what you've read, I was just another person doing his job."

"With all due respect, sir, that's not quite true. You were a lot more than that."

"It *is* true, son. I've known a lot of heroes in the service, and the real heroes all share one thing."

"What's that, sir?"

"They're all dead. They died in the line, and their

names cover a very large wall in the lobby at Starfleet Command."

Parmet was silent for a moment as he absorbed that. Fuller saw that the young man in front of him had a lot to learn. Fuller had known many young officers like this one, and too many of them hadn't lived long enough to get those lessons. Fuller was once again glad that he had not accepted Solow's offer of a section chief position. He didn't want to be responsible for any more young men and women who would have their education so brutally cut short.

"I was sorry to hear about your son, sir," Parmet said.

"My son? How do you know about Sam?"

"I've sort of followed your career. I knew you had a son in the service and heard that he was lost. I'm sorry."

"I appreciate that."

"Sir, it would be an honor if you would have lunch with me."

Fuller nodded. "You have some more questions for me?"

Parmet smiled. "Yes, sir." *Sir.* There it was again. Fuller let it go. This was going to take some time, he knew. As he got up, he caught the look on Parmet's face. It was admiration bordering on awe. It was a look that he had seen before. He had not deserved it then either.

As it turned out, Ensign Parmet did look a bit like Sam, after all.

Chapter Five

I.K.S. D'K TAHG
IN ORBIT OF QO'NOS
2267

"Ship moored and secure, Captain," First Officer Faal said.

Captain Koloth nodded and said, "The crew can exit to the base."

"Senior officers, inform your warriors," Faal said.

Karel leaned down to the bridge weapons console and gave the order for the first group of his warriors to depart. The rest would follow, according to the schedule that Karel had made. He was still getting used to his new position as a bridge officer. He found that much of his time was given over to tasks like making schedules and monitoring everything from equipment to fights among his subordinates.

He wondered what his father would think of him now.

Karel's father had served aboard a Klingon warship, but had died honorably in battle before he had risen higher than a junior officer. As such, he had probably never even set foot on the bridge of the vessel he served. Karel had seen the records of his father's career. He had showed promise, and—had he lived—Karel thought he might have earned a command of his own eventually. Karel had seen that with command came opportunities for battle and great deeds in the service of the empire.

However, there were also mundane administrative tasks. To his surprise, Karel found that he was good at them, better than that bloodless fool who had been bridge weapons officer before him. Karel had always believed there was honor in any service to the empire, even if that service didn't mean fighting in a battle and instead meant, say, deciding at what time and in which order the warriors under him were able to sleep or eat or take shore leave.

Still, he took no pleasure in these tasks he performed well. He took no pleasure even in the battle he had seen in the last few weeks. Since he had taken his brother's life in the fight with the Earthers he had begun to question whether there was honor in serving the empire now. As it stood, the empire was no longer the one forged by Kahless the Unforgettable with his own blood and strength—Kahless, who had once battled his own brother for twelve days and twelve nights because his brother had lied and brought shame upon his family. Now the High Council stripped Klingons of their identity, made them look like Earthers, changing them down to their very blood.

These Klingons had been told lies about the Earthers—*no, humans,* he reminded himself. The infiltrators had been called *betleH 'etlh*, the Blade of the *Bat'leth*, but they were intended to be skulking assassins who would hit the humans from behind, dishonoring Kahless's teachings and themselves because they would never show their true faces in battle.

The High Council sought to use these infiltrators to weaken the humans and their Federation so it would fall to the empire. However, the humans were not the cowardly, dishonorable foe most Klingons had been led to believe. And even if they had been, there would have been no honor in a victory won by stabbing an opponent in the back. If an enemy could not be beaten face-to-face, blood for blood, then there was no real victory.

Karel's younger brother Kell had been one of the Klingons sent to live as a human. They had stripped Kell of everything that made him Klingon, everything except his honor. That he had kept, and he had fought with honorable humans against the Klingons of Karel's own vessel.

Kell had fought bravely until Karel's own hand had dealt him a mortal blow. Karel had only had a moment with his brother before Kell succumbed to his wounds. In that moment, Kell had handed him a recording that contained his story, which he had made because at the end Kell had known that his mission was false and would lead inevitably to his death.

And then Kell had died, by his brother's own hand. Shame still burned in Karel's veins. *Do I even have blood anymore, or do my veins carry nothing but the shame? Yes,* he realized after a moment's thought. There was something else there, something that burned.

It was a rage against those bloodless Klingons who had sent his brother down the honorless path.

Reflexively, Karel reached for his father's *d'k tahg*. Now the recording Kell had made him sat on top of the blade's hilt so that the knife would remind him of both his father and his brother, two Klingons who had been better than he, who had died on paths of honor.

"Bridge officers are dismissed," Faal said. There were grunts of ascent as the bridge began to clear out. With the *I.K.S. D'k Tahg* moored to the station, the ship was secure. The Klingons on the bridge knew they had precious little time to enjoy home.

Karel gave a quick glance at the main viewer and saw Qo'noS hanging beneath them. He had dreamed of returning home covered in the glory of battles fought and victories won in the name of the House of Gorkon. They were mostly childish fantasies, but he had indulged them. Now, the birthplace of Kahless and the empire seemed to judge him, not welcome him. Yet, that judgment was nothing, he knew, compared to what would come in a few short hours.

Still, he did not delay to meet his fate. Shamed though he was, he was still his father's son and he would face his destiny. Karel got up and headed for the door to the bridge. A moment after he left, he heard footsteps behind him. Their sound told him it was Faal.

"You," Faal said, and Karel turned around. "You are a bridge officer now, you can take the transporter down to the surface." Most of the crew would have to wait for transports from the station. The transporter meant more time home, a bonus. Still, Karel shook his head reflexively.

"I can take a transport," he said. The additional time on the surface would do him no good.

"You are a bridge officer, you will take the transporter," Faal said, a threat in his voice. It would serve no purpose to refuse the second-in-command's offer.

"Yes, sir." Karel did not know Faal well, but the Klingon seemed a capable first officer. He did his job reasonably well, even if he did not excel. Though he was not a great leader like Koloth, neither did he try to keep the Klingons beneath him at each other's throats to keep them from challenging his position.

With a grunt, Faal took a turn toward his quarters. Karel headed straight to the transporter room. He had everything he needed with him, once again touching his father's *d'k tahg*. There was a line of Klingons waiting outside the transporter room. Two of them turned around when he approached, and Karel recognized them as two of Faal's personal guards.

There was something odd about that. Reflexively, Karel put his hand on his father's *d'k tahg*, but before he could draw it out, the two Klingons rushed him and pushed him into a transporter systems control room. As Karel found himself reeling backward into the dark room, he realized what had bothered him about the situation: the two low-ranked guards were mere *bekk*s, who would not have been permitted to use the transporter. They belonged on the station, waiting for a transport vessel down to the surface.

The room he was pushed back into was both small and dark, which was no accident, he realized. Whoever had planned this knew that Karel was experienced in the *Mok'bara*, the ancient fighting art. The *Mok'bara* could be a deadly weapon in the right Klingon's hands, but it required room to maneuver, to strike.

Karel knew he had less than seconds to live unless he did something remarkable. However, all he could do as he fell back into a control panel was raise his right hand and thrust it toward his attackers. Karel was already off balance, and the blow was far from full-force.

However, it made deadly contact.

He heard one of the Klingons cry out, and he felt a wet spray on his hand. It was then Karel realized that the hand he had raised to strike out with was the hand he had used a moment before the attack to grasp his father's *d'k tahg*.

His head and shoulders were screaming in pain from the force of his collision with the control panel. The pain gave him clarity of thought, and the realization that his father's knife had just saved him from instant death brought him joy. As he gave a battle cry, he rushed forward, shoving the injured attacker out of his way as he swung at the place where he sensed the other attacker was standing.

Though his eyes had adjusted to the darkness, there was still too little light to see. Nevertheless, he launched another attack, thrusting forward with his *d'k tahg*. The attacker was no fool, however, and, though Karel had surprised him by striking his partner, he was already launching an attack of his own.

Karel's ears told him that the other assassin had moved at almost the same instant as he had himself. Which one of them would strike a serious blow was more a matter of chance than anything else. Karel felt his knife meet resistance, then shoot off to one side. The momentum of his movement carried him forward, and he felt a sharp pain high in his chest.

He knew immediately that he had been struck, seriously if not mortally, and he had landed perhaps a glancing blow on his opponent. Karel struck the wall near the door and realized that this fight would be over in seconds if he did not do something immediately.

He acted on this thought before it had fully formed in his head. Using his knife hand, he tapped the button that switched on the room lights. As the light flashed Karel could only see for an instant as the light hit his unaccustomed eyes.

The figure in front of him was illuminated, its position burned into his brain. Karel threw himself forward, holding his *d'k tahg* in front of him. He made satisfying contact with the Klingon, hitting the spot he was aiming for right under the warrior's rib cage.

As Karel's eyes adjusted to the light, the assassin fell backward, unable to counterstrike. Then he hit the rear wall of the room and Karel's body was pushed up against his, the knife driving in further. The assassin's wild eyes looked at him for a moment, then he fell to the floor with Karel collapsing on top of him, drawing breaths in large gulps.

Karel took a moment to make sure that the Klingon was dead, then spared a glance for the other assailant, who lay motionless in his own blood. Karel saw that his lucky blow at the first Klingon had gone straight through his rib cage and penetrated his heart.

Karel's own chest felt like it was on fire. Looking down, he saw that the Klingon's knife had struck him just below the collarbone on his left side. Although the wound was bleeding freely, the weapon probably hadn't hit anything vital.

As he got up, Karel wondered why in Kahless's name Faal's two *targs* had attacked him. As a bridge officer, he expected challenges from members of his own staff who were looking for advancement, but why would *these* attack him?

The answer came as a single word: *Koloth.* Faal was making a move against his commander. Letting the pain in his chest focus his thoughts and energy, Karel sprinted out the door. He hit the corridor and looked for signs of his captain. There was still a line of Klingon officers waiting for the transporter. Karel checked the transporter room quickly, then headed for Koloth's quarters.

Faal had no doubt seen Karel's loyalty to his captain and wanted him out of the way before he moved against Koloth. That meant Faal's attempt on Koloth would be neither honorable nor fair. It would, however, be well planned—as the attack on Karel had been. It had been clever to make the move when the ship was docked and the crew lax as it prepared to leave for home.

For all Karel knew, Koloth had already been caught unawares. He sped up on his way to his captain's quarters. Turning a corner, he saw Klingons at the end of the corridor. There were two on the ground and three with their backs to him. Karel was sure that those three Klingons had Koloth trapped at the end of the corridor.

"Captain!" Karel shouted. Then he gave his warrior's yell as he sprinted down the corridor. His *d'k tahg* had never left his hand, and he held it high. The three Klingons turned in surprise to see Karel baring down on them. It was a mistake to take their eyes off their prey, because Koloth immediately struck the one closest to him as the three Klingons turned toward this new attack.

There was a moment of confusion as the other two

turned back to the immediate threat of Koloth and tried to snatch glances back at Karel. Forgetting the pain in his chest, Karel felt his blood run hot. In a few seconds they would see how these Klingons who brought five to fight a single warrior fared when the odds were even.

Karel whooped once and noted with satisfaction that the Klingon who had turned to face him started in surprise. Then Karel was on him, bringing his father's knife down. The Klingon didn't have the sense to block the blow and tried to strike out himself. Even with his injured left side, Karel was able to deflect the blow easily and drive his father's honored blade into the chest of the cowardly, bloodless Klingon before him. The Klingon had strength enough for a single, strangled cry, then he fell to the deck.

A kick confirmed that the Klingon was dead. Karel looked up to see Faal a few paces in front of him and Koloth standing against the wall. The captain had a few superficial wounds but looked sound. He had obviously taken two of Faal's co-conspirators before Karel had gotten there.

Now all of Faal's Klingons were lying dead on the floor. The first officer shot Karel a quick glance, and Karel was tempted to end his pitiful honorless life immediately. However, he stayed his father's blade. If he killed Faal now, the insult to Koloth would be great—and Koloth would have to answer it.

Karel wiped his father's knife on the uniform of the Klingon at his feet and reattached it to his belt. Koloth gave him a barely perceptible nod and said, "Commander Faal, do you wish to formally challenge my command of this vessel?" Faal didn't speak, and Karel could see uncertainty in his eyes. "Come, I am injured, strike your blow."

"You are weak," Faal said, his voice uncertain. Looking at the two Klingons on the deck who had died at Koloth's hand, Karel laughed.

"Then you serve the empire by replacing me?" Koloth asked. "Certainly, your strength will add to the glory of our people."

Now Faal didn't just look uncertain, he looked afraid. "Captain . . ." he muttered.

"Enough," Koloth said. Then the captain was a blur of action. He feinted once with his own *d'k tahg*. As Faal tried to parry, Koloth raised his knife and brought it down hard into the Klingon's chest. Faal immediately dropped his own knife and looked up at Koloth in surprise. Looking down at Faal, Koloth said, "You insult me." Then he pressed the knife deeper into the Klingon's chest cavity and gave it a sharp twist. The ship's soon-to-be-former second officer gave a strangled cry and went limp on the deck.

Koloth pulled out his knife, wiped it on Faal's uniform, and replaced it at his own side. "Lieutenant Karel."

"Captain," Karel said, nodding.

"You were dismissed. Why aren't you on Qo'noS?"

"I met some of Faal's guards outside the transporter room. They attempted to . . . *detain* me, and I thought Faal might be planning a dishonorable promotion for himself."

"Faal was a fool, and the ship is lucky to be rid of him," Koloth said. "I am pleased to see you, *First* Officer Karel."

Karel began to protest. "Sir, I am not—"

"Qualified?" Koloth finished for him. "More than Faal, I would say." Karel didn't respond. The two Klingons had had a similar discussion when Koloth had given him his promotion to weapons officer. "Are you refusing my offer?"

The challenge was clear in the question. If Karel refused, he would be questioning his captain's judgment. They would fight. Both Klingons were injured. Both had training in the *Mok'bara*. The captain would be a worthy opponent. It would be an interesting test, yet Karel had no desire to spill honorable Klingon blood with his father's weapon. "No."

"Good," Koloth said.

"Do you have orders for me?"

"Do your wounds require attention?"

"Yes," Karel replied. The bleeding had slowed, but he was feeling weak from the amount he had already lost.

"Tend your wounds, then visit the surface. You deserve the trip," Koloth said.

"I do have pressing business at home."

"Then go, but do not bleed to death. That is an order." Koloth smiled. "I do not wish to replace my second-in-command twice in one day."

"Yes, Captain." Karel turned to go. He headed back to the transporter room, feeling unsteady on his feet. Still, he knew that he had enough strength for his next task. After that, bleeding to death would be the least of his concerns.

When he reached the transporter room, the operator nodded and said, "First Officer Karel." Immediately, the Klingon waiting inside stepped away from the platform and Karel took his place. As the transport beam took him, Karel prepared himself for what he had to do next: tell his mother that despite what she had heard in the official Klingon Defense Force report, his brother had not died at the hands of Earther scum. Her son Kell had died by his own brother's hand.

The transporter beam deposited Karel on the path leading to the estates of the House of Gorkon. He could have used the transporter to save himself the walk, but he did not want to deny himself the chance to look at his family's house as he approached it from the road—as he had done countless times in the past. He had walked the same path with his brother Kell often times, once when Kell had been grievously wounded in a *targ* hunt but had insisted on walking up the hill unaided.

Karel felt a stab of grief. The weeks since Kell's death had not softened the pain of his passing. Karel was his father's son and so had trained himself to silently endure physical pain great enough to make proud warriors cry out. Yet his brother's death pained him in a way that he had never experienced before. He had no defenses to shield him from this loss.

For a moment, he imagined his brother walking beside him. Then for an insane moment, he *felt* Kell's presence. It was impossible—a trick of the mind, he knew, but a convincing one. He did not deserve to walk with his brother's spirit, and not simply because he had killed Kell, but because his brother had walked a path to honor that Karel had not had the courage to see, let alone follow himself. Kell had confronted the deficiencies of the empire and had chosen honor even over his own people. Kell had died defending humans because it was the only honorable choice.

Karel had seen much dishonor in his career, yet he had not truly faced it. Instead, he had hidden behind his desire to pursue a career. Perhaps, he had told himself, if he served the empire well, he might get the command of a Klingon warship. Then he would be in a better position to help guide the empire back to a path of honor. What good would it have done to get himself arrested or killed because he questioned a policy or protested a decision by Command?

Perhaps he had even been right, but such a course was not honorable. And now the High Council would likely lead the empire into a war that it might not win—and worse, a war that was based on lies and deception. Karel knew there was honor in fighting a battle lost from the beginning if the cause was just. This cause, however, was anything but.

Kell had been sent to kill the human James T. Kirk and had ended up owing Kirk his life. And more important, he had seen Kirk's honor and courage and had taken Kirk's side in battle against Klingons—against his brother. Kell had done the impossible. He had found a path of honor on a mission that had been false from the beginning.

The House Gorkon estate loomed large above him. Dev'ghot, his grandfather had named it when he had built it years ago. The name meant "chieftain," and Karel's mother had always told Karel and Kell that they had been born to lead the empire along Kahless's path of honor. In their childish dreams, they had both believed it and had spent many nights discussing the great victories they would win for the empire.

Then the Klingon Defense Force had rejected Kell because of his size. It was a foolish decision, because

Kahless taught that a warrior's body was merely a shell, that his strength came from his heart and his blood. And Kell had more of both than any warrior that Karel had met in the Klingon service.

Those childish dreams were finished now. Kell was dead and Karel did not expect to survive the day. He would never take up his post as first officer on board the *D'k Tahg.* Koloth would have to replace his second-in-command twice in one day after all.

As he approached the front door, he hesitated and took a deep breath, perhaps his last breath of the air outside his home. Then he opened the door. His mother had no doubt heard the noise and was coming down the hall. Karel saw surprise then pleasure register on her face at seeing him. She rushed to meet him and embraced him.

"Karel, my son," she said, squeezing him fiercely. The embrace put pressure on his wound and he winced, though he did not cry out. Sensing something, she pulled back and immediately spied the blood beneath his collarbone.

"You're injured," she said.

"I am fine," he protested, but he felt light-headed from the loss of blood and knew he was far from fine. From his mother's expression he could see that she knew too. "Mother, there is something I need to tell you about Kell."

A shadow of grief crossed her face, but she held firm. "I received the message from Command," she said.

"I received the same message on board ship. It said he was killed—"

"By *Earthers*," she finished for him, making the word a curse.

94

"Yes, that is what the message said, but it is not true," he replied. She was immediately hyperalert. "Let us discuss this in Father's office."

She nodded and led him to the office, which was near the entrance to the house. In his father's room, Karel took a seat. His mother hesitated and said, "One moment."

She came back with bandages, clothing, and a few other supplies. Karel sighed, which did not escape her notice. "It will do us no good if you do not live to finish your tale," she said brusquely.

Karel took off his uniform tunic and saw that a large portion of his chest was covered with either dried or fresh blood. His mother shook her head. "You and your brother," she said, clearly remembering the tusk wound that Kell had sustained in almost the same place in a *targ* hunt so many years ago.

First she washed off the blood and pressed a bandage to the raw wound. "It has stopped bleeding?" he asked.

"Yes, but from the looks of your uniform, it is only because you have so little blood left," she said, a rebuke in her voice. Karel thought that he should stop her from treating him further, but he needed to tell his whole tale and he did not want to spend precious time arguing with her over his injury.

His mother dabbed the wound with a disinfectant. Karel winced but kept silent. Then she began closing the wound with the same device that she had used on Kell years ago—and then on her two sons countless times since. Her hand was practiced and she finished quickly. Karel accepted the pain as a small measure of punishment for his crimes.

"Here," she said, holding out a fresh shirt. As Karel

put on one of his old shirts, she disappeared with his uniform tunic and came back a moment later.

"What is it?" she asked, sitting down behind his father's desk. All maternal concern was gone from her face as she looked at him expectantly. Karel reached to his side and grabbed his father's *d'k tahg*. Lifting up the knife, he reached for the hilt and pulled off the recording he had placed there.

"Do you have the package I sent?" he asked. She nodded and quickly produced a small box that he had sent. As he had instructed, she had not opened it. He opened it now and pulled out the human sensor recording device. His mother was openly surprised.

"It is an Earther . . ." she began.

"Tricorder," he said. Then he put the recording inside. "Kell made this and gave it to me before he died. It will explain his last days better than I can." Karel hit a switch, and Kell's voice sounded from the alien piece of equipment.

"My honored brother Karel. It is your brother Kell. When I began this mission . . ." The sound of his brother's voice made his grief fresh again, and by her face, Karel could see that it was doing the same thing to his mother. Yet they both were silent.

Karel listened to the recording for the second time. It told of how Kell had been offered a chance to volunteer for a dangerous mission to strike a deadly blow against the greatest enemy of the empire. Stuck at a bloodless post in Imperial Intelligence, Kell had accepted, hoping to bring honor to his family and finally serve the empire as his father had done and his brother was doing on a Klingon warship.

Kell had undergone surgery to make him look like a human Starfleet officer who had been kidnapped by Klingons. Then Kell had learned English and had received extensive training on behaving like a human.

He had become an infiltrator, or *betleH 'etlh*, the Blade of the *Bat'leth*. He and dozens of others would live and move among humans until it was time to strike. When the time came they would hit the Earthers in Starfleet from within, meting out a thousand cuts until the Klingon fleet dealt the killing blow.

Uncomfortable with the mission of deception, Kell had asked why the clearly superior Klingon Empire would use such tactics. The leaders of the program had told him that human treachery made true honorable combat with them impossible. It was distasteful, but Klingons would have to use some of the Earthers' own tactics to defeat them.

Kell had accepted that answer and had received a post to the *Enterprise,* where his first orders were to kill its captain, James T. Kirk. Before very long he had found that much of what he had learned about Earthers was not true. And Kirk, in particular, was both an honorable person and a great warrior himself. Kell fought with the humans against Orions twice and realized that the coming war would be a terrible mistake. Not only was it predicated on lies, but the empire might actually lose. And then he had learned that the empire was behind an Orion mining operation that had nearly destroyed a planet full of primitive Klingons living on a world in Federation space near the border. In his last entry, Kell said that he would do whatever he could to stop the madness and reveal the truth about the empire's dishonorable path to war.

Karel and his mother listened to the recording in silence. When it stopped, Karel continued the story. "Kell's ship was protecting a human starbase when it was attacked by a Klingon vessel. Kell fought with his human companions and died in that battle."

His mother's face, which had been nearly unreadable since the recording began playing, was openly surprised at that. After a moment she nodded and said, "He chose honor."

Karel stood and went to the shelf on the wall. There he put down the *adanji* incense he had brought with him. After he lit the incense, he reached for the *mevak* dagger that his family kept on the wall. "There is something else. I know the Klingon who took Kell's life." Walking around the desk, he handed the *mevak* to his mother. Confusion was clear on her face, but she took the knife. "It was me. I killed my brother, your son, the son of my father." Keeping his eyes on hers, Karel waited for his mother to complete the *Mauk-to'Vor* ritual. It might not restore his own lost honor, but perhaps it would repair some of the damage he had done to his family's. Karel's mother made a groaning sound as she stood up. For a moment, she could not speak.

She could, however, raise the knife.

When she found her voice, it was strong. "Did you know you were fighting your brother?"

Karel shook his head. "No."

Understanding dawned on his mother's face. Understanding mixed with grief and pain. A terrible wailing sound emerged from her throat. She raised the knife higher. Karel found that he welcomed the relief that would come shortly. His mother screamed and brought

98

down the knife, but drove it into his father's desk. Now it was his turn to be confused.

"Mother, I invoke *Mauk-to'Vor.* I do not deserve to live," he said.

His mother drew in air in gasps, then said, "These bloodless cowards who sent your brother on this mission of lies, *they* still live?"

For a moment Karel did not understand the question. Then he said, "I do not know who they are."

His mother's face had set harshly. "Then they live," she said. When Karel didn't respond, she said, "And you would end the life of your father's last son before these *petaQpu'* lie rotting in their graves."

"Mother . . . those orders would have had to come from the High Council."

"Is your father's last son afraid of a fight?" she sneered.

Something crystallized inside of him. He saw it now, his own path to honor, or as close as he could come after all the things he had done and failed to do.

"No. They will die," he said finally. His mother studied him carefully for a long moment. Then her control vanished and she reached out for him, clutching him as she gave long, open sobs. Kell did not deserve the embrace, but his mother gave it anyway.

Such was the nature of mothers.

Chapter Six

"THIS IS A JOKE, right, Jim?" McCoy said.

"I'm afraid not," Kirk said. "The Klingon diplomatic team has made the request. They want the proto-Klingon race in System 7348 to make the choice for themselves. They will either continue as a Federation protectorate, join the Federation outright, or become part of the Klingon Empire."

Frustration clear in his voice, McCoy asked, "Did you explain to the admiral that as per our report, the Klingons were using Orion fronts to perform spectacularly destructive deep-core mining? That if it had been allowed to continue, they would have certainly destroyed the planet, which they then tried to do when the *Enterprise* put a stop to the mining operation?"

Kirk understood the doctor's irritation, which everyone else in the room—except perhaps Spock—shared. "The admiral understands the situation perfectly. However, the Klingon Empire has tied the issue to the peace proposal, and the Federation diplomatic team wants to let them make their case to the Klingons in the system."

"But, sir," Scotty chimed in, "that will not only give the Klingon access to the dilithium on the planet, it will give them a foothold in Federation space. The system would be an excellent launching point for an invasion."

"Admiral Solow and Starfleet Command understand that, which is why we're being sent to monitor the activity in the system." Seeing the disgruntled looks on the faces of his senior staff, Kirk added, "President Wescott himself wants to give this peace proposal a chance. It may be our last."

Spock said, "Captain, I must point out that there is a logical contradiction here. Though this is a Klingon peace proposal, until now the Klingon delegation has denied that they are even preparing for war."

"Diplomacy, Mister Spock," Kirk said, "is an art that may be beyond our simple understanding."

McCoy muttered something under his breath.

"Bones?" Kirk prompted.

"I said, 'How stupid is the Federation diplomatic team?' "

"I presume your question is rhetorical, Doctor," Spock said, raising an eyebrow.

Kirk cut off McCoy's no-doubt-testy reply. "That will have to be a topic for another day. For now, we have a mission. It will be up to us to keep the Klingons out of any more mischief."

"Aye, and something tells me there will be plenty of that," Scotty said.

"The Klingon delegation is scheduled to arrive in one week. How soon can we be under way, Mister Scott?" Kirk asked.

"*With* the scheduled upgrades?"

"Those are Admiral Solow's orders, and I suspect we'll need them," Kirk said.

"The systems upgrades should have at least eight days," Scotty said, and then he saw the look on Kirk's face and added, "*But* if I can pull qualified staff from other departments, we can be ready in four."

"You have my authorization. Coordinate with Mister Spock," the captain said. Kirk could see that Scott wasn't happy about the prospect. A refit of this scale was delicate and meant using new systems that had never been tested outside of a lab. Scott preferred to use only his own people for this sort of work, and Kirk knew his chief engineer often performed an unusual amount of the actual work himself. This crash schedule meant that Scotty's own role would be mostly supervisory. Sadly, it couldn't be helped.

"Mister Spock?" Kirk said.

"We can reach System 7348 in thirty-seven point three five eight hours at maximum warp," Spock said.

"So we can be there more than two days before the Klingons?" Kirk asked.

Spock nodded.

"Any other thoughts?" Kirk asked, scanning the room. Giotto, Uhura, Farrell, and Sulu had been silent, but their faces told Kirk that they were as worried as he was himself.

"In my medical opinion, we're walking into serious trouble," McCoy groused.

"I concur with the doctor," Spock said.

If McCoy and Spock were in agreement that the situation was serious, it was definitely dire.

Kirk kept his own expression neutral. "Then caution will be the order of the day," he said.

"We'll need more than caution, Jim. We're going to need a good deal of luck," McCoy said.

"Then luck is so ordered. Dismissed," Kirk said.

By chewing quickly, Fuller managed to finish his food while Ensign Parmet was speaking.

"But the Klingons had complete control of the ship. What made you think—"

"Excuse me," a voice said from Fuller's right. He turned to see Lieutenant Parrish looking down at him. He knew what she wanted. Indeed, he had been prepared for this conversation. It wouldn't even be the most difficult one ahead of him.

Parrish directed her eyes at Parmet and said, "I need a word with Mister Fuller."

"Yes, sir," Parmet replied, getting up from the table and grabbing his tray.

Parrish took his seat and said, "Mister Fuller."

Fuller noticed that she seemed impossibly young. She was attractive, though she had cut her dark hair short to try to hide that. There was a set to her jaw that told Fuller she had seen a few things in the service already. And the no-nonsense way she carried herself told him that she was cut out for leadership. She would have a future in Starfleet if she wanted it, and if she survived long enough to see it.

"Lieutenant Parrish," Fuller said.

"Mister Fuller," she said, "I have something to discuss with you."

Fuller steeled himself. He knew what was coming.

Parrish continued, "A few months ago there was an incident aboard ship, and the officer in charge of teaching Federation history to new officers was dismissed."

Fuller wondered where this was going. "Benjamin Finney," he said.

"You know the case?"

"I knew the man, and I followed the case." Fuller had made a point of reading all reports that involved the *Enterprise* since his son was posted on board. The habit had continued even after his son's death. He had been sorry to hear about Finney. They had served together on the *U.S.S. Republic*. He was a good man. *Had been* a good man. They had seen a few things together. Fuller surmised that Finney had changed after their experiences on the *Republic*, but he had never guessed how much.

Finney was still in custody now, and Fuller made a mental note to visit him when he was released. Then he realized how unlikely it was that he would be able to do that, given what would probably happen in the next few weeks.

"The *Enterprise* needs a new Federation history instructor, and according to your records you are more than qualified," Parrish said.

That was a surprise. She hadn't questioned his motives for being here or expressed surprise at his taking a position beneath his station, as it were. Still, he didn't like where this was going.

"I'd rather not," he said.

"Why?" she asked seriously.

"I'm here to serve because I see what's happening out there. I made a conscious choice to forgo a leadership role in the service after my reenlistment. I would like to remain a simple grunt for the foreseeable future." He let out a breath; he had used some of his prepared speech after all.

"I understand and appreciate that," Parrish said. "I've seen your record, and I know who you are and what you've done. The ship is lucky to have you in any capacity, and I am very fortunate to have you in my squad. However, since you've limited yourself to the life of a simple grunt, you've also left yourself with absolutely no say about your assignments. You're required to follow the orders of your superiors, and I just gave you one. Your first duty on board this ship will be to report to the multipurpose room at 0700 to begin your class. You will find the current curriculum on the computer terminal in your quarters." After she finished speaking, she merely looked at him expectantly.

It wasn't what he had wanted, but as she so plainly put it, he had no choice. "Yes, sir," he said simply.

Parrish nodded as if she had expected no less. Then her face softened and she looked uncomfortable for a moment, as if she were looking for the right words. From what Fuller had seen, he did not think that was something that happened to her often.

After a moment she said, "I served with your son."

"Oh," was all Fuller could say, taken by surprise for

the second time today by this woman. Of course, he shouldn't have been surprised—no doubt there would be quite a few people on board who had known Sam well.

She spoke quickly. "I just wanted to tell you that he was one of the best and bravest men I ever knew. I served with him quite a bit in his last weeks. We fought together, and I wouldn't be here if it weren't for him. I just wanted you to know that and to thank you for, well, for him."

Something came loose inside Fuller and for a moment he knew it showed on his face. He locked it back down—locked Sam back down. He nodded, and when he could trust his own voice he said, "Thank you."

"There are a few of us, a few survivors from Sam's last missions, who would like to talk with you a bit when it's possible, tell you a few things about what it was like serving with him."

Fully in control now, Fuller nodded and said, "Of course. I would appreciate that."

As Parrish stood up, she put her commanding officer face back on, and nodded at him.

"Sir," he said. Parrish left the dining room. It was several minutes before Fuller realized that he had been sitting and staring across the room for some time. He shook off his haze and got up to dispose of his tray.

Fuller headed back to his quarters and saw that Parmet was there. Fuller had no doubt that the young man had been waiting for him. Time and duty permitting, most new officers on their first posting on a starship would be exploring the ship. There was something else going on here.

Parmet got up as soon as Fuller entered the quarters and said, "Sir."

Fuller lifted one hand and said, "You don't need to stand when I enter the room, we're just roommates. And for the tenth time, don't call me sir."

"Yes, si—" Parmet stopped himself, then shrugged and shot Fuller an embarrassed smile.

Fuller headed straight for his computer terminal. He had barely an hour before he had to assemble for orientation and the official tour of the ship that would be conducted by Parrish. He would have little time to prepare for his class tomorrow and would need to take a look at the curriculum before the morning. Of course, he would do most of that tonight. Under normal circumstances that would have cost him sleep, but he had been doing precious little of that lately.

"Is there anything—" Parmet began.

"No," Fuller said before he could finish. "I've got to prepare for tomorrow."

Fuller was grateful that Parmet didn't ask any questions. He simply nodded and pulled a book off his shelf. It was odd enough to see someone reading a real, paper book that Fuller almost asked the young man about it. But he stopped himself. He had very little time as it was, and he didn't want to get into a long conversation with Parmet, especially since Parmet was likely to ask questions that Fuller didn't especially want to answer.

As it was, he only had a few minutes before the door beeped.

"Come," Parmet said, getting up. Fuller turned to the door to see it open just as his roommate reached it. James Kirk stood in the doorway. Fuller could hear Parmet's deep intake of breath.

Fuller stood up also as Kirk said, "Ensign . . . Parmet, is it?"

The young man was silent for a few seconds. Fuller understood why. A ship's commander—or any of the command crew, for that matter—virtually never visited a low-ranking crew member in his or her own quarters.

"Ensign," Kirk prodded, his voice patient but firm.

Parmet seemed to wake suddenly from his daze. He took one step back and said, "Captain, sir, please come in." Kirk nodded and stepped inside.

"Captain," Fuller said, nodding.

Kirk turned to Parmet and said, "Ensign, give me a few minutes alone with Mister Fuller, please."

"Yes, sir," Parmet said, stepping toward the door, which opened obediently for him. Parmet shot a quick look over his shoulder at Fuller as he left the room. The look showed both admiration that the captain had come to see Fuller personally and concern about what that might mean for him. Fuller knew that the admiration was unwarranted, but he appreciated the concern, which he knew was definitely warranted.

As soon as Parmet was gone, Kirk gave Fuller a warm smile and extended his hand, which Fuller shook. "I'm here off the record, Michael. I just wanted to tell you how sorry I was about Sam."

"Thank you," Fuller said. Despite the fact that he had rehearsed this conversation, he found his voice surprisingly tight. He had prepared himself for the words, but not the sincere anguish in Jim Kirk's eyes. Fuller steeled himself. He could not afford any mistakes now.

"I can't brief you yet on his last missions, but I can tell you that a number of people, both Starfleet personnel and civilians, are alive today because of him. He was . . ." For a moment, Kirk was at a loss for words, something Fuller had rarely seen in the man, even when the captain was a fresh-faced young officer on the *Republic*.

Fuller came to the captain's rescue. "I know what my son was, but thank you. Lieutenant Parrish already talked to me a little."

Kirk leaned against the edge of the desk. Fuller leaned back against his own bed. "I planned on seeing you on Earth at the end of the *Enterprise*'s mission. I'm glad to see you, Michael, but under the circumstances I have to ask you about your state of mind and intentions."

"Getting the business out of the way?"

Kirk smiled grimly and said, "I do my most difficult and uncomfortable tasks first. Something I picked up from one of my teachers."

"I presume you've read my psych report."

Kirk nodded. "And so has my chief medical officer, but I'm not concerned about the findings of the report, which were fine, or you wouldn't be here. As we both know, psych reports are not foolproof."

Was that a reference to Ben Finney? Fuller wondered.

If it was, Kirk didn't pursue it. "I'm concerned that you might be a danger to this crew, this ship, or yourself. You just lost your son, Michael." Kirk was direct as usual. And the comment was a fair one.

"Captain, anyone can see from the civilian press what's going on. The Federation will be at war with the Klingon Empire in a very short time. I'm out here to contribute in any way I can. We both know that there is a real chance that the Federation will not survive the conflict. I intend to have something to say about that."

109

"You know how Sam died," Kirk said, making it a statement and not a question.

Fuller nodded. "I know that he was probably killed in a conflict with Klingons or their agents."

"And you realize that there is no room on this ship for personal vendettas."

"Captain . . . Jim . . . my son died for something. He died upholding his oath and the values of the Federation. I only want to make sure that those things still have meaning a year from now. I'm here to make sure that Sam's sacrifice wasn't for nothing."

Kirk held his gaze for a moment, and then nodded and said, "I'm glad you're here, Michael." The captain stood up, signaling that their meeting was drawing to a close.

"I was sorry to hear about the situation with Finney," Fuller offered.

"You heard?"

"When I was still on Earth. He was a good man."

"Yes, it's a real loss to the fleet," Kirk said. From the look on Kirk's face, Fuller could see that the loss was a very personal one as well. How could it not be? Kirk and Finney had a friendship that went back to the Academy. Finney had even named his daughter Jamie after James Kirk. Then, passed over for promotion, Finney had tried to destroy Kirk by framing him for Finney's own death.

"The Starfleet doctors will help him," Fuller said. Kirk nodded. The doctors *would* help him, but Ben Finney would never serve on a Starfleet ship of any kind again.

"It is good to see you, Michael," Kirk said, shaking his hand again.

"You too, sir."

Then Kirk was gone. When Fuller was alone in the

room, he felt a moment of relief as he realized that perhaps the hardest part of this mission was finished. He had dodged a phaser blast and would stay aboard the ship.

However, he felt his mind dwelling on Finney. He had been a good man, and a good officer. But somewhere along the way he had seen things that he couldn't forget, things that had changed him, affected his mind.

Fuller had served with both Finney and Kirk on the *Republic*. The three men had seen quite a bit there together. Was that where Finney had begun to have his problems? Had his future been sealed on the decks of that ship? And had Finney seen his breakdown coming, even then? Did anyone see that kind of thing coming? Could you feel your mind begin to crack, or did the cracks make that perception impossible?

Suddenly, Fuller found that he did not want to be alone. He left his quarters and decided to take a walk through the ship.

Lieutenant Kyle had to jog for a moment to keep up with Lieutenant Commander Scott.

Kyle caught something in the chief engineer's face, something he had only seen a few times—something possibly no one else on the engineering staff would recognize: Mister Scott was nervous.

On more than one occasion, Kyle had heard Scott angry or frustrated. He had also seen Scott remain cool under the worst kind of pressure—when the ship was in immediate danger and Scott held the lives of everyone on board in his hands.

Kyle knew that Scott's nervousness wasn't due to pressure, despite the growing rumors about the coming conflict with the Klingons. This was about a starbase engineering crew having the run of the *Enterprise*.

Of course, Scott had worked with base engineers in the past for repairs and refits. But time had always allowed him personally to review the specs for all upgrades and modifications, discuss them with his own staff, and then perform much of the work himself.

Someone who didn't know better might think that the chief engineer's hands-on approach was pointless and unnecessary, but Kyle knew from experience that work done or supervised by Scott always exceeded original specifications by a wide margin. It shouldn't have been true, but it was. Just as it shouldn't have been possible to detect by visual inspection that impulse reaction exhaust ports were out of alignment by a couple of hundredths of a percent, yet he had seen Scott do that as well.

"Did you find out the name of the base engineer, Mister Kyle?" Scott asked.

"Yes, sir," Kyle said. "Security was tight and they didn't want to transmit any information until we docked." Kyle understood the security protocols there. No open transmissions, only hard lines between the station and the ship through the moorings that now attached the *Enterprise* to Starbase 56. "It's Lieutenant Commander Steele, sir."

There was a flash of recognition in the chief engineer's eyes. "Toni Steele?" Scott said.

"Yes, sir," Kyle said. "Apparently she was just posted to the base from—"

"Earth," Scott finished for him. The chief engineer seemed genuinely surprised.

"Do you know her, sir?"

"By reputation only, lad. She rewrote the book on warp core tolerances. She's also on the board of directors for the next major starship refit and redesign project. And she was the head designer for the new spacedock out there. But what is she doing out here? She's one of our top engineers, and she's been at Command . . ." Scott let his voice trail off. His face went immediately thoughtful.

"What is it, Mister Scott?" Kyle asked.

"They moved her from Earth and from Starfleet Command because of security."

Security? Kyle took a moment to process the word. He couldn't believe it. "Do you think that Command isn't sure that Earth will be safe?" Kyle wondered if other important personnel were being spread throughout the Federation for security reasons.

"Just a precaution, I'm sure," Scott said, but his face said otherwise. "But there's real danger here, and we have important work to do." The two men reached the transporter room.

"Ensign," Scott acknowledged Jawer, standing behind the transporter console. The young man had been on the ship as a security officer for only a few months. He had been on Starbase 42 during the siege. Kyle had been there as well. He still spent far too many nights there . . . in his dreams.

Now Jawer was cross training with the engineering staff. He had talent, but he seemed young to Kyle, though Kyle knew he was just a few years older than the man.

"Someone from base engineering is standing by now," Jawer said.

Scott nodded, then gave the order: "Energize."

Kyle felt the familiar momentary disorientation of the transporter beam taking him, then he was looking out at a starbase transporter room. This one was a new design. The walls were a flat gray. At first, Kyle thought there was no one in the room, then he saw a protective barrier that stood in front of the transporter console. The barrier told him that the base transporter was one of the new units. It was supposed to be much more powerful than current transporter systems . . . and still in prototype.

"I thought these were still experimental," he said to Scott.

"Aye," Scott replied.

Then a woman stepped out from behind the console. She was of average height, with long, straight black hair that was just starting to gray. Kyle guessed that she was a few years older than Scott. The braiding on her uniform sleeves told Kyle that, like Scott, she was a lieutenant commander. Following her was a young lieutenant.

She stepped forward and extended her hand, "Mister Scott, I'm Lieutenant Commander Steele." Scott shook her hand. Then she gestured to the lieutenant standing next to her and said, "This is Lieutenant Anthony."

"And this is Lieutenant Kyle," Scott said.

"I read your paper on impulse tank variance," Steele said to Scott.

"Really?" Scott said, his face showing his surprise.

"Excellent work," Steele said.

Scott looked both pleased and . . . flustered. He was both the best practical and the best theoretical engineer that Kyle had ever seen. Yet, Kyle saw that there were people that even he looked up to.

Steele's face set, and Kyle realized that the pleasantries were over. "I've checked your records, and there is one thing we need to get straight, Mister Scott: I am in charge of this refit."

"Excuse me?" Scott said, and Kyle could see the color rise in his cheeks.

"I know how you usually work, and I've seen the results of your personal methods. However, time and security demands that we do things differently this time. You're going to have help here," she said.

"I have put together enough staff from *Enterprise* personnel," Scott said. "We can have the job completed in four days. Captain Kirk has approved the plan."

"I'm afraid that your plan just changed," Steele said. "My people have been training for this refit for weeks. We developed the system, and we know it better than you do. You and your staff will be able to contribute, but I will supervise and my people will be performing a good deal of the work."

Kyle knew that playing out in front of him was a common scenario for starship engineers dealing with Starfleet Command and starbase engineers. New systems were designed by research engineers, many of whom never served on a starship. They wrote detailed procedures and specifications and expected them to be followed.

Starship engineers, on the other hand, made their careers on their abilities to improvise their own repairs, upgrades, and improvements. And no one Kyle had ever seen was better at that than Montgomery Scott.

"Mister Scott, I don't expect you to like it, but I'm afraid that you have no choice," Steele said, her voice firm. "These orders come directly from Admiral Solow at Starfleet Command."

Scott was silent, and he had a set in his jaw that Kyle recognized. Kyle realized that this was going to be a long refit.

Fuller turned his attention from the airlock to the Klingons and back again. "Ten, nine, eight . . . ," the computer voice said. It was impossible. It had to be a bluff. They wouldn't do this. It wouldn't even serve a purpose.

The assembled crew members all seemed to have the same thought at the same time, and the room seemed ready to erupt. The Klingons held their disruptors on the assembled crew members in the cargo area. Their faces held a feral glee that told Fuller that they were not bluffing.

Fuller was the first to shout, "No!" By now you could see the officers in the airlock desperately trying to escape. Fuller rushed to the window and pounded on it. One of the young officers looked at him through the transparent aluminum.

There was motion around him. Someone was rushing one of the Klingons. There was weapons fire. Fuller couldn't turn around.

A voice behind him gave an order in Klingonese. Turning his head for a moment, he saw one of the Klingons hit the button that controlled the force field that was now protecting the officers from the vacuum of space. There was only a split second now. Fuller turned back to find the young officer, but he wasn't there.

Sam was in his place.

Fuller had time to pound the window once and scream his son's name. Then the force field flashed once and disappeared. Sam was pulled out of the ship in slow motion. He caught his father's eyes. Sam was fright-ened. Fuller's son was screaming as he flew into the void. Fuller couldn't hear him through the window, but he could see that his son was calling for him.

As his son tumbled out into space, Fuller screamed again and threw himself at the window.

Fuller woke with a start. For a moment he didn't recognize his quarters. They were much bigger than his room on the *Endeavour* . . . because, of course, this wasn't the *Endeavour.* He was on the *Enterprise.* It had been a dream, a nightmare.

Fuller found himself gasping for air, feeling the loss of his son wash over him again.

Someone was calling him.

"Sir . . . sir," the voice said. Then the light flashed on and a concerned Parmet was looking down at him. Fuller shook off the remnants of the dream and sat up in his bed. Now he was simply embarrassed. He had spent decades in the service. There had been nightmares almost since the beginning—the Battle of Donatu V had seen to that. And in the years after the battle there had been other worlds and other missions that had left their mark on him and had visited him in his darkest dreams.

Nevertheless, he had never woken up screaming while he served in Starfleet. *No, that didn't happen until Sam died,* he thought.

"Sir," Parmet said again.

Fuller raised his hand and mustered a thin smile that he knew was not very convincing. "I'm okay . . . I was just having a dream." With any luck Parmet would accept that and go to sleep. For a long moment, Parmet didn't say anything. He just looked Fuller over carefully. Fuller realized that Parmet was very young and very naive, but he was a long way from stupid.

Fuller managed a more natural smile and said, "I'm fine." Then he added, "Sometimes the old missions come back to you." That touched something in Parmet, and he nodded without saying anything. Then the ensign turned around and got back into his bunk.

Then Parmet spoke. "I'll be here if you need anything, sir."

"How many times do I have to tell you not to call me that, Parmet?"

"Sorry, sir," Parmet said with humor in his voice.

Fuller was relieved when Parmet shut his light off. Fuller knew it would be some time before he went to sleep, if he slept at all. The dream had been bad. He had dreamed of Donatu V many times in the past, but not recently, and not since Sam died. Since his son's death he had had many nightmares about him. They all ended the same: with Sam calling for him as he died. Mixing that with his memories of the Klingons at Donatu V was an inventive, if cruel, trick of his subconscious.

Donatu V had been his first real mission. It should have been his last. In a rational universe it would have been, but better men and women than he had somehow ensured that he lived to see another day. . . .

Chapter Seven

EARTH
2242

WHEN THE ANNOUNCEMENT CAME, Ensign Michael Fuller grabbed his canvas bag and headed for the designated waiting area of the shuttleport. It wouldn't be long now. He felt the excitement rising in his chest and had to work to keep himself from grinning.

"Maybe we'll use the transporter to get from the starbase to the ship," Andrews said next to him. Fuller nodded. He certainly hoped so. He had hoped they would transport directly to the ship from Earth, but they had been assigned shuttles instead. It made sense, of course, given the energy expense of matter transport; still he had hoped.

"We'll get a chance on the transporter soon enough," Fuller had said. He tried to keep his own disappointment out of his voice.

They had almost reached the waiting area when Andrews said, "Uh, Michael, I think you have a visitor." His tone was somewhere between teasing and sympathetic. Fuller was immediately alert as he turned to see where Andrews was gesturing.

Alison.

She was standing there looking at him with a worried expression on her face. She was wearing the yellow flower print dress that had been his favorite. Fuller had to try to keep his expression neutral when her eyes caught his. He understood why she was here, but her presence wouldn't make things any easier. In fact, it would only make things harder.

"I'll just be a minute," he said to Andrews, and headed to meet her. Fuller was struck by how good she looked. Her curly light brown hair was loose, spilling over her shoulders. She looked nervous but mustered a smile for him.

"Hello, Alison," he said, leaning down and kissing her on the cheek. It was an absurdly formal gesture, but it was the only thing he could think to do. "It's nice to see you, but you didn't have to come see me off." He was actually surprised that she had. They had ended things almost two weeks ago. Actually, he had ended them. And he had made sure that the break was complete. It had been hard for her, but he knew it was the kindest approach in the circumstances.

She hadn't offered to wait for him, but he knew that she had wanted him to ask her to. That wasn't going to happen. His father had been in Starfleet, and his parents' relationship had not survived it. As a result, he had seen far too little of his father while he was growing up.

If and when he had a family, he wanted things to be different.

"Come here," he said to her, gently pulling her to an empty corner of the waiting area. When they had a bit more privacy, he looked at her and without thinking said, "You look wonderful." She did, he realized, and she smelled good as well. Very good, actually.

There was an awkward silence, and then Fuller said, "I'm glad you came." It was all that he could think to say and it was kinder than the truth. She looked up at him as if she was just noticing him. She was more than nervous, he realized. Something was wrong.

"What is it?" he asked, almost relieved that there would be a point to this meeting, something other than the awkward interaction of two people who needed to be finished with one another. If there was something real going on, it also meant that she wasn't holding out hope for their future.

"I didn't come here to see you off, Michael," she said. Both her gaze and her voice were remarkably even. She had been upset when he ended things, but had kept her dignity, showing some of the strength that had attracted him to her in the first place.

"What's wrong?" he asked.

For a moment, she looked as if she didn't know how to proceed, then she said, "It's just that something has happened . . . and I thought you might want to know."

He felt the seconds ticking by. The call to board the shuttle would come soon. "What is it?" he asked, managing to keep the impatience out of his voice.

"Michael, I'm pregnant."

Starfleet had trained Fuller for every possible shipboard or planetside contingency. He had scored high marks in his response times, and he was cool under fire. Yet nothing in his training or personal experience had prepared him for this. He felt his throat getting tight, and the floor seemed to move under him.

Then a firm hand was around his upper arm and Alison said, "Michael." The sound of her voice brought him back to his senses.

He looked at her dumbly and said, "How did this hap—?" He didn't finish the question. In any case, the answer—had he needed one—was clear on her face.

"Michael, we don't have a lot of time," she said. Now that she had gotten the news out, she seemed perfectly calm. "I wasn't going to tell you. Maybe I shouldn't have. I certainly didn't mean to spring this on you now. In the end, I just thought you would want to know."

"Of course, I'm glad you told me," he said. Then he couldn't think of another thing to say. There were a hundred different thoughts screaming in his head. He wasn't able to give voice to a single one of them.

"I'm going to have the baby," Alison said.

Fuller felt his stomach turn. "Alison, I'm shipping out . . . *right now.* We talked about this. Starfleet is my future."

The public-address system called for his squad to assemble and prepare to board. Fuller felt sweat forming on his brow. "Alison, I can't give up . . ." was all he could say.

"I haven't asked you, have I? I haven't asked you for anything."

It was true, but the question had been on her face when he had ended things. It had been on her face when he had first seen her a few minutes ago in the assembly area. Yes, the question had been there, but she had been too proud to ask it.

What was she asking him now? Did she want to know if this new situation made a difference? It was just impossible.

"Fuller." Someone called his name. His squad was getting ready to depart. He felt more cold sweat on his forehead. And she was looking at him expectantly. What did she want?

"Alison, this is impossible. I'm shipping out right now. I can't have a family. We've talked about this."

Something in her eyes shut off. The change was both subtle and profound. "Of course," she said, her voice and expression amazingly neutral. "I know how you feel about having a family now, but you will be having a child."

"We will . . ." Fuller began. Then he saw something in her eyes and before he could stop himself he said, "Did you do this on purpose?"

"What?"

"To try to keep me here?"

Her eyes widened in hurt and anger. For a moment, she didn't speak. Then she said, "You arrogant . . ."

"I'm sorry."

His squad was called again on the loudspeaker, but he was lost in his own thoughts. Then he realized that Alison was speaking again. Her tone was cold. ". . . we *will* be having a baby."

For the tenth time in the last few minutes, that fact stunned him. He tried not to show it and said, "And I want to help in any way I can," he said, feeling embar-

123

rassed by the emptiness of his words, given the circumstances.

"Of course," she said.

Someone tugged at his arm. Andrews was there, looking embarrassed for him. "They're holding the shuttle, but we have to leave now."

Fuller nodded and said, "I'll be right there."

Andrews nodded and turned away to give them some privacy.

"You have to go," Alison said.

"Yes, but I'll contact you as soon as I can."

"Sure," she said. Then Fuller leaned down to kiss her again, but took one look at the stony expression on her face and pulled away without completing the gesture. As he pulled back, she said, "Good-bye, Michael," and turned away.

Andrews gave him a tug, "Come on. They're holding the shuttle, but the *Endeavour* can't wait. It's shipping out immediately." Fuller barely heard him. He felt light-headed, and his stomach was still in knots. "We've got our first mission," Andrews continued.

That got through.

"What is it?" Fuller asked.

"Resupply for a border colony. The Donatu system."

"Never heard of it."

"You'll never see it if we don't hurry," Andrews said, breaking into a jog. Fuller followed him, feeling guilty that his growing excitement over his first posting was already pushing away thoughts of Alison and her news.

Chapter Eight

"ENSIGN FULLER AND ENSIGN PARMET, report to the brief-ing room in thirty minutes," the voice said over the in-tercom. Fuller was immediately alert, roused from his twilight haze—you couldn't call it sleep. He checked the time: it was 0700. He would have to go directly from the briefing to his Federation history class. Fortunately, he had reviewed the material already and would be ready to teach without any more preparation.

Parmet stirred and woke slowly. He was still young and inexperienced enough to sleep heavily. That would change quickly. Anyone who spent more than a few months in security learned to sleep lightly and wake quickly.

"What is it?" Parmet asked.

"We've been summoned to the briefing room," Fuller replied.

"What's going on?"

Fuller shrugged. "We'll find out at 0730."

Fuller was out the door a few minutes later as Parmet was still getting into his uniform. In the last few weeks at home he had often forgotten to eat for as long as a day, but he knew he could not afford to do anything like that on board. Someone might notice. So he ate quickly and mechanically, though he noticed the onboard food had improved since he last served on a ship.

Fuller arrived at the briefing room to find Giotto and Parrish waiting for him. "Fuller," Giotto said, nodding and gesturing for him to take a seat. Fuller had never crossed paths with Giotto, though he knew of the man's reputation. Giotto had served with Captain Garth and had been part of the debacle that had ended Garth's Starfleet career.

Fuller took a seat and waited. Moments later, Parmet arrived, along with the others from his squad. As soon as everyone was seated, Giotto started speaking. "The captain has authorized me to brief you on two of the ship's recent missions that bear directly on the current situation between the Federation and the Klingon Empire."

Makes sense, Fuller realized. The ship's recent missions were highly classified. However, there were over four hundred people on board who had been there. The new recruits would have to be briefed, even if the information was far above their security clearance. Fuller was instantly hyperalert. He realized that he was going to get some of the answers he had been looking for in the next few minutes.

Giotto pointed to the viewscreen that showed an image of a planetary system. A stardate appeared on top. "Several weeks ago, the *Enterprise* responded to a distress call from an unsanctioned colony in System 1324, where a small group of Anti-Federation League squatters had settled. Three security squads were dispatched and came under fire from a group of Orions. At the same time, Orion vessels engaged the *Enterprise.* There were some heavy losses among the security personnel, and the ship suffered considerable damage. However, almost all of the colonists were rescued and the attacking Orion vessels were destroyed. Remarkably, the second planet of System 1324, which suffered the attack, did not have any strategic importance or resources of any significant value."

Some of those details Fuller already knew, but that last piece of information caught his interest. Why take on a starship if there was nothing to gain? The answer started to formulate in his head even as Giotto spoke the words. "We had reason to believe that the *Enterprise's* capabilities as well as the weapons and tactics of Starfleet security were being tested by the Orions. Since that information would be of little use to the Orions, we think they were working for another government. Now, given the current political climate, you might be tempted to jump to the conclusion that the Orions were working for the Klingons, but I can tell you that we have no conclusive evidence that this was the case. Personally, however, I have no doubt that that is exactly what happened, because a short time later the *Enterprise* was sent to investigate illegal Orion mining activity on the third planet of System 7348. We found a large core-mining operation that threatened to destroy the planet, as well as an indigenous group of intelligent humanoids who were genetically identical to Klingons. The *Enterprise* shut down the mine and prevented the Orion fail-safe system from destroying the planet."

Giotto paused for just a moment and said, "On that planet, we found conclusive evidence that the Orions were operating the mine under Klingon supervision to provide dilithium for the Klingon Empire's military buildup."

Everyone in the room seemed to hold their collective breath at that revelation. Parmet was the first to speak, "But you said the indigenous people on the planet were genetic Klingons. Yet the mining operation threatened the entire planet?"

"No," Giotto said, "the operation did not just threaten the planet. It would have *definitely* destroyed the planet and all beings on the surface if it had been allowed to continue." There was silence again as the new recruits processed that.

Fuller had fought Klingons and found them ruthless in their treatment of humans in battle. He had also studied their history to the extent that you could by looking at Federation and Starfleet records. It was both brutal and violent. Even so, to destroy a planet full of their own people to gain some dilithium . . .

Klingons, he thought. Like the ones who had killed Sam.

But his son had not died on either of those missions—the dates were wrong—though Sam had probably served on one or both of them. Then the image on the viewscreen changed again, showing a starbase that

Fuller recognized. The date was what really struck him. It would have been right about the time Sam died. "Then there was an incident on Starbase 42, which had been set for decommissioning until a significant amount of dilithium was found in the core of the planet it was orbiting. Due to a significant security breach, the Klingons had apparently learned of a secret program to extract the dilithium. Presumably, in an effort to replace the supply lost during the incident at System 7348, the Klingons attacked the starbase and tried to take the dilithium from the planet. Through the combined efforts of the *Enterprise* and the starbase personnel, the Klingons were repelled, but there were heavy losses."

Heavy losses . . .

The words echoed in Fuller's head. He had been on many missions where his ship had suffered heavy losses. He knew what the words meant in both abstract and all too real terms. Yet those same words seemed shallow and empty now. For a moment he wanted to get up and scream. Sam wasn't "heavy losses." Sam was his son, at one time his little boy. He had been brave and good and then he had been murdered by Klingons in their lust to attack, to take, to rule.

Using all of his will, Fuller kept himself perfectly still, carefully controlling his breathing and every muscle in his face.

Giotto kept speaking, his words fading out for a moment, unable to compete with the roar in Fuller's head. ". . . further details are now available to you on your personal computer terminals. You are cleared to access relevant logs and computer records."

These were records that Fuller was now sure would

show that his son had died defending Starbase 42 from Klingon animals. What had Sam's sacrifice bought them?

Fuller knew the answer to that: It had bought the Federation and Starfleet a few extra weeks to prepare for the coming Klingon onslaught. The *Enterprise* had kept precious dilithium from the Klingons twice, no doubt forcing them to delay and change plans.

Sam had given them all a chance, an opportunity to live that was paid for with his own blood. He had also given his father a chance to see justice done, to give his son's life and death more meaning, to see that the sacrifice was not wasted. His son had given him an opportunity to atone for his own failures as a father and a man, a final chance to redeem himself.

Fuller vowed not to waste it.

"Unacceptable," Scott said.

Kyle could see that Scott was angry. His jaw was set and his eyes were blazing as he looked at the parts strewn around them in the phaser control room.

"Some of these components weren't in the specifications I received." Scott's voice was tight. Kyle instinctively stepped closer to Scott and saw that Steele's aide, Lieutenant Anthony, did the same with his superior.

When angry, Scott was very intimidating to both his staff and anyone who happened to be in the area. Lieutenant Commander Steele, however, was not intimidated. She leaned toward him and said, "There are some late additions, but we've run simulations on the entire system. They check out."

"Simulations?" Scott bellowed. "This is not a lab,

lass—a starship is the real thing. Mistakes get people killed. If something fails, people die—and there's no reset button to rerun the simulation. Out there systems have to work, every time."

"And every one of those systems was designed in a lab and refined in computer simulations," Steele countered. Kyle noted that her southern accent became more pronounced when she was angry. Similarly, so did the chief engineer's Scottish accent.

"And then it's tested and retested in the *field* before the final specifications are written," Scott said, his voice rising another notch. By now, all work had stopped as the combined group of starbase and *Enterprise* engineers did their best not to look at their two leaders.

"Specifications? Don't throw specs at me. Correct me if I'm wrong, but you are the man who cold-started your warp engines, yes?"

For a moment, Scott was at a loss for words. Then he recovered. "That was a different situation, we had no choice but to try it or burn up in an atmosphere."

Steele's face softened. "And we have no choice here. We need this new phaser system, and we both know why." She took a breath and added, "You starship engineers love improvisation—as long as it's yours."

Kyle saw that that one had hit home, and Scott was silent for a long moment. Finally, he said, "We do what we have to do, and we're right because we have to be. And the upgrades we make in the field often work better than the stuff you dream up in your labs."

Now it was Steele's turn to be silent. It was true. Many of the important advances made in engineering were made on the fly by starship chief engineers. The cold-start technique for warp engines was only one example.

The room went completely silent as the two engineers stared at each other. Then, as if by unspoken communication, they both softened, and Kyle could feel the tension in the room dissipate like the final moments of an ion storm.

To Kyle's surprise, Steele smiled and said, "Then, once it's installed, it will be up to you and your people to make sure that the new design works, however flawed it may be."

Scott smiled grimly at that and said, "Aye."

Suddenly, the confrontation was over and Steele walked over to the control panel to talk to one of her staff. At the same time, Scott turned to him and said, "If I didn't know better, I would have said it was impossible for all this to fit."

Kyle noted that the chief engineer's voice was even, as if he hadn't been nearly shouting a moment before. It was typical of his commanding officer; he was quick to anger and quick to calm down again.

Shaking his head, Kyle looked at the components strewn about the phaser control room. There were more components in the corridor. It wouldn't all fit in the space they had. Logic told him that they would need a bigger ship for the new phaser bank system, but the blueprints on the computer terminal viewer told him it would work on the *Enterprise*.

"Even if it works, we'll be giving up a lot of flexibility in the system," Kyle said. He knew that it was one of the trade-offs that was bothering Scott. The phaser banks had more energy within a fairly narrow frequency range—the frequency range that would be most effective against Klingon shields. The new phasers would be very effective against Klingons, though less effective against other threats. Of course, the Klingons were the only major threat on the horizon at the moment.

"Aye," Scott replied. "But the power gain is something." It took a lot for Scott to admit that, Kyle knew. The new system did manage a huge increase in phaser power and was a good piece of engineering—if it worked. At its heart was a power shunting system that would draw phaser power from other systems on the ship.

Steele approached and said, "We're looking at war, gentlemen. It is serious business, but if we come through this all right, we'll be able to apply the energy across the whole spectrum. Imagine what that power would do against an asteroid threatening a colony. Now imagine the whole system drawing power from the warp engines."

"What?" Scott asked.

"It's the future, gentlemen. Let's get to work and I'll tell you all about it," Steele replied, giving him a quick smile.

Kyle grabbed his tools and started on the cooling system console in front of him. The new system really was incredible, a miracle of miniaturization and layout, packing a remarkable amount of equipment into the available space.

"Commander Steele is very good," Kyle said to her aide.

"No, she's not, she's magic," Anthony said, his voice and expression neutral. "The great ones always are."

133

Kyle nodded. It was as good a description of Mister Scott's abilities as he had ever heard.

Fuller was the first to arrive. The others came moments later. Once the squad was assembled, Lieutenant Parrish said, "There will be no shore leave on the starbase." There were groans of complaint that echoed in the ship's gymnasium.

Finally, one of them spoke. "Where does that order come from?"

"From me," Parrish said. The room was deadly quiet after that. "I may have very little time left with you." Parrish had told her squad about her pregnancy. It was unusual—unheard of, actually. The father had been part of her squad and they had both served under Sam. In fact, the father of Parrish's child had died with Sam on Starbase 42. There was a strange look in Parrish's eyes when she talked about it. Fuller had the feeling there was more to the story, but he wasn't going to ask.

Taking an appraising look at Parrish, Fuller saw that she was not yet showing, but he knew it wouldn't be long. "In the time I have left I am going to try to give you the benefit of what I have learned in my time in Starfleet. You know what you will likely be facing. And if you come face-to-face with a Klingon warrior, you will be glad you gave up a little off-duty time to learn a few things that might save your life. Come with me." She led them to the matted area in the rear of the gym.

Fuller's eyes went immediately to the equipment rack, and his blood went cold. Instead of the regular equipment, there were Klingon weapons, blades of different kinds that Fuller recognized. In fact, though it had been more than twenty-five years since he had last seen them, he found that he remembered those weapons very well.

A chill ran down Fuller's spine. For a moment he found it hard to breathe. Then he sensed movement nearby and looked to one side to see that Ensign Parmet had taken a step toward him and was watching him closely. Fuller cleared his throat and smiled once at the younger man. Then he turned his attention forward again.

"In close fighting situations—say, on board a starship or inside a starbase—Klingons favor bladed hand weapons. The obvious advantage blades provide is that they present a far smaller risk of damage to the hull of a ship that might lead to decompression. Hand weapons have allowed Klingons to take ships virtually intact. Now, I know you have all had Starfleet's hand-to-hand fighting training, which includes techniques to use against blades. Think of this as an extension course that will deal with a few things I have learned about Klingons. I was able to find out a little from the Starfleet database. We also have among us a veteran of a battle with a Klingon boarding party, Michael Fuller."

Suddenly, all eyes were on Fuller. He kept his face neutral and simply nodded. Looking directly at him, Parrish said, "Mister Fuller, much of what I found in the Starfleet training database came from you. Please show us what you know, and also the defenses you developed."

Without hesitation, Fuller stepped forward. He headed for the equipment rack and picked out the largest blade. It was a heavy, two-sided blade shaped like a semicircle. It actually looked like two blades stuck together with one larger, outer edge and one smaller, inner edge. The dual-bladed design gave the weapon four points, which Fuller knew from experience were very deadly. There were three evenly spaced grips on the outer edge. Fuller used two of them to pick up the weapon.

"This is a *bat'leth*," he said, "a Klingon weapon that is widely used. It holds great cultural significance, with weapons staying in Klingon families for generations." *Some weapons kill hundreds of beings over decades,* he thought but did not say.

Testing the weapon, he was surprised to see that whoever had made the mock-up had kept the weapon's heft. He had handled a number of Starfleet-made ones in which lighter alloys had been substituted for the Klingon metal. The result was never the same. Part of what made the weapon deadly was its mass, which helped make its blows more powerful.

He ran the weapon through a few movements and found that it was also very well balanced, again better than the other simulations he had seen. It was almost as good as the *bat'leth*s created by Klingon weaponsmiths and by far the best human-made representation he had seen. Of course, there were some overt differences. The blades were left dull, not razor-sharp like the ones on Klingon-made weapons. And the four killing points were covered with small squares of padding.

Still, it came very close to an authentic Klingon *bat'leth*. He had felt the real thing once many years ago. And while he knew there was a limited market for such artifacts in the Federation, he had been glad to put the weapon down and never touch one again. He much preferred the Starfleet simulations, which had never tasted blood and did not carry the stench of death.

"It's good," he said to Parrish, who had rejoined the squad and was watching him.

"Courtesy of the engineering department," she said.

"I need a volunteer," Fuller said. Parrish immediately stepped forward. Fuller nodded, but he was a little taken aback. He had no problem serving under a pregnant woman, but he had an instinctive aversion to swinging a weapon at one—even a weapon that had been made safer by Starfleet engineers. *Well, I know for a fact that the Klingons won't be so squeamish,* he thought.

Swinging the weapon in a quick arc, he watched Parrish roll under it against the motion of its movement. She came up on his now unprotected side and immediately threw a quick punch at him, pulling the blow at the last moment so it made only glancing contact with his ribs.

He turned to her in surprise, and she gave him a tight smile. He addressed the rest of the squad. "That was an example of an important concept when using hand techniques against a *bat'leth*. The weapon is heavy, even for a strong person. By ducking counter to the movement of the blade, Lieutenant Parrish was able to come up on my unprotected side before I could redirect the weapon. That will be a good place to start—why don't you each try it in turn."

Parmet was the next to step up. Fuller was immediately concerned. Parmet had struggled through his physical training. Still, the Klingons would make no allowances, so he did not. The ensign eventually rolled successfully under the blade, but was not able to land a blow himself before Fuller brought the blade back around.

Quickly, Fuller repeated the movement with the four

137

other members of the squad. Then he showed them a foot sweep movement, again with Parrish. He brought the blade down in a low arc, made contact with her lower calf and brought her to the ground. In an effective but ungainly movement, she rolled out of the way before he could bring the blade down on her while she was on the ground.

"Good," he said. Then he turned back to the squad. "The last place you want to be when you're facing a Klingon with a *bat'leth* is on the ground. Those fights tend to end very quickly. If you do find yourself there, get as far away from your opponent as possible. Then get up and, if possible, run. If that's not possible, we'll talk about some ways to improvise counterattacks."

Parrish got up, and he could see that her face was flushed—flushed and healthy looking. He realized she had had some additional training to go with plenty of natural ability. If not for the baby, she would have a good career in security. *But probably not a long one,* his mind supplied.

She was genuinely attractive, Fuller realized, and more so now that she was . . . glowing. Part of the pregnancy, he surmised. He had noticed that she was usually a little green around the gills first thing in the morning and looked better later in the day. *Another part of the pregnancy.*

He had missed almost all of Alison's pregnancy. Alison had been rounder, softer than Parrish. Had she looked sick in the mornings? Did the same glow come later in the day?

He thought that would have been something to see.

Chapter Nine

U.S.S. ENDEAVOUR
2242

FULLER STARED AT the viewscreen for a long time. *The most difficult tasks first,* he thought.

"Dear Alison," he said into the microphone. "I have been thinking about you a lot as we begin our mission on the *Endeavour.* Life on board ship keeps me busy, but I have been thinking about you a lot." Fuller realized that he had already said that. No matter, if he didn't continue, he didn't know how long it would be before he started again.

"I wish things had been different for us. I wish they had ended differently, but I made a commitment to Starfleet and I need to see it through to the end of my enlistment. I don't really have a choice in the matter." There it was, the lie. He could go see his section chief

139

right now. They would talk, then they would meet with Captain Shannon. In a few months, Fuller would be back on Earth. And if he chose, he could even remain in Starfleet, with a posting somewhere at headquarters. It would not be difficult, but Fuller knew he would not do it—because the *Endeavour* was what he wanted. And he wasn't prepared to give that up, even for Alison, even for the baby that would come in nine months no matter what he did.

"I meant what I said. I want to help you as much as possible. I want to be as involved as I can." *Finally a truth, but how involved will I be when I am rarely less than dozens of light-years away?* "I hope you're well, and I'll contact you again soon. Recording off."

He stared at the blank screen again. The door behind him opened and he heard Andrews's footsteps. He looked down at the computer terminal and said. "Computer, delete message."

"Did you just delete the message you've been working on for an hour?" Andrews asked.

Fuller wished he had a little more privacy. He shared the room with five other people. Because the ship ran three shifts, there were usually only two in the room at any one time. Through luck, he and Andrews had pulled alpha shift.

The last thing he wanted to do was explain his situation to anyone, even Andrews. "I was just sending Alison a message," he said.

"Not a very good one, apparently," Andrews said.

"Well . . ."

"No need to explain. I understand everything, and I have some advice for you: make the break clean and permanent. Don't torture yourself, or Alison. You know there's no room in this life for relationships, particularly not with people back home."

Fuller just nodded. It wasn't that simple, but he wasn't going to tell Andrews that now.

"Come on," Andrews said, "We're due in engineering. I'm sure that Commander Woods has something special planned for us."

Fuller got up and headed out the door, glad for a moment that Andrews was dropping the subject. In the engineering section, they were greeted by Lieutenant Commander Derek Woods, a tall, thin man in his thirties with thinning blond hair. Fuller had met him once during his orientation tour of the ship and a few times after that to receive assignments when Fuller was on loan to the engineering department. Woods was quiet, but he had a great reputation as an engineer. Fuller hoped to have a chance to get to know him.

Assignments like the one they had pulled today gave him the chance to work with almost all divisions of the ship. Though there were drills and training exercises, security work allowed officers free time to cross train in a number of different areas. He had an interest in engineering and thought it might be something he would want to pursue.

"Reporting for duty, sir," Fuller said.

"Good," the chief engineer said, and then he pointed at two hand scanners lying on a nearby console. "I need you to perform a manual warp coil inspection on the port and starboard nacelles when we come out of warp." Andrews made a sound like a cough next to him. Fuller made a point of keeping his gaze forward and his face expressionless. "Is there a problem?" Woods asked.

"Well, sir, we already pulled this duty . . . twice," Andrews said.

"And you did an excellent job, which is why I specifically requested you for this assignment," Woods said. "You do realize that these upgraded engines have less than one hundred light-years on them."

"Yes, sir," Andrews replied.

"And you do realize what would happen if there was a failure of one or more coils while the warp drive was engaged?"

"Yes, sir, but with all due respect, an intelligent ten-year-old could do that inspection," Andrews said.

A hint of humor appeared in Woods's eyes and he said, "That's the problem with intelligent ten-year-olds, they're never around when you need them. So I'm afraid that you two will have to do."

The chief engineer looked expectantly at Fuller and Andrews. "Yes, sir," Fuller said quickly before Andrews could say something else stupid. "Thank you, sir."

Fuller picked up his scanner as Andrews did the same. "And don't worry, gentlemen, you won't be new forever," Woods said as they headed across the engineering deck to the accessway that led to the starboard nacelle. The warning light above the hatch was on, which told Fuller that the ship was still at warp.

"Keep that up and we'll be doing this until we retire," Fuller said.

"But this is three times in two weeks," Andrews protested.

"And it'll be three more if you don't keep quiet."

Andrews snorted and then the warning light above

the hatch went off. Fuller hit the button and the hatch opened. He climbed inside and started up the access-way. The going was awkward. The space was cramped and the deck pitched forty-five degrees inside the support strut that connected the engineering hull to the nacelle. Fuller had to climb using the steps notched into the deck. It would have been much easier if he had both hands free, but one hand was holding the scanner.

As he climbed, Andrews muttered below him, "You know it's a triple redundant check. The nacelle's built-in sensors would pick up any problem. It's just for the engineers at headquarters, so they can pat themselves on the back." Then there was a banging sound and Andrews said, "Owww."

"All right down there?" Fuller asked.

Andrews ignored the question. "They didn't say anything about this at the recruiting office. Where are the strange phenomena, alien races, and exotic ports where no man . . . ?" Fuller didn't hear whatever Andrews said next because it was drowned out by the sound of the hatch at the top of the accessway opening in front of him.

Fuller climbed through and was glad to have his feet on a level deck again. A moment later, Andrews climbed through, still speaking. "You know, everyone else is going to be watching while we make orbit and we'll be stuck up here."

"Mmmm," Fuller said, adjusting his scanner. That thought had occurred to him. The *Endeavour* was making orbit for the first time since he boarded. He had hoped to see that. "I'll take this side," Fuller said, taking a position at the first coil. Dozens of warp coils sat in rows on each side of the nacelle's interior.

As he performed the first scan, he remembered his first time inside the nacelle. He remembered thinking, *This is where it happens, where the incredible energy that makes space travel possible is focused and used. Without this remarkable technology, a trip to the closest star would have taken decades, if not centuries. And if not for the first successful warp drive test, humans would not have met Vulcans when they did and the Federation would not exist as it does today.*

Fuller well remembered the feelings of pride and wonder. They had lasted him the entire shift as he scanned the coils for the first time. They had even lingered through the second time he performed the scans.

Now, as he scanned the warp coils for the third time, an hour into the job he had to work to remember that sense of wonder. Well, at least he and Andrews had made some progress. Looking at the remaining coils, he saw that they were about one-quarter of the way through the job . . . for *this* nacelle.

There was still the other one.

This job would take the whole shift. Well, he knew that Starfleet wouldn't be all excitement all the time. Perhaps this assignment would help him learn patience. *Or tolerance for tedium.*

"Ready for a break?" Andrews said, and for a moment Fuller thought he had spoken that last thought out loud.

"We can stop for lunch when we're through with this nacelle," Fuller said.

"Yes, but we'll miss the orbital approach."

Fuller thought about that for a moment. The first vessel he had been posted to was about to make orbit for the first time on his tour of duty. This *was* why he joined Starfleet.

"Okay, but we work through lunch," Fuller said.

"Sure," Andrews replied immediately.

When Fuller turned around, Andrews had already put his scanner down. He was smiling broadly. Fuller realized that there was a matching smile on his own face.

Andrews opened the hatch and started down the accessway. Fuller was right behind him. "We'll have to hurry," Fuller said.

A few moments later, both men were back on the engineering deck and heading for the door.

"Gentlemen," a voice sounded from behind them.

Fuller turned to see Woods looking at them. "Finish early?" Fuller felt his face flush.

"Well, sir . . . we . . ." Andrews began.

Woods studied them silently for a moment, then he said, "The best view for this approach is in the starboard mess, two levels down." For a moment, Fuller wasn't sure he had heard correctly. "You'd better hurry or you'll miss the show."

"Yes, sir," Fuller said, and headed out the door at a trot with Andrews beside him. Outside, they grabbed a turbolift and were in the corridor outside the dining room within seconds. Inside the dining room, there were a number of crew members standing in front of the three large windows. Fortunately, there was still room on the far right. Fuller and Andrews took their positions in silence.

The officers nearby nodded to them, but no one said a word. Fuller took one look out the window and immediately saw why. The ship was on its final approach to the planet, which seemed to be growing as he looked at it. Donatu V was positioned to the right of their field of view. Because they were looking out the starboard side of the ship, that meant the planet was "in front of" the ship's present course.

They were on the night side of the world, but the system's sun was peeking out from behind the dark planet. It was Fuller's first sunrise from space. And it was amazing.

The ship quickly swung around into orbital position. For a moment the sun disappeared behind Donatu V, which had grown huge from their perspective but remained dark. Then, with incredible speed, the planet was illuminated beneath them in a rush, as a line of daylight chased the darkness away. Of course, it was an illusion created by the speed of the ship as it slipped into orbit, but the effect was nonetheless dramatic.

In less than a minute, the blue-green world was brightly lit beneath them. Their orbit was high, placing them over the northern continents. Fuller could make out cloud cover, water, and land. There were no artificial structures visible from space, but that made sense, given the fact that the colony on the surface was less than ten years old.

There were also, he realized, no large orbital structures around the planet, at least none that he could see. No space stations, and no other vessels. Undoubtedly, there were satellites, but the ship's approach did not take them near enough to any to make them visible.

Overall, the view seemed to be of an untouched Earthlike planet, what Earth must have looked like before space travel, or even before industrialization. The effect was quite beautiful. Of course, the view would change in just a few short years. Donatu V was rich in resources. It was also the first colony world in this sector. In perhaps another ten years, it would be a major hub, with many more people on the surface and large orbiting facilities.

That was good. It was progress, and progress held a different kind of beauty.

Fuller didn't know how long he had stared out the window, but eventually he remembered that he and Andrews still had a lot of work to do. In fact, they wouldn't eat until it was done, and the job would take them the rest of their duty cycle.

Fuller turned to his friend and said, "Andrews, we have to be getting—"

"What's that?" Andrews said, pointing out the window.

Fuller looked where his friend was pointing and saw that there was something in orbit after all. Two somethings, in fact. Large satellites, he guessed. No, they were moving too fast, seeming to come from Donatu V's northern polar region. That was significant, he realized. It would make them difficult for sensors to see.

"There aren't supposed to be any large ships out here," Andrews said.

But these ships weren't just large, they were huge. He didn't recognize the type until the ships changed course slightly, showing him a three-quarter angle instead of the head-on view he had seen initially. His Starfleet training kicked in immediately, and he had no trouble identifying ships with that silhouette.

"Oh my God, they're Klingon," Fuller said. There were loud gasps from the other people in the room as they made the same identification. His first thought was that it had to be a mistake. The ships had to be off course, or in some kind of trouble.

Two of them in trouble? His mind replied. *Two Klingon* battle *cruisers?*

Then he saw that the ships were on an intercept course with the *Endeavour.* His mind did a quick calculation: they were almost in weapons range.

All of that took barely seconds. *Does the captain know? And where's the red alert?* he thought. Then he saw a telltale flash outside the window. The shields were being raised. A split second later, two things happened virtually simultaneously. Red alert sounded, and the nose of the lead Klingon vessel lit up.

What happened next happened very quickly. Fuller saw the torpedo emerge from the Klingon ship. He did another quick calculation, trying to figure the range, the speed of the torpedo, and the time it would take the *Endeavour's* shields to fully deploy. In the end, there was no time to finish the mental calculation.

And no need.

Fuller saw a flare as the torpedo tore through the ship's emerging shields and continued, unaffected, straight for the *Endeavour.* Fuller had an instant to think, *The ship is going to get hit.* Then he realized that the torpedo was heading straight for him and the others in the dining room. Instinctively, he started to duck. Before he could finish the movement, there was a blinding flash outside the window as the deck shook under his feet.

They've hit us, he thought. The torpedo had missed the dining room, but it had come close. In fact, a loud hiss of air told him that the dining room would not be safe for long. "Everybody out, we're decompressing," he said. Fuller could see that the bulkhead had buckled slightly near the ceiling. "Engineering," he said to Andrews, who nodded. Fuller scanned the room quickly to make sure that everyone was on their feet.

"Move!" he shouted, then he and Andrews headed for the door and were out in the corridor, which was filled with people racing for their stations. The turbolifts would be packed, if they were even working. Andrews turned and grabbed the nearest ladder and started climbing up. Fuller immediately smelled smoke.

Fuller passed the deck above him quickly. The smoke got thicker as he neared the engineering deck. And the smell wasn't just smoke. There was coolant in there and other things he couldn't identify but knew couldn't be good for the ship. They were in serious trouble.

Stepping onto the engineering deck, Fuller saw that the *Endeavour* was indeed in trouble. Emergency lighting made the deck dim, but Fuller could see well enough. Bulkheads and flooring were bent and twisted in a number of places. And power was flashing and arcing from open panels and conduits. There were at least four dead people on the deck, their bodies burned severely—and in one case beyond recognition.

He noticed then that an emergency bulkhead had closed off access to the port nacelle. Emergency bulkheads were made of thick alloys that were supposed to be nearly indestructible. This one was bent and battered, more than Fuller had thought possible. There was also a telltale hiss that told Fuller that the engineering deck was slowly decompressing.

There should have been chaos on the deck, but the uninjured members of the engineering staff were staffing their posts with a calm that Fuller would not have thought possible. He was surprised to see that his own mind was working with an analytical detachment that meant he would also be able to function.

"Oh my God . . . oh my God," Andrews said beside him, his voice cracking.

Fuller put a hand on his friend's shoulder and pulled him toward Woods, who was manning one of the stations with a female lieutenant whom Fuller didn't recognize. "Sir, reporting for duty. What can we do to help?"

Woods merely raised a hand to silence him.

"Michael, that can't be right," Andrews said, pointing to the viewscreen above the engineering station in front of them. Fuller looked up and saw a view of the rear of the ship from the point of view of the rear of the saucer section. The view clearly showed the starboard nacelle . . . and a gaping hole where the port nacelle should have been.

"It's gone," Fuller said. It was true, though it should have been impossible. "That's where the torpedo hit us." Fuller was surprised by the calm in his own voice.

We should have been inside that nacelle, he thought, feeling a surge of guilt. He and Andrews had left their post for a frivolous reason. *And that's the only reason we're alive.*

"But, Michael, if the nacelle's gone, how can the ship still be here?" Andrews said.

It was a good question. There were alarms going on at every functioning station on the deck. It was a miracle that the warp core had not immediately been breached. *No, not a miracle, it's people doing their jobs,* Fuller thought, watching Woods's hands work the panel in front of him.

"We have communications," the woman next to Woods said.

"Bridge to engineering. Status?" Captain Shannon's voice said, his tone calm.

"The port nacelle has been severed; we're minutes away from a warp core breach," Woods said, equally calmly.

"We're showing that the main energizer is still online."

"Yes, you'll have limited shields and weapons right until the end," Woods said. "I recommend you prepare to separate the main hull. I can buy you some time if a few of us stay with the equipment."

There was silence on the intercom and from everyone within earshot. Woods was proposing buying the ship a few more minutes by staying behind in the doomed engineering hull.

"Thank you, Commander, and thank your people," the captain's voice said. *"I'm authorizing you to trigger the saucer separation from your position. Give us as much time as you can to move everyone we can to the main hull."*

For a moment, Fuller couldn't believe his ears. Separating the saucer section from the engineering section was a desperate move, one a captain would make only when his ship was already dead.

Like we are . . .

"Yes, sir," Woods said evenly, then the deck underneath all of them shook as the ship took weapons fire from somewhere. Fuller was mildly surprised when nothing exploded.

No, that will come in five or six minutes, he realized. *And it* will *be* big.

"Derek . . . good work," the captain said. *"I want you to know that it's not over."*

"No, sir," Woods said.

"Bridge out."

Woods immediately turned to the crew behind him and said. "There are two Klingon battle cruisers out there and the warp core will breach in a few minutes. We can give the captain a few more minutes of power to keep up the fight if we continue our work here. A few more minutes or even seconds of power might mean the difference in this battle. I need a few of you to stay behind. Volunteers only."

There was a chorus of offers from everyone on the deck. Woods nodded and something moved on his face. "I want the injured out of here immediately."

There were a few protests from some of the barely standing and barely conscious crew members. "No argument," Woods said.

"What can we do, sir?" Andrews said.

Woods looked at Fuller and Andrews for a moment and said, "You can get the hell out of my engine room." He raised a hand to stop any protest. "You can't do any good here. The injured need help, and the captain will need all his security people in the main hull."

"Yes, sir," Fuller said.

Before they turned to go, Woods said, "Whatever happens, don't let the Klingons take you alive." Fuller nodded. He had heard stories, ones that he hadn't completely believed. Looking at Woods's face, he realized that all of those stories had been true.

Fuller took one look at the engineers at their posts and felt shamed by what they were about to do, because whether the captain managed a victory or not, it would be all over for these people in less than ten minutes. Nevertheless, they were calmly going about their work, sacrificing everything so that the rest of the crew would have a chance.

Another blast struck the ship and reminded Fuller just how thin the *Endeavour*'s chances were against two fully functional Klingon warships.

"All nonessential crew to the saucer section. Emergency saucer separation imminent," the communications officer's voice sounded through the intercom. There were two people lying on the ground, one man and one woman. Fuller had seen them around the ship but didn't know their names. The four ambulatory wounded hovered over them, not leaving.

"We've got them, get out of here," Fuller said. The four crew members looked unsure. They were clearly unwilling to leave their friends.

"Do it now," Andrews said, his voice booming. They immediately turned and headed for the door. Andrews quickly examined the unconscious man on the floor; he was severely burned on the right side of his body. Without hesitating, Andrews leaned down and put the man over his shoulder. Though the injured man was easily one hundred and eighty pounds, Andrews lifted him with little trouble.

Fuller saw that the woman who remained on the floor had a burn on her right leg. "I think they're both broken," she said, a trace of embarrassment in her voice as she pointed to her legs.

"It's okay, I'm Michael Fuller and I'm going to help you."

She nodded, clearly in serious pain and said, "Lieutenant Caruso, Eileen Caruso."

As gently as he could, he leaned down and picked her up. For a moment, he was glad that Andrews had lifted the man. Fuller didn't have his friend's bulk. Caruso was maybe one hundred and twenty-five pounds and felt light in his arms. She groaned in pain as Fuller put her in position over his shoulders.

Andrews had waited for him and was at the door when Fuller reached it. The large double doors opened—for which Fuller said a silent prayer of thanks—and he headed out into the corridor. Walking a few steps ahead, Andrews reached the turbolift first. He turned back and said, "It's out."

They continued forward. There was another lift far forward on the deck, where the engineering hull met the connecting dorsal that led to the main hull. If that lift was out, that meant they would have to take ladders. Fuller did not want to think about how they would do that with two injured people on their backs.

Andrews was still in the lead. Fuller saw him take one large hand and smack the turbolift control panel in frustration. There was no doubt, this one was out as well. Rushing ahead, Fuller said, "I'm going to have to put you down." Then he reached the ladder well next to the turbolift and put her down. As he moved, his mind kept track of the passing time.

Less than a minute had passed since they received their order to go from Woods. At best, they had maybe four minutes left. It wouldn't be enough for what he had planned, but he wasn't leaving anyone behind. He scrambled up the ladder and said to Andrews, "Lift him as high as you can, I'll pull him up."

Then he was sitting on the next deck and reaching down with both hands. Andrews was more than two meters tall, which put the injured man at about just under that off the ground now. With a little over three meters separating the decks, the man was just out of Fuller's reach.

Then he heard Andrews straining and saw him lift the man, who rose the precious centimeters up. Then Fuller was able to reach under his arms and pull. The engineer weighed just a bit more than Fuller himself, and for a moment he didn't know how he was going to perform the lift from a sitting position. Then he felt Andrews pushing from below.

The injured man rose and Fuller was able to pull him to the deck. His instinct was to check the man's pulse, but there was no time. Andrews was already lifting Caruso. Fuller grabbed her under the arms and lifted her as gently as he could. Unfortunately, there was no way to keep her legs from hitting the deck as he lifted. She groaned through gritted teeth. When she was lying on the deck, she breathed in large gasps.

Then Andrews was on the deck with them. Fuller looked into the ladder well to the next deck up. He shot Andrews a glance, and his friend merely nodded. They would make their best effort to get the two injured people up the three levels to the primary hull. They would almost certainly fail, but they would try and they would not leave anyone behind. Andrews picked up his man and Fuller headed for the ladder.

155

"Wait," a thin voice said behind him. Fuller looked at Caruso, who was gesturing to the turbolift door. "Try the lift," she said. Fuller nodded and raced for it. To his surprise it opened, and there was light inside. That meant there was power and that meant they had a chance. Caruso had just saved their lives.

The deck moved underneath his feet, telling him that the captain was using high-speed impulse maneuvers. Like much of what had happened since they had first been hit, it should have been impossible. He realized that he had not felt many weapons hits on the ship since that initial blast, and he understood why: the Klingons knew they had dealt the *Endeavour* a fatal blow and were just biding their time until the ship exploded.

Picking up Caruso, he headed into the lift. "Deck four," he said. The turbolift didn't move, so he hit a button on the panel. Immediately, the lift began moving up. It started up, went a few feet . . . and then stopped dead. For a moment, the small space went completely dark, then the dim emergency lights went on.

Andrews was frantically hitting the manual control panel. They were still in the dorsal that connected the two hulls of the ship. And in two minutes, maybe three, Woods would separate the circular main hull from the rest of the ship. Fuller, Andrews, and the two injured people would be stuck in the dorsal, which would still be attached to the engineering section. And then when the warp core went critical, they would all be dead.

As dead as those people in engineering, he thought. Fuller's mind rebelled against the thought, not because he was afraid of his own death but because he wanted to contribute something to this mess of a mission—something to justify some small part of the sacrifice that the engineering staff was making. Fuller couldn't do that trapped here until the final blast came. His only chance to make a difference was in the saucer section, which was less than twenty-five feet away, but in their current circumstance may as well have been in another galaxy.

Andrews was still working the controls to no effect. Fuller put a hand on his. They had done their best. He was pleased that his friend Andrews had done well. It was a pity, he thought. He would have liked to see what kind of officer Andrews became in the long run.

"It's okay, we're almost out of time," Fuller said.

"But, Michael . . ." Andrews said.

Fuller smiled at him and said, "You did everything you could."

Understanding crossed Andrews's face, then the beginning of acceptance. Fuller remembered something and winced.

"What is it?" Andrews said.

"I just realized that I never sent Alison that message," Fuller said. Then he shrugged.

Andrews put a hand on his shoulder. "I'm sure she knows how you feel."

Fuller shook his head. "No, I don't think so. When she came by the shuttleport it was to tell me that she's pregnant. We didn't part well."

Surprise and then sympathy showed on Andrews's face. He nodded and said, "I'm sorry, Michael." Then Andrews turned and pounded once on the wall of the lift.

Chapter Ten

**QO'NOS
2267**

THE AMOUNT THE KLINGON in front of Karel had requested would have represented more than half a year's pay as a junior weapons officer. Karel had haggled fiercely with his new and unsavory business partner, but he had disputed the amount only because accepting it too easily would have brought more attention to himself than was necessary. The fact was that he would have paid twice the amount.

"Half now," Karel said, "and half when the information is in my hands."

"Agreed," the Klingon said, handing him a data spike. "This contains the necessary programs to allow you to decrypt the transmissions I will send you."

Karel nodded. "You had better send that information."

The Klingon looked at once wounded and angry. "Do not insult my honor as you rob me of any reasonable fee."

Karel studied the small, nondescript Klingon in front of him. This was no warrior. He looked exactly like what he was, an information clerk. And yet the Klingon was right: Karel should not doubt another Klingon's honor unless that Klingon gave him reason to. Unfortunately, he had seen too much dishonor lately among his own people.

Interestingly, this Klingon had used the term "honor" casually. Was he a follower of Kahless? Could a follower of Kahless walk the path of honor while trading in secrets and stolen truths? Well, Kell had walked that path wearing the face of a human, so anything was possible. And if this Klingon found the truths that Karel sought, he would go a long way toward helping rid the empire of a great stain on its honor.

Nodding, Karel said, "You have my faith."

Then he turned and headed out of the dark alley that had been the location of their meeting. He took public transportation home, as he had taken it there. No one would be able to trace one of his family vehicles here if someone was watching.

Walking the last leg of his journey, he saw Dev'ghot rising in the distance. Even Karel's own guilt and shame over his brother's death could not dispel all the pleasure of that sight. Here, he felt closest to the spirits of his father and brother.

In the last few years, each time he saw the house, he wondered if that view would be the last. Had his brother had the same thought the last time he had seen the estate of the House of Gorkon?

Karel was still several minutes away when he felt the transporter beam take him. He had a second to look at Dev'ghot before it faded before his eyes only to be replaced by the interior of the transporter room of the *D'k Tahg*. He shot the transporter room operator a look and said, "Explain yourself."

The Klingon looked nervous. "Captain's orders, he wants you now. You did not have your communicator with you. I scanned your home until I found you."

That was fair enough. He had left his communicator behind so that no one could track his movements during his meeting. Now he saw that it had been a wise precaution. Still, he could not let the transporter operator know any of that, so he merely grunted at the Klingon and headed for the bridge.

There, he found the bridge crew assembled and Koloth studying reports. The captain was unhappy, that much was obvious.

"Captain," Karel said.

Koloth acknowledged his presence with a wave of his hand and then hit a series of buttons on his command chair. Then he stood and headed for the exit. "Come," he said to Karel. When they reached Koloth's quarters, the captain scowled openly and said, "We have an urgent mission, and we must set out in a few hours."

That caught Karel by surprise. They had been home for less than a day. The ship would not even have been completely refueled and resupplied. "An urgent mission, where?" Karel asked.

"I have not been told." Koloth was barely holding in his rage. "And I will not be told until we are under way."

That was not just unusual, it was unheard of. There

were a dozen problems that Karel could see immediately. He picked the most pressing. "We are still awaiting replacement warriors." The mission that had claimed Kell's life had claimed a lot of warriors as well. The humans had fought as well as Klingons in defense of their starbase. The High Council would not admit it, but it was the truth and Karel would not deny it.

"Oh, we will have additional crew in minutes," Koloth said. That was impossible. The captain and first officer always had time to carefully choose replacement fighters. Seeing the question on his face, Koloth didn't keep him waiting for an answer. "We will be transporting Councillor Duras. He has volunteered his own security forces to bring us up to full strength."

If it had not been Koloth speaking, Karel would not have believed it. He knew that members of the High Council often maintained large security forces of their own—and not unreasonably, considering how often they were attacked by political rivals. Yet those forces were not technically active warriors in the Defense Force. To put them into service on a ship like the *D'k Tahg* was unprecedented.

Koloth waved off Karel's next remarks. "I have protested, but our orders are clear. We do not have to like it, but we shall have to make the best of it."

Karel did not know of any tactful way to ask his next question, so he chose the direct route. "Captain, who will be in command of the *D'k Tahg* when the councillor is on board?"

Koloth produced what Karel could only describe as a disgusted smile. "The High Council has graciously allowed me to remain in command of the ship, but Duras will be in command of the mission."

Immediately, Karel saw the essential problem here. A ship could have only one commander; warriors could have only one leader. Under the guise of directing this secret mission, Duras could assume command at any time. And even if Koloth and the crew of the *D'k Tahg* resisted, Duras's security forces could back up the councillor's authority. Add to that the fact that Duras's mission was secret—something that made any Klingon of honor uncomfortable. Battle should be direct. A warrior who hid his true face was no warrior at all.

That was one of Kahless's teachings, one of his many gifts to the Klingon people. It was a lesson that Karel's brother Kell had learned on his mission among humans. Karel's blood called out a warning.

Koloth nodded as if he understood Karel's unspoken thoughts. "Make no mistake, we are in the nest of a Denebian slime devil."

"You have my blade, and the blades of the Klingons you command," Karel said, hoping he meant it.

Koloth smiled. "Good, if we are fortunate it may even be enough. Now, we must get ready to receive Councillor Duras and make final preparations to get under way."

Karel nodded. As first officer, he had much to do. He would have to speak to all of the department heads to make sure the ship was ready. He also made a mental note to have a special talk with Gash, the ship's *QaS DevwI'*, leader of the troops on board.

Karel had taken the big Klingon's eye in a dispute when he was under Gash's command in the port weapons room. At the same time he had somehow gained the *QaS DevwI*'s loyalty. Gash had fought at his side in the bloodbath that was the siege of Starbase 42. He trusted Gash now as much as he trusted any Klingon.

And he sensed that he and Koloth would need every advantage they had in the days to come.

Chapter Eleven

U.S.S. ENTERPRISE
STARBASE 56
2267

THE DRILL WAS OLDER than Fuller himself, and he suspected that it predated his own father's service in Starfleet. It was an intruder alert simulation. New recruits were given phasers that were rendered harmless and told there was an intruder in engineering. They had no idea that it was a drill, and so they rushed to the engine room where they found themselves facing a large creature dreamed up by the engineering staff. In this case, the "creature" was a technician in a suit designed to look like a large reptilian alien. The illusion was convincing only in dim emergency lighting.

Since Fuller had performed the drill many times as a security section chief, Parrish had arranged for him to be one of the first "casualties" when the squad reached engineering.

He had fallen to the creature as he climbed the staircase to the upper level of the engineering deck. From his position lying on the floor, he could safely and secretly watch the rest of the squad's performance. The emergency lights cast an eerie red glow in the engine room, but let him see clearly enough. As someone who had graded more of these exercises than he could count, he watched them with a professional eye. He saw that the squad remembered their training and were cautious.

Then they began the cat-and-mouse portion of the exercise that always came near the end. The creature dipped behind the large control panels and led the five remaining squad members on a chase. Parmet and one of the others made clean hits on the creature, but, of course, the phaser fire from the altered weapons had no effect.

Parmet surprised Fuller by immediately taking charge of the remainder of the squad. In a coordinated effort, they corralled the creature into a corner. Parmet quickly organized the others into a direct assault force, rushing the alien monster. Though Fuller knew it was only a drill, his heart rate went up and his breath came in short gasps.

However, Parmet did not know it was a drill as he led the assault on the creature. The five security officers all kept up fire and then, at the last instant, Parmet hurled himself at the monster. As he made contact, the lights went on and Parrish's voice rang out, "End simulation!"

Parmet hit the creature hard and drove it back into the wall. A moment later, an embarrassed Parmet was picking himself up off the ground and apologizing to the shaken technician who was removing the "head" from the costume.

By now, Fuller was on his feet and heading down the stairs. Parmet looked at him and gave him a smile that was both proud and embarrassed. "Nice work, Ensigns," Parrish said. "You dispatched our dragon in good time." Then she smiled at Parmet and said, "Mister Parmet, interesting choice of weapon at the end, but I'm not sure I would want to get into a hand-to-hand combat situation with a creature of that size who is resistant to phaser fire."

Parmet nodded, then he sought out Fuller, who approached the group. Though Fuller tried to return his roommate's smile, he found that he felt sick. The fact was that Parmet had performed very well. He had taken control of the situation and done all the right things to subdue a threat to his ship and squadmates. However, if the drill had been real, Parmet would probably not have survived the encounter.

Parmet had courage. Fuller had known plenty of officers with courage—their names now covered a wall at Starfleet Command.

Chapter Twelve

**U.S.S. ENDEAVOUR
DONATU SYSTEM
2242**

AS ANDREWS BANGED AGAIN on the turbolift wall, Fuller understood what he was thinking. He was angry that they were stuck here while good people in engineering were giving their lives to give the rest of the crew a chance.

"Get me to the control panel," Caruso said.

"What?" Fuller replied.

"The control panel, get me there if you want to live to see your baby," she replied.

Fuller turned and leaned over so that the lieutenant was facing the turbolift controls. It was awkward getting her into position because she was slung over his shoulder and was working upside down. Fuller had to bend his knees so that her hands could reach the controls.

She tugged once at the panel, trying to pry it open. Fuller freed one hand and reached down to help her, but she pulled at the panel with a strength that surprised him—and immediately drew blood on her fingers. Caruso ignored the cuts as her hands raced across the newly exposed wires and internal control panel.

"This might be rough," she said. "There's a chemical propellant under the lift that is activated in catastrophic emergency situations only."

Fuller knew that turbolifts could be used as lifeboats, but initiating the system would blast them through the outer hull of the ship and into the ship's deployed shields. The ride would be very unpleasant and very short.

"I'm going to turn on the system and then shut it off before we break the hull," she said, the strain of the effort and the pain clear in her voice. "It might even work."

Then Fuller watched her grab a bare wire and use it to make contact with a circuit board.

Nothing happened.

She grabbed another wire and repeated the procedure. At once, the deck seemed to rush at him and he had to struggle to keep to his feet. They were moving up. Before the movement had fully registered, Caruso pulled the wire to break the contact. Nothing happened.

Then, with amazing speed considering that she was seriously injured and working practically upside down, she reached into the control panel, grabbed a handful of wires, and pulled.

Immediately, their ascent stopped. But where were they? They were still inside the ship because the artificial gravity was still holding them to the deck. Had they cleared the dorsal? Were they in the saucer section yet? He had no doubt that they would find out very soon.

"I'm impressed, Lieutenant," Fuller said. He thought that Caruso was someone he would like to get to know if they survived this day.

Then the lift shook and Fuller found himself forced into the wall. Caruso cried out at the abuse of her broken legs. "That's it. We're separating," she said. There was a steady vibration in the floor, then another jolt. "That was the last of the explosive bolts."

Then the floor was still. They had either made it up to the saucer section or were still in the engineering section. If it was the latter, their fight would be all over in a few moments. Woods would have very little time before the warp core went critical—just enough for the main hull to get a safe distance away. That meant one minute, maybe two.

However, it was only seconds before he heard a noise outside the turbolift doors. Then he heard the screech of protesting metal as someone used clamps to force the doors open. Fuller found himself looking down at concerned faces and extended hands.

They had made it.

The turbolift had come to a stop a meter above the deck. Andrews put his injured man carefully down on the floor of the lift, jumped to the deck, and then passed the man to the medical personnel outside. Fuller did the same with Caruso, who gritted her teeth but was silent as they moved her. Then Fuller and Andrews jumped down and watched as Andrews's man was loaded onto a waiting stretcher.

"I have a pulse," one of the nurses said, and then raced the stretcher down the hall.

Two more nurses put Caruso on a stretcher. One of them leaned down and said, "We're going to get you right to sickbay."

"No. I need to see," she said, pointing to the observation room behind them. One of the nurses scanned her quickly and nodded, immediately understanding what she wanted and why.

Suddenly, Fuller realized he needed the same thing. "I'll take her," he said, as he and Andrews pushed the stretcher into the observation room. Since they had entered the saucer section at the very rear of the ship, they had a good view of the engineering hull as it seemed to float away from them. The damage was horrific, and seeing it through the window was much worse than seeing it on a monitor. The nacelle was gone, and there was a large black pitted hole where it had been attached to the hull.

Beyond the slowly shrinking engineering hull, Fuller saw the two Klingon ships in battle formation, waiting with a patient menace. Then the engineering hull started to move, pitching and yawing. He could see the exhaust of thrusters. Was Woods trying to move the ship? Why? With the warp drive down, the hull had no propulsion other than the maneuvering thrusters, since the impulse engines resided in the saucer section.

Again, the thrusters flared, and Fuller realized that they must have engaged as all systems began to fail. The misshapen hull shook.

Then the hull moved slightly. At first, Fuller thought that it was coming apart, then he saw that it was definitely moving, or more accurately, its position was being adjusted, though he couldn't fathom why. Thrusters wouldn't get them anywhere. What they should be doing now, he realized, was getting to the escape pods while they still had a few seconds. In the pods, they would be sitting ducks for the Klingons. It would not be much of a chance, but staying in the dying engineering hull had even worse short-term prospects.

Slowly, the hull began to spin. The movement might have been a product of the failure of various systems in the moments before the warp-core breach, but something told Fuller that that wasn't it. There was something oddly deliberate about the positioning of the hull before the spinning began. Then, in scant seconds, the spinning became too fast to follow, making the hull and its single nacelle a blur.

And then Fuller realized what was happening. For some reason, the chief engineer and his people had brought the warp core up to full power, or as near to it as the damaged systems would allow.

Fuller was no expert on warp field geometry, but he knew that the enormous energy of the two engines and their warp field coils were delicately bound and balanced between a ship's twin nacelles. When both nacelles were working, they pushed the ship's center of gravity—and the ship itself—forward at faster-than-light speeds. Turn one of those nacelles off—or blow it into space—and you had an uncontrolled warp field that became incredibly elongated as it drove the ship into a spin.

The rotational speed was incredible, yet Fuller had no doubt that the engineering hull's artificial gravity and inertial dampers were compensating. He was certain that Woods and his staff were very much alive at that moment.

He wondered what the Klingons were making of the odd movement of the dying hull. Because they didn't fire at the ship or move out of position, he guessed that they did not see the danger they were in.

Fuller did.

Under normal circumstances, a warp core breach on an *Icarus*-class vessel's main reactor would cause an incredible explosion and a subspace shock wave that would radiate in all directions. But Woods was creating circumstances here that were far from normal.

In a few moments, the elongated warp field would focus the energy of the blast along the plane of the hull's rotation. In this case, that plane of rotation was a direct line to the two Klingon ships. Clearly, someone in the main hull of the *Endeavour* knew what Woods was doing because he could feel a vibration in the deck that told him the saucer section was shifting position, taking it even farther from that plane of the engineering hull's rotation.

What Woods and the others were doing was damn clever, he realized. It would also be a small group of engineers' last act in this universe.

The hull was perhaps a few thousand meters from the Klingon vessels when it exploded in a brilliant flash, its blast radiating three hundred and sixty degrees along the plane of the hull's rotation. The explosion was red-orange on the outside, white-hot in the center. Before he reflexively closed his eyes, he could actually see the circular shock wave moving out as it was fed by huge amounts of matter and antimatter annihilating each other instantaneously.

Enough of the energy of the blast reached the main hull to make the deck rock under Fuller's feet, and he opened his eyes to see the remnants of the explosion glowing brightly against the shields of the two Klingon ships. No, not just glowing against them, it was enveloping them. For a crazy moment, Fuller hoped that the sacrifice would be enough and the Klingon vessels would be obliterated.

Then the glow died down and he saw the ships were fine . . . no, not fine. They were intact, but the one on the right—the one closer to the explosion—was listing relative to the other ship. Fuller felt a glimmer of hope. Perhaps that vessel was out of the fight.

Of course, one fully functional battle cruiser would—under almost any circumstances—make quick work of the saucer section of an *Icarus*-class ship. The hull that Fuller and the surviving crew now occupied was more a lifeboat than a fully functioning vessel. The saucer could operate at reasonably fast impulse speeds and did have shield capability as well as phasers. However, power to all systems was limited.

Outnumbered as they were, their best chance would be to run. But the *Endeavour*'s warp capability was destroyed, as were the bravest people Fuller had ever seen in his life. Their only hope was that Woods and his people's sacrifice had crippled the Klingons.

Then, as if on cue, the listing Klingon ship righted itself. And Fuller saw a flicker of energy dance around the vessels. That told him that the Klingon ships' shields were already back online. Yes, the explosion had hurt them, but not critically.

"Come on," he said to Andrews. Then he looked down at Caruso and said, "We'll come see you in sickbay when this is over." She nodded, and he gestured for the medical personnel to take her away. Fuller spared another glance at the Klingon ships outside the window. The lead ship was already moving. Fuller knew that it was coming into attack position.

Watching the ship pull away from the other, Fuller was nearly hypnotized by the cold elegance of the maneuver. However, he didn't need to watch to know what was going to happen next, and he had duties to perform—duties that were possible only because of the sacrifices of his crewmates. He would not waste this chance and whatever time Woods and the others had bought him.

Intellectually, he knew that the Klingons would probably take the ship. The entire crew would do their best, but it would not be enough. The best Fuller could hope to do was to make the Klingons pay a heavy price for their victory. If this was the beginning of war, he had a duty to reduce the number of their enemies to give Starfleet a better chance in the fighting to come. If this was an expeditionary force testing Starfleet's resolve, perhaps he and the rest of the crew could make the Klingons think twice about taking on the Federation again.

Fuller hit the ladder first and scrambled up. He didn't even bother to try the turbolifts now. The ship would be locked down in preparation for Klingon boarding parties. The turbolifts would be permanently disabled to make it harder for Klingon warriors to make their way around the ship.

A blast struck the ship. Fuller held his breath, waiting for another.

None came.

Fuller was mildly surprised by this. He was certain that they had been hit hard enough to tear through the main hull's underpowered shields. A single torpedo or a sustained disruptor blast would be enough to destroy the unprotected remains of the *Endeavour*, but no further attack came.

They want the ship intact, he realized.

"Don't let them take you alive . . ." Woods's words came back to him. Whatever the Klingons' plans were for the *Endeavour* and its crew, Fuller doubted that he would have much choice in that matter. If he followed his training and did his job to its logical conclusion, he and the rest of the security forces wouldn't last long against a Klingon boarding party. He remembered the quiet dignity of Woods and his staff as they faced their end. He hoped that he died as well. And more important, he hoped that he managed a final surprise for the *Endeavour*'s attackers, as those brave engineers had done.

Fuller stepped out onto the deck and sprinted down the corridor, hearing Andrews behind him. The ship was quiet, with few people in the corridors. That made sense. He and Andrews had been the last to leave the engineering section. Everyone else had had time to get to his or her post.

Their final posts, his mind supplied.

Fuller reached the armory and saw an officer there. The man tossed him a laser pistol, which Fuller caught easily. Then Andrews arrived and caught his pistol. The officer behind the counter thought for a moment and handed both Fuller and Andrews another pistol each.

"Take the extras," he said, then Fuller saw that he had two more pistols laid out on the counter for himself.

Extras . . .

The ship maintained a store of additional weapons. And now, of course, there were a number of engineers who no longer needed theirs. Fuller felt the weight of each weapon in his hand and decided that he liked the idea that one of these weapons actually belonged to one of the fallen crew. He found the thought gave him strength. Next, the armory officer handed each of them a communicator.

Nodding to the officer, Fuller checked his lasers to make sure they were set to heavy stun. Even given the high stakes of the coming battle, regulations forbade setting a weapon to high within a space vessel. The danger of a hull breach was too great, and the potential damage too catastrophic. And if Fuller found himself blown out into space, his life span could be measured in seconds—a few very painful seconds.

Another ladder took them down to the level of his squad's emergency duty station. He made his way to the outer corridor of the ship and followed it to the rear section, where the impulse engines were housed. The impulse level was two decks high and, as a result, had four potential entry points from four corridors—two on each side of the impulse room on each of the two decks.

Fuller and Andrews's squad was assigned to protect the upper starboard level. As they approached, Fuller could see Section Chief Rizzo and the others were all there. Rizzo smiled openly when Fuller and Andrews came around the bend. "Good to see you two. Commander Woods called in to say that you were helping wounded get out of the secondary hull. I'm glad to see that you made it."

"Thank you, sir. It was close," Fuller said.

"You know what we're up against?" Rizzo asked.

"Klingon boarding parties."

Chief Rizzo nodded. He gave the two lasers in each man's hands a look and said, "I'm glad you came prepared. Take your positions."

The impulse reactor deck was a large room and looked like a smaller version of the engine room. Fuller was in a corridor that was level with the upper portion of the impulse deck. His corridor connected to a walkway that ringed the inside of the impulse room and overlooked the deck below as well as the large reactor equipment. Fuller could see the catwalk system that gave technicians access to the tops of the reactors as well as the hydrogen tanks.

Inside the impulse room, Fuller could see crew members going about their business with a quiet coolness that he recognized. These people, he remembered, had worked very closely with Woods and the others who had been lost already.

Fuller and Andrews walked to their designated positions behind one of the support pillars that ran next to the walls in this section of the corridor. These structures would provide the security teams with their only cover from forces advancing in their direction. Being the smaller of the two men, Fuller crouched down as Andrews took a standing position above him. They were in one of the rear positions across from the entrance to the impulse room. Directly across the corridor were two more people from their squad. And a few meters ahead of them were another pair on one side and Chief Rizzo on the other.

There was a loud click behind him, and Fuller turned to look inside the impulse room. Everything looked normal as the engineers went about their business. Then a computer voice sounded over the intercom, temporarily replacing the red alert Klaxon, *"Clear impulse room emergency doors."* Almost immediately, the thick blast door began to close. The door was large, covering the entire width of the opening to the impulse room, which was easily seven meters.

There was a steady hum as the door moved slowly into place. Fuller could also feel the vibration in his feet. He knew the blast door was nearly indestructible. In fact, an enemy would have an easier time cutting through the surrounding decks or bulkheads than attacking the door directly. That level of protection made sense. The only chance the ship had in a battle situation like this one lay in the power generated by those impulse reactors. Their weapons, their life support, their only hope, lay in maintaining that power.

Clearly, the Klingons had caught the *Endeavour* by surprise, but there would have been time to get out a distress call. That meant that help was on the way. If they could hold out, if they could maintain that power a little longer, there was a very slim but very real chance. Fuller only hoped that if help came, it came in force. There were still two battle cruisers out there.

As the door slowly passed Fuller's position, he caught a last look at the men and women working inside. He knew they were the real strength in that room, the real source of the ship's power now. Protecting them was the single most important thing he would do in his life. He might die doing his job, but he was glad that he had found a task worth giving his life to accomplish.

A few seconds later, there was a large metallic clang that told him the blast doors had met the floor of the deck below them. The impulse room was sealed.

Less than a second later, the computer's voice sounded over the comm system. *"Intruder alert. Intruder alert."* The computer's tone was calm and measured, though Fuller knew that they were facing more than mere intruders. This was a Klingon war party.

Nevertheless, Fuller felt a calm descend on him. Part of it was his security training, which had prepared him for every possible contingency. And part of the calm came from somewhere else inside him. He had often wondered how he would behave under real fire. Now, he was pleased to find that his mind was clear and his body ready. He knew that he would do his best to make sure that the sacrifices already made by members of the *Endeavour's* crew were not in vain.

There was complete silence in the corridor for long seconds. Fuller could hear only the hum of the ship—louder than usual now that he was so close to the impulse room—and the sounds of his own breathing and heartbeat. The silence was finally broken by sounds of shouting and running. He wasn't sure, but he thought that some of the shouting was not in English.

"Let them know they've been in a fight," Rizzo said.

"I'm ready to give them hell," Andrews whispered down to Fuller from his standing position. Fuller only nodded. Then he saw a green energy blast strike the wall of the corridor ahead of them. He recognized the color of Klingon disruptor fire, and his grip tightened on his laser pistol as he waited for the inevitable. Fuller kept his right hand and the pistol that he held in reserve behind the column, keeping only his left hand out and ready to fire.

In training, Fuller had scored high in marksmanship with both his left and right hands. Andrews was left-handed. This allowed them both to shoot effectively with their left hands while keeping themselves partly protected by the cover of the support beam in front of them. Suddenly, Rizzo's choice of placement for him and the others during training drills made perfect sense. Every edge, every advantage would be exploited now. And they might actually make a difference.

The sounds down the corridor got louder and Fuller found that he could make out words spoken in English, as well as shouts and grunts that were definitely Klingon. Then a barrage of fire came his way, seeming to hit the corridor all around him.

"Fire!" Rizzo shouted.

Immediately, the laser weapon came alive in Fuller's hand. He fired blast after blast, trying to aim the blue bolts at the source of the enemy fire. A thin haze of smoke started to form in the corridor around them as more Klingon disruptor blasts hit all around them. Fuller felt a blast shake the column in front of him. Then another. And another.

Still, he had not seen any other signs of the enemy. And as more and more smoke filled the corridor, it became more difficult to see anything. The smell of smoke and scorched metal grew stronger. Fuller could also feel warmth on his face. The release of large amounts of energy from the weapons was increasing the temperature in the corridor.

Fuller caught a glimpse of movement ahead of him. Before his brain registered the event, his hand had aimed and fired. More movement, another series of shots from his laser. His eyes became more and more useless as visibility decreased, but his ears told him that the enemy was not advancing. For a moment, he felt a faint hope that he and the others were succeeding, that they were somehow holding the Klingons off.

He felt a vibration through the deck plating beneath his feet. Then he realized that some of the sounds of fighting he had heard were mostly coming from beneath them. It made sense: the Klingons were making an all-out attack on the saucer section's primary power source—of course they would hit both decks at once. Though Fuller didn't dare take a moment to turn his head, his ears told him that the squad a few meters to his rear who were protecting the other entry point on this deck were still coming under heavy fire. The same was happening on the deck below them.

Suddenly, he realized that the Klingons must be hitting all four points as hard as they could. And they had the crews of two ships to draw from. Since the attackers had no doubt planned this attack in advance, they could have loaded their ships with warriors. In effect, they probably had a very large number of fighters to draw from—whereas the *Endeavour* had only its limited number of surviving crew. There would be no replacements, no relief. If it became a battle of attrition, the Klingons would win because of their sheer numbers.

Unless they did the impossible. Unless they held out long enough for Starfleet to even the odds. Unless help arrived in time.

Fuller had noted that the Klingons firing on him still had not advanced, and that was something. However, he knew that he and the others had to turn the tide of this battle to have some chance at survival.

Leaning his body out farther into the corridor, Fuller brought his right hand and the laser pistol it carried into the open. It put him at greater risk, putting more of his body in harm's way, but there was no helping it. He sensed Andrews doing the same and saw a flash up ahead as one of their beams hit something other than wall. Then a beam from one of the Klingons did the same.

Fuller knew that his sense of time had been altered, and though the battle had seemed endless, it had probably taken only a few minutes so far. Still, he found it odd that he had yet to see an actual Klingon. From what he knew of Klingons, they were brutal and ruthless fighters who advanced quickly in battle by using overwhelming force. He had even hoped that their aggressive behavior would allow the defenders to inflict serious casualties early on. Yet here, the Klingons seemed content with the stalemate that had been achieved. Of course, they could afford to wait.

Something about the situation bothered him, tugged at his consciousness. However, his attention was too focused on what was in front of him to worry about what might be driving the Klingons now.

Fuller noted that the sounds and vibrations coming from beneath his feet were increasing in volume and intensity. The fighting on the lower deck must be more intense, he thought. Then it seemed to stop abruptly. Though the boarders firing on his position kept their attack steady, the deck beneath him went almost completely quiet. There was something odd about that, something troubling. He guessed that the defenders down there had been overrun. He remembered the chief engineer's warning: *Don't let them take you alive.*

Had his crewmates just a couple of meters below his position been taken alive? He found himself hoping that they had made the Klingon attackers pay for their victory.

Almost all at once, the enemy fire on them stopped. He saw movement through the haze but rejected what he thought he saw as impossible: the Klingons seemed to be falling back. Wary of a trick, he kept his fire up and saw that the rest of his squad was doing the same.

But the tugging on his mind remained and he realized that something was very wrong. His instincts were screaming now.

"Chief Rizzo—" he called out, but his next words were drowned out by a strong explosion, slightly muffled because it was coming from beneath him. The floor shook and then rocked beneath his feet. A moment later he found himself lying on the floor, still clutching both laser pistols. He quickly scrambled to his feet, not wanting to meet whatever came next while he was lying on the ground.

He was at a crouch when the floor gave way beneath him. He was surprised that he remained both calm and aware as he went down. He realized immediately what the Klingons had done: they had used overwhelming force on the deck below and had then used simple charges to collapse the upper deck and take out Fuller and the Starfleet officers above. It was more clever than he would have given the Klingons credit for, given what little he knew of their tactics.

Fuller chided himself for underestimating an enemy. He knew now it would likely be the last mistake he would ever make, because of all the hostile races in known space, Klingons were perhaps the least forgiving of error in warfare.

Fuller felt himself falling for barely a second. Then he struck the floor hard and was immediately thrown back down to the ground. Without bothering to check himself for injuries, Fuller forced himself to his feet. He realized that the deck under his feet was now resting on the deck that had been below them. The floor around him was torn and uneven, and Fuller found that his legs were unsteady. Shaking his head, he refocused his mind and lifted his lasers. Then, scanning quickly through the smoke and haze, he got his first look at Klingon warriors.

They were approaching his position quickly, shouting something that sounded like a battle cry. Fuller didn't wait. He picked a target and fired both laser pistols simultaneously at one of the advancing figures. Then another. Then another. He depended on his peripheral vision to tell him that the Klingons had gone down since he knew that he had very little time and would not allow his vision to linger on a target.

The same peripheral vision told him that there were a few other members of his squad on their feet now and joining the fight. He was pleased to see Andrews's familiar figure among them. A shot came from behind him and Fuller turned, choosing and firing at another target as he did.

It was then that he realized that he was standing in the center of the ruined corridor, with no cover at all. He ignored the danger and kept up his fire, sensing by now that Andrews was behind him firing in the other direction.

Two targets emerged from the smoke. He got off a shot at one of them and was noting with satisfaction that he had made a hit, when he felt a burning hot sensation in his shoulder. He realized instantly that he had been hit. As he felt his body flying backward in space, he remembered the talk among the cadets at training. Conventional wisdom was that Klingons had only one setting on their disruptors: Kill.

Then the world was a swirl of color and movement that quickly went black. His last thought was that he had taken Woods's advice—he had not let the Klingons take him alive.

Chapter Thirteen

U.S.S. ENTERPRISE
STARBASE 56
2267

IN THE SHIP'S GYMNASIUM, Fuller repeated the hand blows and kicks that made up the combination. Then he stepped aside as Parmet tried to perform the same movements. The ensign was making a serious effort, but he was slow and his coordination a bit off.

"Watch me again," Fuller said, and repeated the movements as Parmet studied him carefully. Parmet tried again and did marginally better. Parmet looked up at Fuller with frustration in his face. Frustration, and something else Fuller couldn't quite place.

"Sir, I appreciate your taking this time with me, but if you want to stop, I'll be fine. I will just work by myself for a while," Parmet said. Then Fuller recogonized the look that he had seen in Parmet's face: determination.

Fuller thought of his empty quarters and shook his head. He would rather keep himself occupied. And he might be able to teach Parmet a few things.

According to Parmet's Academy record, Fuller's roommate had struggled through his physical training, but had scored at the top of his class in every academic area. That raised questions for Fuller. Why would someone as smart as Parmet, who was obviously suited to computer work or the sciences, choose security? Some of the most intelligent people he had ever met were security officers, but usually people with Parmet's particular mix of gifts sought other assignments.

Fuller found he was curious, but not curious enough to ask Parmet—it was simply not worth the conversation that would follow. Parmet had been respecting Fuller's privacy, and Fuller did not want to initiate any closer contact. He had even considered declining when Parmet had asked him to go to the gym to pick his brain on hand-to-hand combat. In the end, Fuller had gone simply to avoid staring at the walls of his empty quarters. Now, he realized that he would be able to teach Parmet a few things that might actually save his life.

"Listen, Ensign, have you heard of Krav Maga?" Fuller asked.

Parmet shook his head.

"It's a martial art developed by the Israeli Defense Force in the twentieth century. It's excellent for developing your speed and coordination. Would you like to learn a few basic movements?"

Parmet nodded eagerly and Fuller had to look away from the excitement in his face. Then he began. Of course, Parmet would need weeks or months to make any real progress, but anything he learned in the meantime would only help him.

Given the time constraints, Krav Maga was a good choice. The point of the art was to finish a fight fast by quickly disabling an opponent. Even a few moves would give Parmet a much better chance against a Klingon warrior. And a few moves might be all they had time to cover.

Considering the way things were now, Fuller had a feeling that the chances that he and Parmet would both be alive to complete any real course of training were slim. At a different point in his career, he might have done something like this as an act of faith. Now, it was just a way to pass his off-duty time.

Chapter Fourteen

FULLER AWOKE INSTANTLY, going from unconscious to alert in less than a second. Even before he could see properly, he tried to get to his feet. As his eyes began to clear, he felt a hand on his back. Someone was helping him up, he realized.

And I'm not dead, he thought with genuine surprise.

As his vision cleared he heard a voice. "Michael," someone said. It was Andrews. Fuller turned to see his friend and roommate looking at him with concern. "Are you okay?" Andrews asked. Fuller nodded. His shoulder burned a bit from where he had been hit, but otherwise he felt fine.

He had been hit by a Klingon disruptor. But he thought

189

their weapons didn't have a setting for stun. *Obviously they do,* he realized.

"We're in the cargo bay," Andrews said, as Fuller's eyes registered the same information. By the look of things, more than half the crew was there as well. He noted there were few security people in the large room, and none above the rank of ensign.

"Rizzo? The others?" Fuller asked.

Andrews shook his head solemnly. "I don't think any of the others made it." Then, after a moment, he added, "We were lucky."

It was true, the entire squad had fallen through the deck into a fortified Klingon position. By all rights, he and Andrews should have died too. Scanning the room, Fuller saw a group of Klingons guarding the two large entry doors in the front of the cargo area. They carried weapons Fuller didn't recognize: long, curved blades that looked very heavy and very deadly. They also wore large knives that looked equally dangerous.

Looking around him, he noted that many of the crew had sustained injuries that looked like cuts and puncture wounds. Yet, like himself and Andrews, they had all been left alive.

"How long was I out?" he asked.

"Just a few minutes more than me, and I woke up as they were dragging me in here."

Moving slowly through the crowd, he took a closer look at the Klingon guards. On average, they were taller than most Starfleet crewmen—though most of the Klingons were not as tall as Andrews.

Their attackers had known the *Endeavour* was coming and had waited to launch a sneak attack. The Klingon battleships had lain in wait for the *Endeavour* and had struck by surprise.

No Starfleet vessel would ever have done such a thing, no civilized or human ship would launch a sneak attack. Clearly the Klingons were not human. They were—quite literally—inhuman.

Stepping as close as he dared, Fuller glanced at the Klingon guards. He saw that they all wore disruptor sidearms. That was unfortunate. The Starfleet personnel in the cargo hold outnumbered the half-dozen guards by a large margin. If not for the disruptors, the crew would have a chance at rushing the intruders.

"I know what you're thinking," Andrew whispered. "I had the same idea, but those disruptors could cut us all down before we did any damage." Then he seemed to read Fuller's mind and answered the question that was there. "They haven't said a word to us. No announcements, nothing about what they want."

"They haven't killed us," Fuller said. This was not a small point. In Starfleet, one of the most frequently repeated notions about the Klingons was that they did not take prisoners.

"They haven't killed us *yet,*" Andrews said.

Fuller watched the guards carefully, studying his enemy for anything they could use to their advantage—though advantage was hardly a term that applied to their current situation. Immediately, he admonished himself for defeatist thinking that ran counter to his training and flew in the face of what he had seen a small group of engineers accomplish not long ago. For Woods and his staff, if for no one else, Fuller would keep hope alive within himself. And he would use every last second of his life to try to turn this defeat into a victory.

The guards were alert and rarely spoke to one another, and when they did it was at a whisper. Clearly, they knew their jobs and wouldn't make any obvious mistakes.

Fuller's thoughts were interrupted by a beeping sound by the doors. He didn't recognize the sound but realized what it was when one of the Klingons—the leader, he supposed—took some kind of communicator from his belt and spoke into it. Seconds later, one of the sets of doors opened and he saw six more of his crewmates being led into the cargo area by two armed Klingon guards.

Four of the officers were medical personnel and two were on stretchers. Fuller recognized Caruso and the burned man that Andrews had carried. Caruso was conscious and alert. The other patient was not, but Fuller was glad to see that he was still alive—otherwise, he would not have been brought here with the others.

Their appearance gave him hope. It meant that there might be more of the crew still out there. Perhaps the engineers in the impulse room were still safely behind the blast doors. Perhaps the Klingons did not have complete control over what was left of the ship.

None of the bridge crew were in the cargo area. Maybe Captain Shannon and the others were still out there, planning something. Well, if he could help them from here, he would.

The medical personnel were moving the stretchers to the rear of the cargo deck when the head guard yelled "Stop!" in perfect English. The foursome stopped, but

Fuller could see reluctance in their eyes. Clearly, they wanted to get their patients as far from the Klingons as possible.

The officers came to a stop in roughly the center of the room, putting them less than five meters from Fuller's own position. The Klingon leader and one other guard approached them. Fuller felt his body go very tense as he realized that the ship's chief medical officer was not among the medical personnel there. He suspected that the ship's surgeon would not be joining them anytime soon.

Two men and two women he recognized as nurses stepped in front of the stretchers, putting their bodies between the Klingons and the injured. This seemed to surprise the Klingon leader.

"Who are they?" he asked, pointing to Caruso and the unconscious man.

"Innocent people attacked and injured by Klingons," the male nurse said, clear defiance in his voice.

This seemed to surprise and then amuse the Klingon, who took a step closer to the stretchers. The nurses tried to block his way and Fuller heard Caruso say, "Don't."

What happened next happened very fast. The Kling-on leader and the other guard grabbed the two nurses closest to them and shoved them aside. Then they did the same with the other two nurses. By now, Fuller was already on the move, heading toward the disturbance.

Before he took two steps, the Klingons had drawn their odd, three-pointed weapons and very quickly plunged them into the chests of both Caruso and the other man, whose name Fuller had never learned.

Though shocked, Fuller kept moving and saw one of the male and one of the female nurses charge the Klingons, who quickly withdrew the knives from the two dying officers and swung them toward the nurses.

Fuller winced involuntarily as he saw the knives strike deadly blows into the chests of the two nurses. Then the two remaining nurses were on the move and others nearby were starting to react. Watching the two Klingons carefully, Fuller saw the subordinate reach for his disruptor. To Fuller's surprise, the leader shouted something that sounded like "No." Then he lifted his large weapon, the one with the double curved blades. The subordinate guard did the same.

The two Klingons swung their blades, the leader's cutting one of the nurses across the stomach, causing him to clutch himself and fall to the ground. The other surviving nurse immediately began to help him. Fuller knew the wound was serious, but probably wouldn't be fatal if he got medical attention reasonably quickly. However, that wouldn't happen as long as the Klingons held them.

The other officers, including Fuller, immediately stopped their movement.

"Cowardly Earthers," the leader shouted. "I have done you a favor and eliminated the weakest among you. Would any more care to join them?"

No one spoke and Fuller felt rage take hold of him. *Weak? Caruso? Injured maybe, but she had had strength enough to save his and Andrews's lives when they were in the turbolift.* Still, he held his tongue and forced his rage back down. It wouldn't help now.

"Weaklings, you will all die today," the Klingon continued. "If you wish, you may challenge me now and I will take your lives in combat."

No one moved. Fuller felt the blood pounding in his ears. The Klingon scanned the room, both a taunt and a challenge in his eyes.

Then he hung his long blade over his shoulder, while the other guard followed suit. Both Klingons kept their daggers out as they made their way back to the doors at the front of the room. The only other movement in the cargo hold was from the officers who stepped out of the way to give them room.

When the two Klingons had rejoined the four other guards, the leader turned and said, "You are all sniveling, bloodless cowards, and it will be my duty and my pleasure to rid the galaxy of you."

Rage rose up in Fuller again, and again he forced it down. He needed his wits now. The Klingon had answered his most important remaining question: as prisoners, they would not be kept alive for long. He had also provided Fuller with another crucial piece of information.

He turned to see Andrews looking at him. The boil of emotions on his friend's face told Fuller what he was feeling. And Andrews's eyes told Fuller that he had caught the same small bit of data. The two men nodded to each other, and an idea began to form in Fuller's mind.

Fuller and Andrews made their plans quietly, trying very hard not to draw attention to themselves—that would come later. Getting the information to the rest of the assembled crew required a simple solution that was both low-tech and would not arouse suspicion. Fuller and Andrews simply whispered the outline of the plan to two people and asked them to do the same. In just a few minutes, the crew would know what to do.

But less than a minute later, four of the guards came through the crowd with their disruptors drawn. "Do not resist," the Klingon leader said. Seconds later, the Klingons had reached the forward door of the cargo area. One of the guards hit the button that opened the inner airlock door to reveal the airlock. It was a relatively small space of maybe five meters square. The outer wall of the airlock was a reinforced door. Beyond that was the void of space.

Immediately, the Klingons began ushering crew members into the airlock. The group included the two nurses, with the injured one barely keeping his feet. Fuller felt a chill run down his spine as he watched it happen.

"Do not resist!" the leader repeated. In just seconds, twenty of his friends and crewmates were inside the small airlock space, looking at the rest of them through the window in the airlock door that shut them in.

One of the Klingon guards hit a button, and a force field crackled to life next to the airlock's outer door. After the flash of energy, the force field seemed to disappear, but Fuller knew it was there, just as he knew what the Klingons would do next.

"Cowardly Earthers, one of your pitiful Starfleet vessels has arrived. You will soon go to meet it in person," the leader said, addressing the crowd. Then the Klingon at the airlock control panel hit another button, and the outer door of the airlock flew open.

For a moment, Fuller was afraid that the twenty people inside the airlock would be blown into space, but it didn't happen, and he realized that the outer force field was still protecting them from the vacuum.

Then Fuller saw it: another *Icarus*-class ship. Like the *Endeavour,* it had a primary and engineering hull, along with two long nacelles that rode just above the vessel's saucer section. Help had arrived, and was now sitting a short distance away. He wracked his brain trying to remember which ships might be in nearby sectors. Quick mental calculations told him that the vessel was probably the *Yorkshire.*

Even as hope began to grow in his chest, he felt a cold fear for the twenty people in the airlock and a growing dread for what he thought was about to happen—what he feared would happen if he didn't do something immediately.

The leader shouted something in Klingon to the other guards, and the one at the control panel hit another button. From that moment time slowed to a crawl.

He heard his own voice shouting, "No!" as he watched twenty of his friends and crewmates get lifted off the floor as if by some unseen hand and hurtled out into the void. His mind tried to reject what he was seeing. It was impossible . . .

Inhuman.

And it was also true. The Klingons had just tossed twenty living beings into space, to certain death. Even before that thought registered, he saw that the *Yorkshire* was in motion, executing a high-speed maneuver as it fired phasers at the Klingon ships. He saw a flash of energy that he hoped might be a transporter beam snatching up the unprotected crewmen. But it was hard to be sure because the figures themselves were carried almost immediately out of sight.

The Klingon vessels didn't even try to strike the *Yorkshire*. When they fired their disruptors it was into what looked like empty space, but Fuller knew it wasn't—they were firing at the people floating in the void.

He immediately saw the cruel cunning of the maneuver, because the Klingon ships then turned their weapons on the Starfleet vessel, pounding it with disruptor fire. The Klingons were tossing people into space, counting on the *Yorkshire* to try to rescue them. And rescue meant lowering the ship's shields to use the transporters.

Fuller watched the disruptor fire strike the *Yorkshire*. Then he saw the *Yorkshire* returning fire as phasers lanced out at one of the Klingon vessels' shields and felt hope rise in his chest. The captain and crew of the *Yorkshire* were good, very good.

Then there were shouts as the Klingons rounded up another group. This time, the Starfleet officers resisted. Some of the people fought, but there were quick flashes of movement and Klingon blades hit at least two people that he could see.

Another twenty-odd officers ended up standing by the inner airlock door. There was near chaos in the cargo room. Of a crew of one hundred and sixty-one, there were now maybe eighty people left, including the twenty who were now by the airlock. If those twenty got thrown into space, there would be sixty . . .

Then forty . . .

It would not take long for the entire crew of the *En-*

deavour to be completely wiped out, no matter what happened in the battle raging outside between the *Yorkshire* and the Klingon vessels.

He had to do something and do it fast.

The unmistakable sound of disruptor fire rang out through the cargo area. Like the others, Fuller was shocked and the cargo room fell silent. The leader of the Klingons spoke and said, "Cowardly humans, my warriors and I will kill you without hesitation. Do not resist. Hold on to your pathetic lives a little longer. Soon enough your deaths will come and serve the greater glory of the Klingon Empire."

Fuller's mental clock told him that the airlock would be repressurized in seconds. There was no time to get the word out on his and Andrews's plan, let alone execute it. Well, he would have to improvise. He shot Andrews a look, and the larger man nodded.

"You take the two on the right," Andrews said.

"Go," Fuller replied. Giving a shout, he raced toward the airlock, aiming his body at the two guards on the right, while Andrews made the same move toward the two on the left. He heard shouts from behind him in Klingon, then he was launching himself through the air at the nearest of the two guards.

As he did so, he saw that the inner airlock door was opening. He hit the Klingon high, driving him into his partner. The move was crude, but he was pleased to see that it was effective. The Klingon had only had time to turn to face him before Fuller hit him with the full force of his body.

Physics took care of the rest and the Klingon fell backward, knocking into the other one. Fuller didn't see what happened next, but he ended up on top of the Klingon he had hit. Both of them were on the ground. Moving quickly, he did two things simultaneously: he started to get up and he grabbed for the dagger weapon on the Klingon's belt.

He felt the cold metal of the knife's handle in his hand and grasped it firmly as he stood up. Before he could make another move his peripheral vision told him that something was wrong. There was a shout in Klingonese, then he saw a flash of metal and he felt something hard and fast strike the back of his head.

The world started to go black as Fuller felt himself falling to the floor. Through force of will, he fought off unconsciousness and held his hands out to break his fall. He ended up on his hands and knees with the world swimming around him. As he shook off dizziness, something hit him hard in the ribs on one side.

He immediately recognized it as a foot as he fell over sideways. Knowing that another blow was inevitable, Fuller tried to scramble back to his feet. To his surprise, the pain in his side helped clear his head. There was shouting he couldn't understand and then he was on his feet, his vision clearing.

The Klingon leader was shouting down one of the guards, who was gesturing at Fuller . . . and Andrews. With his vision finally clear, Fuller saw Andrews holding a gash in his right shoulder. For a moment, Fuller was too pleased to see his friend alive to worry about the fact that their ad hoc assault on the Klingon guards had failed so miserably.

Then he saw one of the guards holding his right arm close to his body. The assault had not been a complete failure. Apparently, Andrews had gotten at least one good blow in. And by the looks of the guard, Fuller guessed that the arm was broken. There were still six other Klingons in the cargo area, and they still had disruptors, but Fuller was glad to see any advantage turn in their favor.

The guards spoke quietly to one another, but Fuller didn't need to hear them to understand what they were saying. The leader was telling the others not to kill him and Andrews because they needed the hostages to keep blowing them out the airlock, to keep the *Yorkshire* off balance and vulnerable.

There were shouts, and Fuller turned to the airlock door and saw that another group of twenty was inside waiting to die. The leader shouted, "Now," and the guard operating the airlock control panel hit the large button that turned off the force field—performing the task with all of the concern of someone hitting a waste disposal button.

Rage and horror bubbled up in his chest simultaneously as twenty more of his crewmates were blown into the abyss. But this time, he clearly saw the telltale flash of transporter beams taking some of them immediately. Looking in the distance, he saw the *Yorkshire* executing high-speed impulse maneuvers. There was a blizzard of weapons fire from the *Yorkshire* and the Klingon ships, and Fuller thought he saw another flash of transporter energy.

At the end of it all, Fuller was pleased to see that the *Yorkshire* was still intact, having given at least as good as it got. Fuller's thoughts were cut short by hands grabbing him roughly and shoving him toward the inner airlock door. He turned to see that one of the guards had one hand around his upper arm while the Klingon's other hand held a dagger over him.

Another group was being put together, in a hurry, he noted. That gave him hope: perhaps the *Yorkshire* was doing well out there. Maybe the Klingons were sweating a little. Fuller decided right there that he would not die out in space. He would fight, right here and right now. He might not get to strike even a single blow, the way Andrews had, but at least he would keep himself from being used as a weapon against the *Yorkshire*.

There was a beep that told Fuller that the airlock was now pressurized. Immediately, the door opened. The guards shoved him toward the open airlock. There wasn't much time . . .

"Wait!" Andrews's voice boomed out.

Fuller turned to see Andrews addressing the Klingon leader. "Let me take his place," he said, pointing to Fuller.

The leader looked at Andrews, then at Fuller. Then he nodded. "You have earned the right to choose your death, and to end the indignity of your captivity." Fuller saw that Andrews's blow against the guard had somehow won him the respect of the head Klingon. The leader pointed to Fuller and shouted to his guard, "That one stays here for now."

"No!" Fuller found himself shouting. But immediately there was another Klingon on his other arm. He struggled, but their grips were firm.

One of the guards leaned into him and said, "Do not worry, Earther, your pathetic life will end soon enough."

Andrews walked past him and Fuller said, "Don't do this."

But his friend only smiled grimly. He looked down at his wound, which was still bleeding freely, and said, "I can't help much now, but you still can." It made sense, Fuller knew. Andrews was stronger and a better fighter when he wasn't injured. Now his left arm was useless, and Fuller could see by the pallor of his skin that blood loss was taking its toll on him.

Still, Fuller shook his head. "No," he said.

Andrews leaned down and whispered to him, "Let them know they've been in a fight."

Then Andrews was standing with the group in the airlock. Two Klingons held disruptors on them. Every face in there was calm; like Andrews, they were facing their deaths with courage. Tears stung Fuller's eyes. Too many members of the *Endeavour*'s crew had done that today.

Now there would be less than forty of them.

"Michael, you go home and see that baby of yours," Andrews said.

"What?"

"Get out of here and see that baby," Andrews said. "Promise me."

For a moment, Fuller was speechless. Then he said, "I promise," nearly choking on the words.

Andrews smiled and then the heavy inner airlock door slammed shut, the sound of it resonating through the room.

Almost immediately, the Klingons holding him released his arms. Fuller rushed to the window of the door. Twenty pairs of eyes were looking at him. He found Andrews, who was standing closest to the window. His friend's eyes met his.

Once again, time slowed to a crawl, but too soon he heard the Klingon leader shout something. There was the sound of a click, then a flash as the force field holding the atmosphere inside the airlock shut off. Like before, Andrews and the others were instantly plucked from the deck and shot out into space.

Fuller prayed that the *Yorkshire*'s transporters were ready, but he didn't stay an instant to watch what happened. Instead, he turned and strode across the deck to the Klingon leader, who watched him approach with amused contempt. He stopped less than a meter from the larger alien and said, "You!"

Then he reached out with both hands and shoved the Klingon backward.

Chapter Fifteen

I.K.S. D'K TAHG
2267

THE PROBLEMS HAD BEGUN even before Duras and his Klingons had arrived on board. First, there was the cargo. Duras had ordered large numbers of containers be stowed on the ship. They all had security seals and were impervious to scans, which made Karel even more suspicious. In addition, they were of sufficient size and number to force Karel to have other cargo removed.

The first category to go was food. It was the easiest to cut, but that would have ramifications for the crew. The ship now had less than a week's supply of food on board. That meant they would have to acquire additional food from appropriate planets on the way. It was a simple enough matter but bad for morale. The fact was that warriors fought better with decent *gagh* and *rokeg* blood pie in their stomachs.

Karel had also had to sacrifice some spare parts for nonessential systems—nothing that would compromise the vessel's battle readiness in the short term, but as first officer he had a duty to think in the long term as well.

Finally, he had had a terrible time accommodating the council member's staff and security people. Originally, Duras was going to contribute only the Klingons necessary to bring the *D'k Tahg* up to full fighting strength, but the soldiers he was bringing actually exceeded the number of replacements they had needed. Worse, their number meant that nearly half the crew and fully half the battle-ready forces were now Klingons loyal to Duras. Karel's blood had called out a warning when Koloth had first told him about Duras; now his blood was screaming its message.

Yet Karel's hands were tied, and so were Koloth's. They had their orders and their duty to the empire.

Karel was now cramming the crew even tighter to make room for Duras's staff. In his final message, Kell had told him that the humans had only two junior crew members to a single room that was spacious by any standard. Now, Karel was placing eight Klingons to a room. That meant more fighting among the crew and a waste of energy and focus that wreaked havoc with efficiency.

Karel had just finished his last reassignment of crew quarters and found Gash waiting at the transporter room. "Commander Karel," the large Klingon said.

"Gash, Duras's troops will be arriving first. See that they get to their assigned quarters and that they understand the rules of the ship," Karel said. As ground security forces stationed at High Command these Klingons had probably never served on a Klingon Defense Force vessel. "And keep a close eye on them at all times."

Gash simply nodded, completely missing the irony of the remark, given the fact that he had only one eye. He was an excellent warrior and even a good leader in battle situations, but Gash was completely humorless. That was fine with Karel. What he and Koloth needed now were Klingons they could trust. Karel was glad he had put Gash in charge of the surveillance of Duras's soldiers.

Karel headed for the bridge, where Koloth and the rest of the bridge crew were assembled. A few minutes later the communications officer announced, "The last of Councillor Duras's troops are here." He waited a moment and said, "The councillor is now also on board."

Koloth acknowledged the information with a nod. The rest of the crew looked at their commander, waiting to see what he would do now. After waiting a moment, Koloth smiled and said, "Tell the transporter officer to give Councillor Duras directions to the bridge."

The bridge crew did not respond overtly, but Karel could feel the tension in the room increase to battle levels.

Honored guests were usually greeted on arrival by the commander or at least a member of the senior crew. At worst, they would be escorted to the bridge. What Koloth was doing would send a clear message to Duras about how he regarded this secret mission. Showing such disrespect to a councillor was a dangerous business and the action of a Klingon who was either foolish or fearless.

Karel decided that he was glad to have Koloth for a captain.

A short time later, the bridge doors opened and a large Klingon entered. Klingons in the Defense Force had a familiar saying: *There are no fat warriors.*

The councillor was no warrior.

Of course, Karel immediately recognized the cassock of the High Council that Duras wore over his portly form, but he had never met this Klingon before. Yet, there was something familiar about the Klingon, and Karel's blood called out a fresh warning. The councillor was taller than Karel himself, with a more rounded shape than any warrior in active service would maintain.

"Councillor Duras," Koloth said as he stood and the bridge crew followed suit.

"*Captain* Koloth," Duras said, putting a subtle emphasis on Koloth's rank.

"The *D'k Tahg* is ready to serve the empire," Koloth said.

"Excellent," Duras said. "Take us out of orbit, Captain."

Koloth nodded to Karel, who leaned down to his own command console, hit the intercom button, and said, "Clear all moorings." There were audible clicks as the mooring and supply lines that connected the *D'k Tahg* to the docking structure were released.

Karel watched his screen for confirmation and then said, "All moorings clear."

"Pilot, take us out of dock and orbit," Koloth said. Thrusters moved them slowly out of the docking structure, and then there was a subtle shift in the hum of the ship as impulse engines were engaged to take them out of orbit. "Heading, Councillor?"

"Out of the system will be fine for now," Duras replied.

The ship was under way, there was no reason to deny Koloth information about their heading. Duras was withholding it merely because he could. Karel watched Koloth's face for some reaction, but there was none.

"Use your discretion, pilot," Koloth said calmly, though Karel knew that his commander must be seething inside. A few minutes later, the ship cleared the system. Turning to Duras, Koloth merely looked at him.

Duras walked to the front of the bridge and stood in front of the viewscreen. Karel suddenly remembered where he had seen that posture before; it looked like the councillor was about to make a speech. "Klingon warriors, you are now called upon by your empire. This is a dangerous time for our people. Even now, cowardly Earthers are plotting the end of the great empire that Kahless himself forged just as surely as he forged the first *bat'leth*. We will now enter Federation space for what may be the first strike in a conflict that has been inevitable since the Earthers' treachery at Donatu V, where they denied us our rightful victory. We will soon see the beginning of the final stage of that conflict that began twenty-five years ago. We shall reclaim the honor lost that day, and we will soon see the day when the Earthers and their cowardly Federation of weaklings fall to the might of the Klingon people."

Duras paused to let the importance of his words sink in. Karel, of course, knew the history of Donatu V. It was often mentioned as a stain on the empire, and the treachery of the humans was usually given as the reason that the empire had been forced to accept the cessation of hostilities without a clear victor.

For much of his life, Karel had accepted what he had

209

been told about that battle, partly because his own father had died in that fight and could not tell his sons what had really transpired. But since he had heard Kell's final tale, he questioned much about what he had been told about humans.

The Klingons on the bridge, however, did not have the benefit of his secret knowledge and pounded on their consoles in reaction to Duras's words. Smiling, the councillor continued. "We head for Federation space to a system the Earthers call 7348. There we will begin our work and there we will strike the first blow."

The rest of the bridge crew responded to the fact that the ship would be once again heading into Federation space. Many of the Klingons on board had lost comrades on Starbase 42 and were eager for revenge.

Karel felt none of that. He knew the attack on the starbase was part of an honorless plot within the empire. And he knew something about the planet that they were heading to—something that no one else in the crew did, not even Captain Koloth. According to Kell's final message, that was the planet full of Klingons living a primitive existence. Someone in the empire had used Orions to mine the world of precious dilithium. If it had continued, the mining process would have destroyed the planet. Then when the human vessel on which Kell had served showed up to put a stop to the operation, the Klingons in command of the operation tried to destroy the world and every Klingon living on the surface.

That was the true stain on the honor of the empire.

Koloth stepped forward and said, "Pilot, plot a course, then give us best speed to Federation space."

Chapter Sixteen

EARTH
2267

LIEUTENANT WEST'S COMPUTER BEEPED, telling him that a priority one security message was incoming. He nearly dropped his coffee in his effort to race across his office and get to his terminal quickly. The message was from Starfleet Intelligence, and West checked it twice. Then, as a triple check, he called up the raw sensor data used to make the conclusion.

There was no doubt. Without hesitating, he jumped to his feet and headed out the door at a run, even as he heard Admiral Solow calling for him over the intercom. West didn't stop to answer the call and instead headed to the admiral's office. He was there in a few seconds.

Though the admiral looked composed, West had

served with him long enough to know that he was very concerned. "Lieutenant, you've seen the report." It was a statement, not a question.

"Yes, sir."

"Come here."

The lieutenant took a position in front of Solow's viewscreen. His heart was pounding in his chest, and a sick feeling formed in his stomach. He knew what was coming next and had his thought confirmed when Solow's assistant said over the intercom, *"Admiral, I have President Wescott."*

The Federation seal appeared briefly on the viewscreen, then it flickered and West saw the president. It was not the same man whom he had met for the first time a week ago. Gone was his easy smile, and he looked more worn than he had just those few days before. West could have sworn that there were more lines on the man's face and that his hair had more gray.

There was, however, no doubt that the dark rings around those powerful blue eyes were new, as were the bags under them.

"Mister President," the admiral said. Then he gestured to West and said, "You remember my aide, Lieutenant West."

The president gave them a grim smile. *"I don't mind saying that I had hoped not to speak to you again so soon."*

Solow returned the smile. "I understand perfectly, sir."

Then West saw it: the president's genuine smile. The smile was something to see, even on a viewscreen and under dire circumstances. Then the president was all business again. *"You're convinced that the intelligence is accurate?"*

"There's no doubt, sir. A Klingon warship has entered Federation space," Solow said.

The president nodded. *"We're trying to reach Ambassador Fox now."*

West felt the seconds ticking by and wanted to scream that they needed to act immediately, that nothing Fox had to say would make a difference. However, he took one look at Solow's face and held his tongue. If the admiral was content to wait, he could too.

Finally, the image on the viewscreen shifted, splitting in half, the president's face on the left and Ambassador Fox's on the right. The slight flickering of the ambassador's image told West that Fox was talking to them via subspace, no doubt from wherever he was conducting negotiations.

The president got right to the point. *"Ambassador, what do the Klingon diplomats have to say about the incursion?"*

"I have not spoken to Ambassador Wolt yet, but in a message he maintained that we had agreed to allow them to send a . . . delegation to the planet so they could begin talks with the genetic Klingons there. As far as they are concerned—"

"They sent a warship!" West found himself blurting out.

Fox hesitated for a moment and then replied. *"It is irregular, and I have lodged a formal protest with the Klingons."*

A protest! West thought. *The Klingons are launching an invasion, and he's lodged a protest!*

"The Klingons have assured me that they have no hostile intent, they are merely taking the action we all agreed upon," Fox said.

"We agreed to a warship?" West asked.

"No, we agreed quite specifically that they would use a civilian transport. However, the ambassador says that there was a miscommunication somewhere within their chain of command," Fox said.

"Do you believe him?" West asked, keeping his voice carefully controlled.

Fox didn't hesitate. *"No."* Then he added, *"However, we have already agreed to send a starship ourselves."*

"Yes," Solow said, "but there is a difference between using the might of a starship to monitor the activities of a hostile alien force in *our* territory and these actions by the Klingons whom we *know* are planning a massive invasion."

"The question is, what do we do now?" the president asked. *"Lieutenant West, what do your Klingon cultural studies suggest?"*

West didn't hesitate, either. "We know that as far as the Klingons are concerned, the hostilities that began twenty-five years ago at Donatu V have not ended. They consider the empire and the Federation to be in a state of war that has had only a temporary pause. In that context, we can see this clear violation of the spirit of our agreement with them on their contact with the people in System 7348 as a first strike. If a Klingon were engaged in a hand-to-hand duel with an enemy, it would be an initial blow designed to test the opponent's reactions."

"What would you recommend as a response?" the president asked.

"We need an overwhelming show of force. Tell the Klingons to turn their warship around or we will blow it out of space. Then, if they do not comply, we need to follow through on our threat."

"Ambassador?" the president said.

"I'm not convinced that we've exhausted all of our diplomatic channels," Fox said.

The president asked Solow, *"Admiral, how far along is your emergency refit program for our starships?"*

"The *Enterprise* was the first ship to begin the refit and it will be the first done. Four more have begun as we speak, with all twelve *Constitution*-class ships completed within three weeks. Most upgrades of major planetary defense networks will be finished within the same time frame."

"Your recommendation?"

"I would rather have all of our upgrades in place, but I don't think we can allow this threat to go unanswered."

President Wescott took all this in, a look of intense concentration on his face. West realized that he had underestimated the man after their first meeting. His face told West that the president knew full well that the decision he was about to make would be the most important one of his political career. The weight of that choice was clear, yet he made it quickly.

"Admiral, dispatch the Enterprise *immediately to monitor the situation in System 7348. We don't have time to wait for their upgrades to be fully installed. And we'll have to trust Captain Kirk to conduct further threat assessment and take appropriate action if necessary."*

"Mister President," Solow said, "the *Enterprise*'s original schedule put them three days ahead of the

Klingons, but that was on the assumption that it would be a civilian transport. Even with the *Enterprise* leaving early, the Klingons may get there ahead of them."

West added, "That may give them time to get hold of the dilithium resources in the system—time to set up their foothold in our space and make preparations to begin a conflict that is inevitable."

The president nodded solemnly. *"You may be right, Lieutenant, but if you are, God help us all. If this war is inevitable, then we may be looking at the last days of the Federation. I will not put us on that path now—not if there's hope for diplomacy."* Then, before West could speak, the president raised a hand and continued. *"And if we are to go to war, then we may be giving the Klingons an advantage now, but we will be sowing an advantage of our own as well."*

West held his tongue. The president had made up his mind and had not done it lightly.

"Ambassador Fox, you have some more time to pursue your channels. Godspeed to you," Wescott said.

"Thank you, Mister President," Solow said. Wescott nodded and the screen went blank.

"Sir—" West began.

"Politicians and diplomats, Lieutenant. Don't blame them. They're a product of their natures, their training, and their experience—just as we are."

"But, sir, there is one important difference in this case."

"What's that?" Solow asked.

"We're right and they're wrong."

Chapter Seventeen

U.S.S. ENTERPRISE
STARBASE 56
2267

MCCOY'S EXPRESSION DIDN'T BETRAY what he was thinking, but his eyes told Parrish something was wrong when she entered his office.

"What is it?" she asked immediately.

The doctor stood behind his desk and gestured for her to sit. "Please," he said.

"I'd rather stand, Doctor." If this was bad news, she would rather receive it standing up. "Is there something wrong with my test results?"

He shook his head. "No, but I did learn something about human-Klingon pregnancies. There were a few case histories on colony worlds that I was able to dig up on the starbase."

"Is a successful pregnancy possible?" she asked, for

a moment not knowing which answer she wanted.

"Yes, it's *possible.*" He raised his hand. "But it won't be easy, especially as you get into the second trimester. Complications are likely."

"Will the baby be healthy?" she asked.

"I can't give you any guarantees, and we don't have enough of a sample to give you odds. I can tell you that most of the danger in these cases seems to be to the mother." After a few moments of silence, McCoy added, "I know this may change things for you. However, you don't have much time to make your final decision. The captain has arranged for the ship to meet with a civilian transport before we reach System 7348. That's in three days. The transport will take you to a starbase. If you are going to have this baby, you need to be on that transport, and I would strongly recommend that you then travel to Earth immediately."

"Earth? But I'm from—"

"Lieutenant, if you are going to have this baby, you can't do it on a colony world in a mining complex," McCoy said. "The best doctor we have for hybrid pregnancies is on Earth. I would want you in her care."

That definitely changed things. Parrish could almost imagine having a child at home, with her family around her. Mining colonies were tightly knit. There would be friends to help her.

But Earth . . .

She had only stayed there for her four years at the Academy. She didn't know anyone outside of the service on the planet.

"I'm sorry that I don't have better news," McCoy

said. Parrish only nodded, her thoughts a swirl in her head. "And I will need your decision very soon."

A question rose up and Parrish asked it without thinking. "Can I remain on limited duty until then?"

"Sure, for the few days you have until the rendezvous. But I need to monitor you closely, understood? You'll have to come see me before *every* shift, and you're only to do one shift per day."

"Of course. Thank you, Doctor." She headed for the door.

As she entered the corridor, Parrish realized that she had no idea what she would do, what she *should* do. For her entire life, she had always been decisive. Her path had always been clear, her goals always in sight. She had wanted Starfleet and gotten it. She had wanted starship service and gotten it.

Now this . . .

And yet the confusing mass of thought and emotion cleared as she realized that she had an immediate duty to perform. She had made a promise that she meant to keep. For the moment, her own situation would have to wait.

As he stood in the phaser control room, tension was written all over Scott's face and Kyle knew why: Scott would not leave the phaser control room until the system had had at least one full-power test, and he had to be in the sensor area when work began there. The problem was that even Montgomery Scott couldn't be in two places at once, and the disassembly of the sensor components had begun twelve hours ago.

The intercom beeped and a voice that Kyle recognized as belonging to one of Steele's engineers came through the system. *"We're ready to begin assembly down here."*

"Fine, get started. I'll be down as soon as I can. Steele out," Steele said.

Kyle watched Scott wince at that, but Steele gave no indication that she'd noticed. In fact, she didn't even look up from the phaser control main console. After a few minutes a green light on the console went on and Steele looked up.

"The simulation checks out," she said, turning to Scott. "Would you like to give the order?"

"Aye," Scott said. Then he leaned over the phaser control officer and said, "Begin power-up sequence."

The lieutenant at the console hit a sequence on his panel, and there was a brief moment of silence followed by a gentle hum as power flooded the system. As with the shields, phaser circuits were designed to reach full power quickly, and the hum rapidly rose in volume and pitch. Kyle noticed that the sound was subtly different than it had been in the past, no doubt because of the new components. That would take some getting used to. Engineers and phaser control officers could often tell the status of the system simply by the sounds it made.

"We're at full power," Scott said, and Kyle let out a sigh of relief. Without looking at him, the chief engineer said, "Mister Kyle, why don't you adjust the power and frequency range?"

As Kyle started work, he was surprised at how responsive the new controls were and how quickly the system could be adjusted. And if those new readings were accurate, he was seeing quite a boost in phaser power. Without a doubt, Kyle knew he was looking at the most powerful starship-based phaser banks in the known galaxy.

Scott muttered something under his breath, and Steele seemed amused. "Surprised it works, Mister Scott?"

"I'll check the control circuits and let you know," Scott replied. A moment later, he turned away from the console and Kyle could see that he was genuinely surprised.

"Control circuits?" Steele prompted.

"Fine," Scott replied, a ghost of a smile on his face. Kyle knew why: in new equipment, dramatic increases in power always meant dramatic increases in magnetic fields, which wreaked havoc on control circuits— though not this time, apparently.

Steele smiled again. "You know, back at command, we do occasionally read the reports sent back from field engineers." Then before Scott could respond, she said, "Come on, let's go see what they've done to your sensor array."

"Mister Kyle," Scott said, and Kyle followed. When he got to the sensor area, Kyle was glad he was not claustrophobic, because space was tight there. In fact, it was without a doubt the most difficult space on the *Enterprise* to do major repair jobs or perform upgrades. Any sort of significant work, he knew, usually required decompressing the whole section and removing the exterior sensor/navigational deflector dish itself and working from the outside in.

That process, however, could take weeks. However, Steele had devised a procedure that made such a drastic step unnecessary. *Enterprise* and station engineers would disassemble major components and remove them a piece at a time. When that was done, the replacement components would be packed into the same area and assembled with more handwork than Kyle had usually seen for this sort of job.

The system should not have worked, for a number of good reasons. For one, the amount of equipment they were building into the sensor array should not even have fit in the space they had to work with. And second, the assembly should have been possible only on a factory floor by sophisticated automated equipment.

But according to the schedule, Kyle saw they would actually save time by doing the work manually because they would be able to field-test individual pieces of equipment as they installed them. Problems would be easier to see and fix on the spot. Once this new equipment was installed, Kyle knew there would not be weeks of shakedown and troubleshooting required.

"Mister Scott," Steele said in her southern drawl, "it looks like we're about to begin assembly. If you're satisfied in here, you and I can move on to the new shield generator components."

"I've read the specs. I'm looking forward to seeing the equipment," Scott said.

Steele nodded. "Then I won't keep you waiting."

"Mister Kyle, help out here and call me when you're ready to perform the system check," Scott said.

"Aye, sir."

Scott and Steele turned to go. Kyle saw that whatever difficulty the two had had before, it was over now. He knew a quick rush of optimism, the first one he'd felt in the weeks since the crisis with the Klingons had begun.

But before Scott could leave the deck, Uhura's voice filled the room, and a dozen engineers stopped what they were doing to listen. *"Mister Scott, please report to the briefing room immediately."* There was a brief pause and then she said, *"Lieutenant Commander Steele, report to the commodore's office at starbase."* And then Uhura repeated both messages.

Scott and Steele shared a silent look as the rest of the engineers watched them. For many hours now, they had all been caught up in the work they were doing. There was a beauty and a symmetry to the new systems that appealed to all of them, so much so that they had forgotten the deadly purpose behind their work.

The silence of all fourteen officers on the deck was the sound of them all remembering that purpose once again.

Steele and then Scott hit the intercom button and said they were on their way. Then the two officers left the deck together. An instant later, eleven pairs of eyes turned from the door and looked to Kyle.

"We have a systems checklist to get through. Let's do this quickly," Kyle said. He didn't have to say anything else. Everyone understood what he left unsaid.

Kyle got to work.

Captain Kirk nodded when Scott entered the briefing room. The rest of the senior staff and the department heads were already present, so he didn't waste time. "There has been an important development in the situation regarding the Klingons and the delegation they are sending to System 7348. They will be arriving in less than seventy-two hours, and the Klingon delegation is being ferried by a Klingon battle cruiser, not a civilian transport, as we had been led to believe."

The captain paused for a moment to let that information sink in. McCoy was the first to speak. "Does this 'delegation' even exist?"

Kirk shook his head. "We have no conclusive proof either way."

"Captain, I must concur with the doctor," Spock said, his even tones providing an ironic counterpoint to the deadly serious content of what he was saying. "We have very little reason to believe that the Klingons have anything but hostile intent. The fact that they have entered Federation space in a battle cruiser is a serious breach of protocol."

"True. There will, however, be no immediate military response," Kirk said. His people were too professional to express their surprise. "With one exception. The *Enterprise* is ordered to make for System 7348 immediately. Mister Scott, I know that is a tall order, given that you are now in the middle of upgrading two major systems, but I need your absolute best."

"We can be under way in ten to twelve hours," Scott said. Kirk could not keep the surprise from his face. "Maybe less, though I can't promise until I talk to Commander Steele." Scott saw Kirk's expression and explained. "The phaser refit is finished, and we're installing the sensor equipment now and about to begin on the shield generators. If I can have Steele and her staff for another ten hours, we can get the basics in place. Then, even at maximum warp we're looking at almost four days to the system. I can have everything online before we get there. Given the time frame, we should be able to beat the Kingons to the system. It will be close but we can do it."

"Mister Scott, that is impressive. Thank you," Kirk said.

"No need, sir. 'Tis the upgrades. Commander Steele and her design staff have done a fine job."

Kirk nodded. That was something. He had seen Scott's initial reports, which showed the chief engineer's doubts about the refit. His new attitude spoke well for the major overhaul the *Enterprise* and the rest of the fleet were due in three years. The captain dismissed the thought. That would come after the end of the *Enterprise*'s five-year mission, and the ship would have to log a lot of star hours before then. For now, their first order of business was survival, for themselves and for the Federation.

"Then I won't keep you, Scotty," Kirk said, and the chief engineer got up to head for the door. Scanning the table, the captain said, "Thoughts?"

"Jim, no one wants war, but if it's coming anyway, why let the Klingons start it in our backyard?" McCoy asked.

"President Wescott feels that there's still some hope for the diplomatic option. If they continue talks, maybe both sides can reach a compromise."

"But if the Klingons want to wipe us out, can we afford to compromise on that? Let them have, say, *half* the Federation?" McCoy asked. "They tried to destroy a planet of their own people. How does the president think they will treat *us* if we lose?"

McCoy was just expressing the frustration they were

all feeling, that even Kirk was feeling acutely right then. "I don't have any answers for you, Bones. What I have now are orders."

"When this is over, remind me that there's a moon I want to sell to President Wescott."

"Noted, Doctor," Kirk said. He looked around the room again. No one had anything else. And he could see that they were all anxious to talk to their own people and make the necessary preparations for departure.

"Dismissed," he said. The room emptied quickly.

Fuller found that his heart was beating loudly in his chest as he approached the dining room. He was nervous for reasons he could not quite explain, yet he wanted to do this—he wanted to hear what these people had to say. As promised, Parrish had arranged it, and what she and the others were offering him was a gift: A chance to know his son better, a chance to better understand what kind of man Sam had become.

A chance to know how Sam had lived. And a chance to know how he had . . .

Died.

That was it. They would tell him the things he wanted to know, the kind of things that no official report would even think to mention. He had thought he was ready to hear it all, to know it all. But the fact was that not knowing allowed Fuller to keep the truth of Sam's death locked away in the same place he had locked away too many others. Andrews, Caruso . . . almost too many to count. Too many names on Fuller's own personal wall.

Confronting the details of his son's death, the reality

of it, might cost him some of the control he needed for his final mission for his son. Well, he could not say no to this now, not without arousing suspicion. And with Parrish shipping off the *Enterprise* as soon as it could reach a transport, there was no putting it off.

Fuller reached the dining room and the doors opened for him. Parrish was there with six others. Seven people who had served with Sam on the mission in System 1324 and at the siege of Starbase 42.

Fuller took a deep breath and stepped inside, giving the waiting people a smile. Seven faces returned the smile, and they all stood up, nearly as one. One of them, a young man—an impossibly young man—stepped forward in embarrassed excitement. The man held out his hand and Fuller shook it.

"Sir, my name is Adam Jawer—" Then something caught in his throat. He waited a moment and continued. "I served with Sam on his last two missions." Then the young man's voice started breaking. "I wouldn't be here if it wasn't for him. I'm very proud to meet you."

Jawer's face was a mix of earnestness, emotion, and excitement that Fuller found hard to look at because it reminded him of Sam as a young officer. In the end, he smiled at the ensign and said, "I'm glad to meet you." Jawer seemed both pleased and embarrassed. Fuller put a hand on his shoulder and turned to the others. "I'm glad to see all of you."

Parrish introduced him to the others one at a time, then she said, "Why don't we sit?" The table was set and food was already out. Parrish put him at the head, and the others took their places.

Parrish spoke first. "Your son was my first commanding officer. I served in his squad with Ensign Jawer. Our first mission was to System 1324—"

She was interrupted by the comm. Fuller recognized Kirk's voice immediately. *"All hands, this is the captain. The* Enterprise *has received new orders. We will be leaving starbase for System 7348 in eight hours. Begin departure procedures immediately. Kirk out."*

Then a voice that Fuller recognized as the communications officer said, *"All security teams report to the ship's theater. All security teams report to the ship's theater."*

Fuller and everyone else at the table stood up simultaneously. Parrish was first to the door. Fuller found that he felt a mixture of disappointment and relief. Then, as he stepped away, both of those feelings disappeared and he concentrated on the new situation. If they were heading to the planet early, that meant something had happened. The Klingons were up to something.

His mind went over a number of possible scenarios as he headed for the theater. Fuller vowed that he would be ready for all of them.

Chapter Eighteen

FULLER HAD CAUGHT the Klingon by surprise and was pleased to see him stumble backward awkwardly. The other Klingons began to shout, but the leader recovered quickly and raised a hand to silence them. Fuller saw that the two at the nearest cargo room door had their hands on their disruptors, stayed only by the leader's gesture.

That was it, he realized. He and Andrews had been right. He knew from his Starfleet training that Klingons had a strong martial tradition and many rules and cultural norms regarding fighting. He had seen earlier that the leader had not wanted his men to use disruptors against unarmed people. Fuller was glad to see that he had been right—his and Andrews's plan depended on it.

Of course, Andrews would have been better able than he was to execute this part of the plan, but that couldn't be helped now. Fuller only hoped he lived long enough to give the others in the room a chance to do something.

"I challenge you," Fuller said to the Klingon leader.

There it was, the look of amused contempt. The Klingon smiled, a decidedly unpleasant sight. Fuller felt an unnatural urge to wipe that murderous grin off the alien's face. *"You,* Earther?" the Klingon said.

"Yes, this 'Earther' challenges you, you *bloodless coward,"* Fuller spat back at him.

The amusement on the Klingon's face disappeared. Now there was just contempt, and fury. Fuller was pleased to see it. Obviously those words that the Klingons used so casually to describe humans had a powerful effect when hurled back at them. Without delay, the Klingon unhooked the meter-long curved blade from his back. He gave it a swing and looked up at Fuller with that unpleasant smile. "You will die slowly, Earther."

"Not by your hand, you pathetic bastard," Fuller replied. He had been half expecting the Klingon to hurl himself at him at that, but the Klingon's fury had gone cold, showing only in his eyes now. This Klingon wasn't going to lose his head, and his calm indicated that he had just become more dangerous.

"Give the human a blade," the Klingon said, steel in his voice.

"No, I don't want one of your *cowardly* blades," Fuller called out, taunting the Klingon some more. He looked around quickly and said, "I need a high-torque maintenance wrench."

A few seconds later someone called out, "Got it,

Fuller." There was movement behind him as the tool was passed from one officer to another. Finally, a woman handed it to Fuller, and he nodded. The wrench was heavy and nearly a meter in length. It had the heft he needed and he would be able to swing it like a simple club. Perfect for his purpose.

Of course, it didn't look like much of a match for the deadly looking blade in the Klingon's hand, but Fuller found he wasn't worried about that now. It felt good to be doing something besides watching his friends and shipmates die. He had a plan now.

And he had some fury of his own.

Automatically, a circle cleared around Fuller and the Klingon leader, giving them five meters in every direction. Fuller noted with satisfaction that the other five guards had come in closer to the center of the room to watch the fight. Fuller gave his wrench a test swing. It had some heft, and he guessed that it was about as heavy as the Klingon weapon.

"I'm afraid that I cannot spare you as much time as I would like, Earther. I have orders to dispose of the cowardly lot of you."

Fuller did not rise to the bait. He saw no point in taunting the Klingon now. Instead, he lunged forward and swung the wrench directly at the Klingon's head. Surprised by the quickness of the attack, the Klingon reflexively jerked back and raised his blade defensively. The wrench hit the blade with a resounding clang, making it vibrate roughly in Fuller's hand.

The Klingon recovered quickly and swung the blade at him. Now it was Fuller's turn to dodge. He pulled his head back and felt the deadly weapon pass less than an inch from his throat. Watching carefully, he saw the momentum of the blade carry it through its arc, leaving him a small opening to attack the Klingon's unprotected left side.

Fuller didn't take it. Not yet.

His plan required the Klingon to swing at him from the other direction. That would be tricky to manage. Of course, the plan also required that Fuller survive another attack, which would be even trickier. He sensed that the Klingon leader was an expert with that weapon. Until now, the Klingon had been testing him, even toying with him, but there wouldn't be much more of that.

"Neither you nor your pathetic *tool* are a match for me. You will die, Earther," the Klingon said. Of course, he was probably right. However, the Klingon didn't know that Fuller didn't need to survive this fight for his plan to work.

Fuller and the Klingon circled each other, holding their weapons out. As he walked, Fuller stepped a bit closer to the Klingon, putting himself just inside the leader's strike zone. As he had hoped, the Klingon swung the weapon high, from right to left.

This time, Fuller ducked and dove into the attack. He felt the blade graze the top of his head as he rolled. Timing his roll carefully, he dropped the wrench and reached up with his right hand toward the Klingon's hip. Then, using instinct alone, he rolled out of the way as he sensed the Klingon's blade coming down at him as he lay on the floor.

Sure enough, he heard the blade strike the deck, missing him by inches. Then Fuller turned and looked up at the Klingon leader, who was staring at him in disbelief. With his left hand, Fuller grabbed hold of the Klingon blade and held it to the deck. With his right hand, he raised the Klingon disruptor that he had taken from the Klingon's side.

Shock registered on the Klingon's face as he stared down the shaft of his own energy weapon. To him, what had happened was inconceivable, made even more so because he had not allowed his guards to use disruptors against Fuller or the others. Fuller had no such compunctions.

Without hesitating, he fired the weapon into the Klingon's chest.

The blow tossed the large alien backward, and Fuller was immediately on his feet. Like their leader, this turn of events took the other Klingons by surprise. Three of them made the mistake of reaching for their blades first. *Endeavour* crew immediately overwhelmed those guards.

Two guards had the sense to reach for their disruptors. Fuller was able to hit one with his own disruptor before the Klingon fired a shot, but there were too many of his crewmates in the way for Fuller to get a clear shot at the other one. So he simply rushed through the crowd, his right hand still holding the Klingon leader's blade.

The Klingon was firing blindly in all directions. In the chaos Fuller noticed that at least two of his crewmates had gone down. Then Fuller was nearly on top of the Klingon. He grabbed the blade by one of its handles and swung it at the guard's legs. The Klingon went down immediately, firing one shot up as he fell. The blast missed Fuller, but passed so close that he felt its heat on his face as it traveled upward.

233

Fuller fired at the Klingon, who immediately went still. One of the ensigns nearby leaned down and picked up the fallen Klingon's weapon. There was the sound of movement all around him as *Endeavour* crew retrieved the rest of the weapons. Others grabbed tools or anything else they could find.

"What now?" someone said to him. Fuller turned to see that it was a security officer from another squad who was holding a Klingon disruptor in his hand.

"Move the Klingons in there," he said, pointing to the airlock. The officer gave him a surprised look. "We're just going to lock them in." For a moment he considered blasting them out into space. It would have satisfied some of that fury that burned inside him, but it also would make him like his enemy, and that was the last thing that Fuller wanted right now.

Without asking any questions, the surviving crew followed his instructions. In less than a minute, the six unconscious Klingons were piled inside the airlock. Then Fuller assigned two of the crewmen who were now armed with disruptors to stand with him on one side of the large cargo room doors. He had everyone else stand behind them, fitting in as best they could.

Fuller hit the button on the control panel that opened the large double doors, which slid open. In less than two seconds, four Klingons who had been standing in the corridor rushed inside. All of them were cut down by disruptor fire before they even saw Fuller and the others.

As people grabbed the fallen Klingons' weapons, Fuller and other armed crewmen poked their heads into the corridor. It was clear.

"And now?" one of the people behind him said.

"Now we let them know they've been in a fight," Fuller said.

Fuller broke the survivors into four groups. One would head for the bridge, one for the phaser room, and one to the impulse deck. The final group would put the four additional guards into the airlock and then scour the ship for remaining Klingons. There was a chance that the captain and crew were still barricaded on the bridge. And if there was any chance of getting power to the weapons, Fuller and the others would have to secure the impulse room.

Fuller's group headed for the phaser room. Almost immediately, they came upon dead Starfleet officers. The Klingons had left the humans' weapons on the deck, and the *Endeavour* crew was quickly able to arm itself with laser pistols. Fuller was uncomfortable carrying the Klingon weapon. He wished there had been enough lasers for him to trade his disruptor for one, but there hadn't been. He'd had to satisfy himself by dropping the Klingon blade on the ground.

They raced through the corridor and met little resistance on this level. The small group of Klingons had been surprised to see them and had not even fired off a shot. Fuller was himself surprised that there were not more Klingons on the deck, but then he realized why: the Klingons had rounded up most or possibly all of the surviving crew and had put them in the cargo room. Obviously, they didn't feel the need to keep many of their soldiers on board to maintain control of what was left of the ship.

They were arrogant and overconfident. And they didn't think much of humans. On the other hand, the battle so far had gone overwhelmingly in their favor. They had had plenty of reason to be confident.

The turbolifts were all out, so they took ladders and stairs to reach their respective decks. The phaser control room was near the front of the ship, and Fuller's instincts told him to proceed with caution. He led his group forward slowly, listening carefully for any sign of the enemy. None came, and soon they were looking at the charred doors of the phaser control room.

"Earthers!" a shout came from behind them. Fuller froze in place, cursing himself for letting the Klingons sneak up on his group. "Do not turn around, just put down your weapons," the Klingon voice said.

Fuller decided that he would just turn and fire. Maybe he would get lucky and hit one of the Klingons before he fell. But before he could move, he heard the sound of laser fire. Immediately, he turned and fired, slamming himself back against a corridor wall. There was a group of perhaps a dozen Klingons caught out in the open while someone behind them kept up the laser fire.

Fuller and his people kept up their own fire, and the Klingons fell quickly. He signaled for his people to hold their fire and called out, "Identify yourselves."

A shaky voice called out, "Lieutenant Fitz."

Fuller raced around the curve of the corridor and saw a young female communications officer sitting on the ground, cradling someone in her arms. No, not someone, the captain.

Captain Shannon had a disruptor burn that covered the right side of his face. His single remaining eye was open and sightless. Fuller saw immediately that the captain was dead. "Oh my God," someone said next to him.

Part of his own mind screamed out that it was impossible. Shannon couldn't be dead. He was the *captain.* And he had just saved them from the Klingons. A louder part of his mind said, *He died to give us this chance.*

Fuller would see that that sacrifice—and Andrews's and Caruso's and Woods's and all the others—was not wasted. "We can't help him. I need everyone to come with me to the phaser room." He reached down and helped Fitz put the captain gently on the deck. Then he helped her up.

"We may be able to do some good in the phaser room," he said to her.

Fitz looked up at him. She was suddenly alert, snapping out of the daze that had been caused by watching the captain die. There was something else in her eyes: Fury. Without another word, she was on her feet and leading the way to the phaser room.

Fuller left four people guarding the door—a pair on each side. Then he, Fitz, and two more entered the phaser room. There were four dead people on the floor. All but one of them, he noted, had been killed by a Klingon blade. As a result there was some damage to the equipment, but the room was surprisingly intact considering that it had been the scene of a battle.

He pulled a dead lieutenant off the main console and tried to power it up. Nothing.

"Communications are out," Fitz reported. Then she tossed Fuller a communicator. "But these should work."

"Fuller to bridge," he said into the device. Nothing.

"Fuller to impulse room," he tried.

"Impulse room, here. Lieutenant Silverman," a voice responded.

237

"Are you secure?"

"Yes, the Klingons were cutting through the door, but then they just stopped."

"We sent some help. I guess they got there," Fuller said. "Can you give us some power to get into this fight?"

"We have power in one of the reactors, but I can't get the phaser control room on my board. We'll need your help to get power to your control circuits. Then we may be able to get phaser banks online."

Fuller looked up and waved over a man in a technician's jumpsuit. "I need you to get power to the main control circuits."

The man looked at him and said, "I'm a junior technician."

"So?"

"I'm only rated on the food service equipment," he said, embarrassment in his voice.

"You just got a promotion," Fuller said. Then he handed the communicator to the young technician. "Have Lieutenant Silverman talk you through it."

"I have visual," Lieutenant Fitz said.

Fuller looked at Fitz, who was working at a console. Above her, the viewscreen showed a star field. "There it is," she said, and hit something on the board.

Suddenly, Fuller was looking at two Klingon ships. He could see that the closest one was damaged. There was scorching on the main hull and, more importantly, on the port nacelle. That was promising. It also gave him a target.

"Where's the *Yorkshire?*" he asked.

"I don't know, sensors are down," Fitz said. She hit a

series of switches and the view changed a number of times. Finally, it settled on the *Yorkshire,* which was slightly above them and a few kilometers away. The Starfleet ship had also taken some damage, but seemed intact. "The Klingons are keeping us between themselves and the *Yorkshire.*"

"They're hiding," Fuller said, with some satisfaction. The *Yorkshire* must have really hurt them, he realized with pride. "Give me a view of the Klingons." A moment later, he was looking at the Klingon vessels again.

He leaned over to the technician working at the main console. "What have we got?"

The technician raised his hand, listened to the communicator. Then he hit a series of switches on the console and a few buttons on the board lit up. One of the buttons was main power and one was manual targeting. "That's it," he said with pride in his voice. Then he frowned, "We have power to one forward phaser bank only, starboard side."

That was a problem, Fuller realized. The Klingons were behind them. The forward bank couldn't make the shot. Fuller took the communicator and asked, "How much power do we have, Lieutenant?"

"One good shot, maybe two if we don't blow up," Silverman said.

"Good, but we can't hit the Klingons in our current position. Can you spin us so that we're facing the enemy?"

"Maybe, with maneuvering thrusters, but we're blind down here."

Fuller tried to calculate the required rotation given what he could see on his screen, the placement of the exterior camera on the hull, and the firing radius of the forward phaser bank. Finally, he gave up and said, "I need approximately a thirty-degree, clockwise rotation. And do it very slowly."

There was silence on the other end for a moment. Then Silverman said, *"I can give you rotation, but I can't promise that I can stop it at thirty degrees. However, I'll time the power-up of the phaser bank so that you have full power at the thirty-degree mark."* That was necessary. They couldn't have the power up for long. The Klingons would see the power surge on their scanners. Once that happened, the ship would have only a few seconds of power at most before the Klingon vessel blew the unprotected remains of the *Endeavour* out of space. *"Begin rotation, mark,"* Silverman said. Fuller could see the slow change of position of the Klingon ship on the viewscreen. *"It'll be less than a minute."*

"Keep the view on the damaged Klingon ship," Fuller said to Fitz, who nodded. With targeting scanners out, Fuller knew that he would have to target the phasers manually. And with maybe one shot, he could not afford to miss. Of course, if he had estimated the rotation incorrectly, the whole issue would be moot and he wouldn't even get that shot.

The room had gone completely silent as they all waited, silently marking the time. The Klingon ship faded out of the view of the camera and Fuller was afraid that he wouldn't get his shot. He held his breath and then he heard Fitz's voice from next to him. "Switching to forward camera."

Fuller knew that the forward camera had roughly the same orientation as the forward phaser bank. Theoretically, the field of view of the camera would be the same as the field of fire of the phaser bank. Of course, Fuller had no way of being sure. He was a new recruit just out of training, with no experience on large weapons systems outside of a simulator—and no simulator he had ever seen had been programmed with this particular scenario.

But he had made a promise to his friend. He had made a promise to a better man, and he would not let Andrews down. Fuller willed the Klingon ship into position and almost immediately saw it appear in the left third of his screen. He could see the damaged nacelle clearly. He lined up the phaser with his target, compensating on the fly for the rotation of the *Endeavour.*

"Power on my mark," Silverman's voice said from the communicator.

Long seconds passed.

"Mark."

There was no hesitation. Fuller hit the main power switch and the room around him hummed to life. There was a split second of nothing, and then a single, beautiful blue phaser beam lanced out at the Klingon ship, striking the shield above the nacelle directly. There was a bright flare where it hit the Klingon ship's shields, and Fuller saw flashing energy, the telltale visual sign of shield failure.

They had hit the Klingons hard. The damaged nacelle was unprotected now, but they had scored no additional damage that he could see.

"Silverman, do we have power for another shot?" he asked. There was silence on the other end. Fuller was mildly surprised that the Klingons had not immediately retaliated. Perhaps he had hurt them more than he had thought. For all he knew, the Klingons were fighting a warp core breach now.

Finally, Silverman said, *"I don't know. We've blown a lot of circuits here."* The ship was still rotating, and the Klingons would soon be out of range of the phaser bank. Once again, Fuller didn't hesitate. He checked his targeting and fired.

It worked.

Another blue beam lanced out, ripping into the nacelle itself. As the beam traveled across the Klingon ship, it seemed to be tearing out large pieces of the hull. Then the nacelle disintegrated in front of him. After that, the phaser beam struck the rear of the ship and then it was out of the camera's view and disappeared from the screen.

"Yes!" someone said behind him.

The Klingon ship lurched. If they had been fighting a warp core breach before, Fuller realized that it was inevitable now. The viewscreen went dark, but Fuller didn't need the screen to tell him what was happening.

The lights dimmed all around them. Then they went out completely, only to be replaced by the dim red lights of emergency power. *That's the end of our power,* he thought. It didn't matter, though. They had done it. At least one of the Klingon ships was finished.

The gravity seemed to lessen, and Fuller felt his stomach lurch. Then it felt as if someone grabbed the ship and tossed it roughly. Fuller hit the console in front of him as he felt the artificial gravity completely disengage and he floated into the air. A moment later, even the dim emergency lighting went out.

Floating in the darkness, Fuller said, "Sound off." One by one, the people in the phaser room called out their names. Everyone was accounted for. He saw a handheld light come on. Then another.

One of the lights floated over to him. It was Fitz, who handed him a light. "Follow me," she said, using hand-holds to float to the door.

Out in the corridor, Fuller saw that the four officers who had been guarding the door were okay. "Come on, we'll make our way back to the cargo bay," he said. Fitz took the rear. They made their way slowly down the corridor, pushing past the floating body of the captain as well as a number of others.

On the way, he flipped open his communicator and said, "Fuller to impulse room."

"Silverman here. I'm sorry, Fuller, but we're all out of power here, and it may be a while before we can change that."

"Thanks, but that's okay. We got them. I'm sure that was their warp core." He didn't mention that there was another Klingon ship out there. He hoped that the reason it wasn't shooting at them was because the *Yorkshire* had it occupied, but there was no way to know. He knew that the end could still come any time now. But until then, he had a job to do. As a security guard, he had to get all the survivors to a safe beam-out point. "Collect everyone you can and meet us in the cargo bay. Fuller out."

He continued floating through the remains of the ship, using hand- and footholds to push himself forward. He occasionally passed dead crewmates who floated in front of him. *The ship is truly dead,* he realized. The *Endeavour* was now a lifeless hulk sitting in space. The blast they had felt from the warp core breach had driven pieces of the Klingon ship through their own outer hull, which would be full of breaches now. They would be lucky if the cargo bay was intact.

Long minutes later, they reached the cargo area. The door had enough battery power to open and there was still atmosphere inside—only because it was not facing the Klingon ship when that vessel exploded, Fuller realized.

Thirty-five other people were assembled there. Thirty-six survivors out of a crew of one hundred and sixty-two. The windows in the cargo bay told them nothing, showing him only star field. Fuller wondered if the *Yorkshire* had been destroyed. And if it was gone, had it managed to destroy the Klingon ship before it went?

If that had happened, all thirty-six survivors of the *Endeavour* would be dead.

Fuller could feel the effects of their zero-power situation on life-support systems. There was plenty of atmosphere, but the temperature had dropped significantly. They would freeze to death before they suffocated.

Just when he had decided to start moving people to the escape pods, Fitz handed him a communicator and said, "I've set it to send out hails on all Starfleet frequencies. We may get lucky."

A few long seconds later, the communicator chirped and she said, "It found an active receiver."

Fuller flipped it open and said, "*Endeavour* to *Yorkshire.*" He waited a moment and said, "*Yorkshire,* this is the *Endeavour.*"

"This is the Yorkshire. *Lieutenant Robert Justman, acting captain here."*

"This is Ensign Michael Fuller. It's good to hear your voice. We were able to monitor some of the battle from here. Is it over?"

"The two Klingon cruisers are neutralized, thanks to your efforts over there. Those phasers came at just the right time. Is Captain Shannon with you?"

For a moment, Fuller was silent, then he said, "No, Captain Shannon didn't make it, but we have him to thank for the phasers."

"Understood. I'm sorry about your losses. How many of you are there? Are there any Klingons on board?"

"The Klingons have been . . . neutralized. There are just thirty-six of us," Fuller said.

"Stay together, we will pick you up shortly. I look forward to shaking your hand, Mister Fuller."

"And I yours, sir. There's one more thing. That last group that were ejected from the airlock . . . were you able to retrieve any of them?"

There was silence on the other end, then Justman said, *"No. I'm sorry to say that we were not able to save any of them. We have eighteen more of your crewmen from the first two groups, though."*

"I understand. Thank you. Fuller out," he said, closing his communicator. That was it. Andrews and the other nineteen people with him were dead.

For the next few moments, Fuller was grateful for the darkness in the cargo area.

Fuller found that he was eager to get off the *Endeavour*. It was dead now, a ghost ship. Before long, the

Yorkshire called and the transport began. The ship's transporter took them six at a time, and soon only Fuller and five others remained. Then he felt the transporter beam take him too.

When it deposited him in the transporter room of the *Yorkshire,* Fuller realized that he had just taken his first trip through a transporter.

Chapter Nineteen

I.K.S. D'K TAHG
2267

"Report," Karel said to Gash.

"Councillor Duras's soldiers are now all in their quarters," Gash said.

Karel saw that Gash had a bruise on one side of his face and a cut on the other side. Yet, he was standing, and that could only mean that the other Klingon or Klingons who had scuffled with him were not. "Have you completed their orientation to ship's rules?"

"Yes," Gash said.

"Are all of them . . . intact and ready for duty?" Karel said.

Gash looked embarrassed. "Two are injured, but they will recover."

"Good work," Karel said. Gash's orientation had no

doubt gotten physical, yet he had showed restraint and not killed any of Duras's Klingons. That meant he had used his hands and not a blade or a disruptor. It was necessary to show Duras's men that they did not run this ship, no matter what sort of behavior they saw from their arrogant superior.

"You are dismissed," Karel said, and got back to the computer console. He noted that their food supply would not even last as long as he had originally calculated.

Duras's Klingons ate more than Klingons on active duty did. It showed Karel that they had not seen battle in the recent past. Warriors facing battle ate to satisfy their hunger, but not so much that it would slow them in actual fighting.

Karel heard footsteps outside, counting three Klingons. He shook his head. He had chosen the main computer control room because it was empty this time of day. Finding empty places on the ship was getting more and more difficult.

As second-in-command, he was entitled to private quarters—a privilege reserved for just him and the captain. But Karel had been first officer for such a short time that he had never been able to enjoy that privilege. And because he had been squeezing the ship's crew tighter and tighter, he had kept the same quarters he had had when he was bridge weapons officer—a post that he had held until just days ago. He still shared those quarters with the relief weapons officer. Duras now occupied what would have been his quarters, and Karel found what solitude he could to do the work necessary to keep the ship running.

The door to the computer room opened, and Karel was automatically alert and getting to his feet. He had locked the door with a command code. Only the captain could override the code and enter without buzzing first.

When the door opened, he did not see the captain. Instead, it was Duras. The large Klingon raised his hand and said, "I wanted to speak to you." No one followed him inside, but Karel was sure that there were two of Duras's guards posted outside now.

After a moment, Karel sat.

Duras smiled. Karel prided himself on his warrior's ability to see another Klingon's intention to kill him on that Klingon's face. That ability had saved his life more than once. Karel did not see that intent on Duras's face now. Yet there was something else there, something he did not trust.

"What do you want?" Karel said.

"I knew your father," Duras said. Then the Klingon paused, letting the silence speak for him. Karel did not know what to expect from the large Klingon, but that comment had genuinely surprised him.

"I served with him at the Battle of Donatu V," Duras said. "He was a good warrior, courageous and cunning."

"And an *honorable* Klingon," Karel added.

"Yes, of course. He never forgot his duty to the empire."

"We all serve as best we can," Karel said, studying the Klingon's face, looking for some sign of what Duras was after.

"Perhaps when we have more time, I could tell you something of what I knew of your father."

That was it. The councillor was offering him something, something that Duras knew he wanted. There were forces at work here that Karel did not see. He decided to answer honestly. "I would like to know more about my father."

"Yes, your father served the empire well. But not all service is the same, just as 'not all blows are struck by the hand.'"

For some reason, Karel was uncomfortable hearing Duras quote Kahless. "That is true. There are many ways to strike an enemy in *open* battle."

Duras smiled at that. "You have much to learn, young Karel, but I think you will have a long and successful career in which to do it, with many glorious campaigns. I am impressed that you have already come so far, so fast. You are first officer on a battle cruiser. I know that just months ago you were toiling at a secondary cooling system console in a weapons room."

Karel did not respond to that. He merely waited to see where Duras would go next. He did not have to wait long.

"Have you thought about your future?" Duras asked.

"My future? I intend to destroy the empire's enemies for as long as I am able."

"True, but you will be even more effective in that endeavour when you have a command of your own."

There it was, the beginning of Duras's second offer.

"I have been first officer for less than a week," Karel said.

"Still, you must have thought of the time when you will challenge Koloth and the ship will be yours."

"Koloth is a good commander."

"If you are stronger . . . it is inevitable," Duras said.

"And there are many kinds of strength. Allies increase a warrior's strength. Weapons also increase a warrior's strength. Weapons like a battle cruiser."

Now Karel understood. Duras had already seen that Koloth would not allow him to rule over the ship. The councillor was planning something, a path he was not sure Koloth would follow. So he was offering Karel help in making a challenge to the captain. If Karel accepted the help and went along with whatever Duras was planning, he would have the *D'k Tahg*.

Of course, it was all subtle. The councillor had said very little of actual substance. Instead, he had suggested and implied. And yet, looking into Duras's eyes, Karel had no doubt of what the Klingon was offering him.

Karel stood up immediately. "Captain Koloth is in command of this ship because he is the best warrior on board. He has *many* kinds of strength, including the loyalty of his crew and the loyalty of his first officer."

"I was not suggesting otherwise."

"Yes, you were. Do not show me a false face. You were offering me help in making a dishonorable challenge to Koloth."

"Do not accuse me," Duras said, raising his voice and standing up himself.

"I only state the simple truths we both know. Anything less would be *dishonorable*."

Duras was shaking in his fury, a vein bulging in his forehead. "I am a member of the High Council."

"And I know my duty to the empire. I will serve my captain until it is clear that he is no longer fit to command this ship. Then, and only then, will I make a challenge. And when I do, I will owe nothing to anyone."

The councillor reached for the *d'k tahg* at his side.

Karel smiled at that and flashed a challenge with his eyes. His blood was boiling, and he welcomed the opportunity to teach this sniveling liar something about honor. Duras saw some of that in Karel's face and stayed the hand at his side.

"You have made a mistake, a very dangerous mistake," Duras said. Then he turned and headed out the door.

Karel was certain that he had made an enemy of the councillor. And he had no doubt that Duras was a very dangerous enemy to have. Yet, if he sat on the High Council, then there truly was great danger to both the empire's future and its honor.

A warrior may be known by the enemies he keeps, Kahless had said. Karel found that he was proud to know that Duras was now his enemy.

Chapter Twenty

U.S.S. ENTERPRISE
STARBASE 56
2267

KYLE AND SCOTT saw off the last group of the station's engineers. Only Steele, her aide, and two other technicians were left. Steele handed Scott a final report on the upgrades. "Thank you for your patience and your indulgence, Mister Scott."

"Thank you for everything you've done for the *Enterprise*. She's stronger now, more ready," the chief engineer said.

Kyle saw something in Scott's eyes. Steele must have seen the same thing. She put a gentle hand on his arm. "She *is* stronger, Mister Scott, because of people like you and people like us." She gestured to her own staff. "These changes are progress. Think of them as practice for the refits we talked about. You think she's been refitted for one purpose, for war, but she hasn't, not really. The Klingons respect strength, and they will have plenty to respect about the *Enterprise.* The changes are just progress. And progress isn't good or bad—for us, it's just inevitable."

"Aye," Scott said. Then the two engineers shook hands. Something passed between them—something Kyle couldn't see but he could definitely feel in the air. Steele took her position on the transporter pad as Scott took the transporter controls.

"Good-bye and good luck to you and the crew," Steele said. Then Scott activated the transporter beam. Steele, Anthony, and the two technicians disappeared a moment later in a burst of energy and light.

Later, Kyle would think about the way the two engineers had said good-bye, the things they had said and the unspoken things that had passed between them. Then he finally put his finger on it. They hadn't looked like two engineers talking about a collection of systems, components, and circuits, they had looked like parents talking about a child they were sending off into the world.

Kirk could hear Spock receiving final status reports at his station. "All stations report that they are ready for departure," Spock said finally.

Kirk nodded. It had been just over eight hours. Scott was as good as his word, as usual. A moment later, Scott and McCoy came through the turbolift doors. Scott took his position at the engineering console, and the doctor took his place beside and just behind the command chair.

"Mister Scott, all systems show ready," Kirk said.

"Aye," the chief engineer said.

"Mister Sulu, clear all moorings."

A few seconds later, Kirk heard the dull metallic clank that told him the *Enterprise* was disengaging herself from the starbase's umbilicals and power cables. A few seconds later Spock said, "All moorings are now clear."

Uhura said, "We are receiving a hail from the starbase."

"Audio only," Kirk said, wanting to keep his eyes forward.

Then a voice Kirk recognized came from the comm system. *"Captain Kirk, this is Commodore Zier,"* the voice said. *"I just wanted to wish you luck. The* Enterprise *will be in all of our thoughts."*

"Thank you, Commodore. We appreciate that," Kirk said. Their departure had been so sudden that there had not been time for the usual formalities and the customary departure visit with the station commander. With so little time to prepare, Kirk had been unwilling to leave the ship. Yet Kirk could tell there were no bruised feelings there, only genuine concern.

"Godspeed," Zier said.

"Thank you, sir. Kirk out. Mister Sulu, all ahead. Thruster speed."

"Thruster speed, aye," Sulu said. Then the lieutenant's fingers danced over the controls and the forward section of the starbase seemed to fall back as the *Enterprise* moved forward. After a few seconds the last of the dock's gleaming struts and supports disappeared as the front of the ship hit open space.

Their mission was dangerous, and there was a high likelihood that the *Enterprise* would soon be tested—for the first time ever in her history—in a full-scale war of unknown duration. These were dark days for the Federation, which was facing the greatest threat to its existence since Kirk was a freshly minted officer. He had gotten his first taste of battle then and had decided that if he never saw it again, it would be soon enough.

Yet he had seen it again, every time hoping that it would be the last. *Once more unto the breach,* he thought. Or into the darkness. The darkness that had swallowed too many of his crew in the last few months. The darkness that had swallowed Sam Fuller and left a grieving father trying to find meaning in a senseless death.

Too many grieving fathers, too many grieving families.

"We are clear of the dock," Spock announced.

"Ahead, one-quarter impulse," Kirk said.

"One-quarter impulse, aye," Sulu acknowledged.

The hum and vibration of the ship changed as the impulse engines engaged. "Accelerate to full impulse and prepare for warp speed on my mark," Kirk said.

"Accelerating now," Sulu replied.

Kirk remembered his excitement as a new cadet shipping out on his first training mission. It was a smaller ship, a less impressive dock, yet Kirk had been barely able to contain his excitement.

A ghost of that feeling remained in Kirk now. The excitement. The possibilities of what they would find out there. Perhaps they would find an answer, a solution that did not require endless condolence messages to endless parents . . .

... and wives ...
... and husbands ...
... and children.

The *Enterprise* was stronger than she had ever been. And the crew was ready. Kirk knew that *he* was ready for whatever was required of him. Ship and crew would give their best, and they had to succeed because, this time, if the darkness came, it might very well swallow everything.

Fuller did not watch the *Enterprise*'s departure from Starbase 56. It was the first one in his career that he had missed, he realized. Instead, he had invited Ensign Parmet to the gym for more training.

Parmet had taken to the new, aggressive fighting style better than Fuller had expected. By all accounts, Parmet was a gentle, almost passive, person. Yet Fuller could tell there was something else at work behind Parmet's eyes. When he fought, he did it from an inner well of ... what? Anger? Pain? Grief? Fuller wasn't sure and didn't ask. Parmet was entitled to his secrets. Fuller was certainly keeping enough of his own.

Parmet had worked hard and mastered some of the more difficult combinations that Fuller had taught him. And he was eager for more, but their workout had been cut short by a voice over the comm that announced, *"All security sections to the recreation room."*

The two men headed straight for the rec room, not even changing out of their workout clothes. They were among the first to arrive, and the room quickly filled with the rest of the security staff, some of whom had clearly worked the night shift and had been gotten out of bed.

Giotto stood at the front of the room with Parrish and the rest of the security section chiefs. Their faces were serious, and for a moment Fuller wondered if the war had already begun. Giotto didn't keep them waiting.

"We have just received an updated report from Starfleet Intelligence. The Klingon vessel that is now heading at high warp speed for System 7348 is the *D'k Tahg*." There was a quick collective gasp from the room and then silence.

"For those of you new to the ship, the *D'k Tahg* was one of the vessels at Starbase 42. I know that many of you lost people close to you on that mission. We lost a lot of good people on that day. However, this mission is to monitor the situation on the planet and try to make sure that the Federation does not have another day like it. I trust that you all know and will do your duty, but I thought that you should know exactly who we will be facing."

Giotto paused for a moment and scanned the room, then he added, "See your section chiefs for your new drill and training assignments."

Fuller's heart pounded loudly in his chest and, once again, blood raged in his ears. They wouldn't just be facing Klingons, they would be facing the same Klingons who had killed Sam.

"Sir?" Parmet said, looking at him with worry.

Fuller was grateful for the ensign's concern. It reminded him where he was. Fuller forced a smile and willed his body and mind to be quiet. He had succeeded, more or less, by the time Parrish arrived.

Looking at her, Fuller remembered that her squad had been especially hard hit during the siege, losing not only the section chief, Sam, but almost all of the others. He saw something in her face, something he thought he understood.

Whatever was in her eyes, her voice was steady as she said, "Get into your uniforms and go to the armory for training phasers. Then I want to see all of you on the shuttle deck in fifteen minutes."

Fuller didn't hesitate. He headed for the door with Parmet on his heels. He found he was glad to have something immediate to focus on.

Chapter Twenty-one

ONCE HE HAD fully materialized on the transporter platform, Fuller felt full gravity for the first time in almost
an hour. It felt odd and left him dizzy for a moment. The
room was brightly lit and he had to squint after the darkness on board the remains of the *Endeavour.* Fuller ori-
ented himself quickly and saw a young officer standing
in front of him.

The officer stepped forward and held out his hand.
"Mister Fuller, I'm Lieutenant Justman." Fuller shook
the man's hand, marveling that someone so young was
an acting captain. Then he saw something in Justman's
eyes. Maybe he wasn't old enough chronologically,
maybe not by the book, but the man's eyes told Fuller
that Justman was more than old enough for the job—a

job he must have gotten because something had happened to the ship's captain.

"I know you've had a rough time and I wish things were different, but I'm afraid that this fight is not over. Sensors show three Klingon ships headed this way. They will be here in less than an hour," Justman said.

"Any Starfleet vessels close enough?" Fuller asked. Justman shook his head. *No.*

It seemed impossible. The destruction of two Klingon ships had taken the combined efforts of the *Yorkshire* and the *Endeavour,* which had not survived. The thirty-six survivors crammed into the transporter room and spilling out into the corridor deserved rest, a few moments of peace after all they had been through. However, it looked like the Klingons were determined to make sure that didn't happen.

To his surprise, Fuller found that made him angry. "What can I do to help?"

"We'd all like to help," Fitz said beside him. She was joined by a chorus of others.

Justman nodded. "Who can brief me about what happened out there?"

Fitz stepped forward. "Fuller was the one who freed us all from the cargo hold. He was also the one who blasted that Klingon cruiser out of space." Fitz gave Fuller a look that bordered on awe and said, "He's a hero. He saved us all."

Shaking his head, Fuller said, "Sir, we all fought. I'm no hero."

"Then you'll have to do until one comes along. You're with me, Mister Fuller," Justman said. Then he addressed the group. "I won't lie to you. We're in trouble, but we've given the Klingons few surprises today. I say we deal them a few more." A lieutenant walked in and then Justman said, "The rest of you check in with the watch officer, then report immediately to the head of whatever department you belonged to on the *Endeavour.* I also need volunteers for the salvage teams we need to retrieve components we can use from your ship. Wait here, and Chief Engineer Watkins will be along to organize you into parties."

As officers stepped forward, Justman turned to Fuller and said, "Come on. I need you in auxiliary control."

Auxiliary? Why wasn't Justman commanding from the bridge? What had happened to the *Yorkshire?* The lieutenant read the question on his face and said, "The bridge took a direct hit during the battle. We lost the captain and the bridge crew."

For a moment, Fuller was too stunned to speak. That meant that Justman and whatever junior officers posted to the auxiliary control room had waged *and won* the battle after what should have been a crippling blow to the ship.

Then Fuller made another realization. "It happened when your shields were down to rescue the people the Klingons blew into space."

Justman nodded. So the *Yorkshire*'s captain and bridge crew had given their lives to save Starfleet officers they didn't know who had been tossed into space by the Klingons. Fuller realized that there had been real heroes here today, but they all shared one thing: they were all dead.

So much sacrifice. So much courage. So many examples of people doing the impossible. And unless they produced a miracle, the three Klingon battle cruisers that were on their way would allow the Klingons to win the fight.

They reached auxiliary control and stepped inside. Because the *Yorkshire* was an *Icarus*-class ship like the *Endeavour,* they were nearly identical, and if not for the strange faces at the auxiliary control stations, Fuller might have thought he was on board his ship.

Justman introduced him to the officers there, and Fuller realized that none of them were much older than he was and no one in the room had a rank higher than lieutenant. And yet these young people had already done the impossible.

Justman took status reports and issued orders. Then Fuller briefed him on what had happened on board his ship. The lieutenant listened and said, "Mister Heller, get Lieutenant Palumbo from security down here." Turning to Fuller, he said, "I'll need you to brief him on the Klingon boarding party tactics."

Fuller nodded. "Sir, I recommend that we avoid having the Klingons board us at all costs."

Justman looked at him for a moment and said, "Noted."

By the time Fuller had briefed the acting security chief, there was less than thirty minutes before the Klingons arrived. By then, the first salvage team had returned from the *Endeavour.*

"I have something on long-range sensors, headed this way," Acting Science Officer Parker said.

"Another Klingon ship?" Justman asked. Parker seemed confused by her readings, and Justman approached her. "Is it the Klingons, Ensign?"

"I don't know . . . I don't think so. In fact, this is impossible," she said.

"What is it?" Justman asked.

"Whatever it is, it's moving fast—warp six-point-five."

That *was* impossible, Fuller thought. But the science officer confirmed that it was true and that the ship was on an intercept course *and* that its origin was Earth. A moment later, there was a face on the viewscreen that Fuller immediately recognized.

"This is Admiral William M. Jefferies in command of the starship U.S.S. Constitution, *designation NX-1700. The people back at Command thought you could use some help out here."*

A cheer went up behind him, and Fuller felt himself smiling. He knew about the *Constitution,* of course, the first vessel in a new starship class. It was supposed to be able to carry a crew of over two hundred, with a very long range, faster engines, and labs to rival any at a starbase. The *Constitution* and her sister ships were the future of the fleet, but she was not due to launch for at least a year.

A few minutes later, the *Constitution* appeared on the viewscreen. Fuller had seen pictures of the design, but it was much more impressive in person. It was more graceful than the *Icarus*-class ships, which had the same basic design but were stockier.

"Five minutes until arrival of the *Constitution,* nine until the three Klingon ships are in weapons range," Parker said.

"Recall all salvage parties now," Justman said to the acting communications officer. "I want everyone back on board."

A moment later, the admiral's face was back on the viewscreen. *"Mister Justman, what is your status?"*

"We have full power to the weapons, eighty-five percent shields. Sir, is the *Constitution* ready to fight?" Justman asked.

"We don't have any weapons on board at the moment, but we have new shields that it would take more than three Klingon ships to breach. And this ship has a few surprises in her. Our security station is establishing a link to your tactical command now."

"I have it," the young man at the weapons station said.

"Do you think we can warn the Klingons off?" Jefferies asked.

"I don't know, sir. When they attacked the *Endeavour,* they had a two-to-one advantage. I don't know what they will do when faced with our current situation," Justman said.

Jefferies nodded. *"If it comes to a fight, I'll be depending on your weapons. Keep the* Yorkshire *moving and use us for cover."* Then Jefferies gave an order to his communications officer and said, *"The Klingon ships are not responding to our hails. I'm afraid this is not over yet, gentlemen. Jefferies out."*

"Parker, give me full magnification," Justman said.

A moment later, Fuller saw three small silhouettes that he recognized. The Klingon battle cruisers were coming at them in attack formation, and Fuller was suddenly sure there would be no discussion. In minutes, the Klingons would start a fight and within the hour it would all be over.

Those few minutes of waiting seemed like the longest

of Fuller's life. He realized that he had no role in auxiliary control. He wanted to join a security squad to prepare for Klingon boarding parties, but Justman insisted that he remain to advise.

So Fuller waited.

"Admiral Jefferies is transmitting to the Klingons. I'll put it on screen," the communications officer said. A moment later, Jefferies's face appeared.

"Klingon vessels, this is Admiral William M. Jefferies commanding the U.S.S. Constitution. *You are in violation of Federation space, which is an act of war. Two Klingon warships that attacked Starfleet vessels have been destroyed. Return to Klingon space immediately or continue at your own peril."*

"No response from the Klingons," the communications officer said.

"And they are not turning around," Parker added.

Jefferies's face disappeared, and the view of the Klingon ships returned. They were getting closer, the viewscreen's magnification making them look even closer. Fuller realized that the last time he had seen that view of Klingon battle cruisers, they were about to deal a lethal blow to the *Endeavour.*

"Two minutes until Klingons are in weapons range," Parker said.

"You have a dedicated audio connection to Admiral Jefferies at your station, Captain," Heller said.

Fuller was standing next to Justman's command chair and heard Jefferies's voice say, *"Looks like we're gonna have to fight. Take position behind us until they fire and then maneuver and fire at will. We're feeding coordinates to your helm now."*

"Helm, follow coordinates provided by the *Constitution*. Ready all weapons and prepare for maneuvers," Justman said.

Fuller watched the scene on the main viewscreen shift as they took position behind the starship. Up close, the vessel was even more impressive. And even though it was unfinished and virtually unarmed, Fuller found comfort in the presence of the ship. It was an example of what the Federation was capable of, what human beings and their partners had accomplished.

Even if they lost the battle today, there would be more ships like the *Constitution* to ensure that the Federation survived, to see that threats like the Klingons were answered.

Past the great ship, Fuller could see the three Klingon vessels grow on the screen as they approached. "Approaching outer limit of Klingon weapons range," Parker said.

The two Klingon cruisers on the outside started to break away from the center ship and fan out. It was a classic attack formation. When they had put enough distance between them, the Klingon cruisers suddenly increased their speed and seemed to leap toward the *Constitution.*

Very quickly, space was full of weapons fire, with the center Klingon ship laying down a spread of torpedoes as the two flanking ships fired disruptors. That many direct hits at that range would have immediately torn through the shields of an *Icarus*-class vessel.

The *Constitution*'s shields simply glowed under the assault, radiating out the incredible energies directed at them. If the Klingon maneuver was an initial pass to test

267

the *Constitution,* they would have something new to think about now.

Before the pass was completed, Justman called out, "Target weapons on starboard vessel. Helm, follow them."

There was a vibration in the floor as the *Yorkshire* leaped into action. As soon as the Klingon ships began to break off their attack and turn away, the *Yorkshire* was following its target.

"Fire torpedoes," Justman called out and an instant later Fuller saw the torpedoes race toward the ship and make a direct hit on the Klingon ship's rear shields. Before the explosion faded, Justman called out, "Fire phasers now. And stay with the target, helm."

They were pursuing the Klingon ship at less than two thousand meters. The phasers hit the ship and the Klingons' shields flared again.

"We have one Klingon vessel taking position behind us," the weapons officer announced. "The other ship is engaging the *Constitution.*"

"Stay with the target," Justman repeated. "Fire torpedoes."

Two more torpedoes and two more direct hits. The Klingon shields had to be weakening.

"Klingons have a weapons lock on our rear," Parker announced. "Incoming torpedoes."

A moment later the ship was hit. Justman said, "Fire phasers."

Two blue beams lanced out and made contact with the shields of the ship in front of them. There was a flash, and Fuller was sure the Klingon ship's shields were about to fail.

"Klingons arming disruptors," Parker announced.

"Fire torpedoes," Justman shouted.

Fuller watched the torpedoes fly toward the Klingon ship as the deck shook under his feet.

Warning bells rang around them as the torpedoes hit their mark. The Klingon cruiser's shields flared briefly as the first torpedo tore through it. It made contact with the battle cruiser's hull, and there was an immediate explosion, followed by another explosion as the second torpedo hit its mark.

"We've lost rear shields," someone shouted.

"Helm, bring us around and back to the *Constitution*'s coordinates," Justman called out.

"Sir, our target is in distress," Parker said.

"On-screen," Justman said.

Immediately, the viewscreen showed a side view of the Klingon ship. Large pieces of the rear hull were missing. Fuller couldn't believe that the ship was that badly damaged and still intact. The thought was cut short by a bright flash as the vessel's warp core went critical and the ship was vaporized.

A second later, the subspace shockwave hit them. Then the screen shifted and Fuller could see the *Constitution* in front of them. The two Klingon vessels sped away and regrouped out of weapons range.

"Damage report," Justman said.

"Rear shields are out. No casualties," Parker said.

Justman hit a button and said, "Engineering. What can you do for our rear shields?"

"I can give you twenty percent if we borrow the power from port and starboard shields, but I'll need a few minutes to reconfigure the system."

269

"Do it," Justman said.

Just then one of the Klingon ships moved forward and two disruptor bolts flared toward the *Constitution.* At that distance they were far from full strength when they hit the starship's shields, which flared briefly. The Klingons were just testing them.

"What's your condition?" Admiral Jefferies's voice came through the intercom.

"Minimal rear shields," Justman said.

"Nice work. They still have more firepower, but we're almost evenly matched now," Jefferies said.

"What now, Admiral?" Justman asked.

"I have a maneuver in mind, but it will require you to engage the Klingon ships and bring at least one of them back here. For this to work, the Constitution *will have to remain in a fixed position."*

"We have rear shields at twenty," Parker announced.

"We're ready to go," Justman said.

"Your helm has the return course now," Jefferies said. *"Begin at your discretion, and good luck."*

"Thank you, Admiral," Justman said. "Weapons at full power. Helm, prepare an intercept course, then swing us around on my mark." He waited a few seconds, then said, "Full thrusters now!"

The *Yorkshire* shot forward.

"Target the port ship and prepare torpedoes . . . wait . . . now, fire!" Justman said.

One torpedo and then another raced for the ship, at least one of them making a direct hit.

"Phasers, now!" Justman said. The beam lanced out at the Klingon vessel, which banked hard to evade the fire. The phasers scored a partial hit, and Justman called out, "Helm, bring us around and put us on a course back to the *Constitution.*"

"Klingons are pursuing. The lead ship is targeting our rear deflectors," Parker called out. "They're firing torpedoes."

The words were barely out when the ship was hit. People were shouting damage reports, but Fuller heard Jefferies's voice boom out through the intercom. *"Come to a full stop and drop shields now!"*

"Do it!" Justman said and the bridge crew immediately complied.

On the viewscreen, one of the Klingon ships was already breaking off, but the other was making an attack run. "They're targeting us," Parker said.

Fuller realized the ship's shields were down but even as that thought rose up, Parker announced, *"Constitution* has extended her shields around us."

That was an impressive feat; it would have been impossible for any other ship. And then Fuller got another surprise when he saw the Klingon ship suddenly thrown to one side even as it bore down on them. Some unseen force simply tossed it to one side and it spiraled out of control, away from both Starfleet ships.

"That was the *Constitution*'s navigational deflector," Parker said as the ship tumbled out of sight. "The other vessel is holding outside of weapons range."

There was silence on the bridge for a moment, and then damage reports began coming in. Rear shields were down for good and port shields were badly damaged. There was some hull damage in the rear of the ship and some minor injuries. And the warp engines would need repair.

"Where is that second Klingon ship?" Justman asked.

"It's rejoining the lead ship now," Fuller could see the two ships in the distance. It was hard to tell if the ship they had hit with the navigational deflectors was damaged at this distance.

"They have no shields, and I'm showing no power to their disruptors," Parker said.

"They're hurt," Jefferies's voice said through the intercom. *"And they've asked for a temporary cease-fire."* Another surprise to add to Fuller's list for the day. *"Captain Justman, I'd like to meet with you on board the* Constitution *to discuss our options."*

"Yes, sir. I would also like to bring one of the survivors of the *Endeavour,"* Justman said with a look at Fuller.

Five minutes later, Fuller found himself walking the impossibly large corridors of the *Constitution* as an officer led them to the briefing room. There he met the admiral and his bridge crew and briefed them on what he'd seen on the *Endeavour.*

Jefferies listened carefully and said, "We can end this all right now. The Klingons have asked for a permanent cease-fire."

"Will we win if we finish the fight?" Justman asked.

"Yes, I think we will. The simulations and my instincts tell me we will. Both Klingon vessels have weapons, but the *Constitution* can maintain its shields indefinitely."

"But we'd need to leave the protection of your shields to maneuver and use our weapons," Fuller said.

"Yes." Jefferies nodded. "None of our simulations have the *Yorkshire* surviving."

Fuller's mind ran through options. They could staff the *Yorkshire* with a skeleton crew, necessary personnel only. He would volunteer, and he suspected that most of the *Endeavour*'s survivors would as well.

"I'm inclined to end this with no more bloodshed," Jefferies said, "but I want your thoughts. You've been in this fight longer than we have. The question is: Can the Klingons be trusted? Will we be able to keep this peace?"

Justman was silent for a moment, then said, "I think enough people have died today."

Then Jefferies's eyes were on him and he said, "Mister Fuller?" Clearly, his opinion was important to the admiral—Fuller had a feeling he wanted a unanimous decision.

In his heart, Fuller felt the day's fury still living inside him. He wanted payback for Andrews, Caruso, Captain Shannon, and all the others. He knew it was beneath him, as an officer and a man, but the call for revenge was strong. And yet he was tired of the loss, the grief, the death. And they could end it now. No more dying. No more wasted lives. No more letters home to shattered families.

"I honestly don't think the Klingons can be trusted, but I say give them their truce and send them packing," he said in the end.

Jefferies nodded again. "A truce, then."

And then Fuller realized that it really was over. This fight was finished. Fuller found relief washing over him. The adrenaline that had kept him going for hours now dissipated and he found that he was tired. He was also sore in a number of places.

He returned to the *Yorkshire* with Justman as Jefferies negotiated the terms of the truce and then called Starfleet to confirm orders and have diplomats begin formal talks with the Klingon Empire. The Klingon ships were gone within hours.

When the Klingons were out of sensor range, Fuller left auxiliary control and headed to sickbay, where some of the survivors of the *Endeavour* were recovering. In the back of his mind he had been harboring a thin hope that Justman had been mistaken and that some of the last group to be thrown into space had been picked up by the *Yorkshire* and that Andrews had been among them.

Of course, Andrews was gone. Still, it was good to see more survivors from his crew, all of whom would recover. The doctor had taken one look at him and insisted that he lie down on one of the examination beds for a few minutes. Fuller agreed, and didn't wake up for nearly twelve hours.

After his rest, he helped to recover the fallen from the *Endeavour,* including those who had died in the unforgiving void of space. All personnel were accounted for. And all of them would be going home. Andrews would be going home.

Jefferies had offered the survivors of the *Endeavour* quarters on the *Constitution* and a quick ride home. About half had agreed. Fuller stayed behind on the *Yorkshire* to help with repairs. He wasn't ready to go—didn't feel that he deserved it yet.

The *Yorkshire* towed the saucer section of the *Endeavour* back to Earth. The journey was slow, but there was plenty to do and Fuller was glad to be occupied.

The trip took six months. During that time, he had tried a number of times to compose a message to send to Alison. In the end, he had to satisfy himself with, "Dear Alison: I have had a lot of time to think and I would like to meet with you when I return to Earth. There is a lot I would like to say, but I would rather say it in person. There is one thing I would like to ask you now, so you can have time to think about it. I lost a good friend on this mission. You may remember him from training, Samuel Andrews. If our baby is a boy, I would like to name him after Andrews. I would like to name him Sam."

In the weeks and months of the journey, Fuller took every duty and every assignment that he could. Even so, there was too much time to think. And even when he managed to completely fill his days, the nights were too long. But as the ship traveled closer to Earth, he felt something like hope rise inside him. He had a plan. When he got home, he knew what he would do. To his surprise, he found that he actually looked forward to doing it. Six months ago, it would have been unthinkable. Now it was the only thing he wanted.

As the *Endeavour* approached Earth, he arranged to meet Alison at a restaurant. On his first day, he visited home, and then there was the Starfleet Command reception and ceremony for the survivors of what was already being called the Battle of Donatu V. There were speeches in which flag rank officers called him and the others heroes. Fuller sat through the ceremony with gritted teeth, keeping to himself what he wanted to scream out loud: They had left the real heroes behind. The best of them had all died, some of them in the engine room of a dying ship, some of them at the point of a Klingon blade, and some of them tumbling out into the cold void of space.

Fuller accepted the medals and commendations with a tight smile, biding his time. The next day, he met with his reassignment officer, a nice lieutenant commander named McCourt. "Mister Fuller, it's a real honor to meet you," McCourt had said when Fuller walked into his office at Command. "I've read all the reports—your personal accomplishments were nothing short of incredible."

"Thank you, sir," Fuller said. It was easier than explaining everything he was thinking and feeling, easier than explaining what had really happened.

"A lot of people in Command have noticed you. I can tell you right now that nothing is impossible. The starship program is the future. The *Constitution* will have its official launch soon, and then there will be eleven more like her. I can tell you right now that if you want service on one of those starships, you can have it."

Fuller knew what that meant. Initially, there would be only a few hundred positions available on the starships. Even when the program was mature, there would be only a few thousand officers in all of Starfleet serving on them. And now he was being offered a position on the first active-duty ship.

"Thank you, sir. I know what that means and I appreciate it, but I have another request," he said.

"If it's in my power to grant it, I will," McCourt said.

"I would like to resign my commission immediately."

McCourt did not even try to conceal his surprise.

"Mister Fuller, I don't know what to say . . . I know things were tough out there, but there's counseling available. There are people you can talk to, people who have been through similar experiences. You have a bright future in Starfleet. Please don't make a hasty decision."

Fuller told McCourt that he was going to be a father, that his decision was more about having a family than about getting away from space. Most of what he had said was even true.

McCourt understood. "If there is anything you need, contact me. Starfleet does not forget its debts." McCourt shook Fuller's hand as he left the office, a civilian again.

Fuller did not take the time to change out of his uniform. It felt like a lie to wear it now, but no less a lie than it had in the last six months. He went straight to the restaurant to meet Alison. He sat at a table outside and waited for her, watching the sidewalk.

He saw her approach, wearing a dress he had never seen before. *Of course, because most of her old clothes wouldn't fit her now.* Even at a distance of a dozen meters, he could see how much she had changed now that she was almost seven months pregnant. Her stomach was showing and she was rounder everywhere. As she came closer, he could see that her blond hair was longer and she really seemed to be glowing.

He thought she looked absolutely beautiful.

Her face brightened when she saw him, and Fuller felt a pang of relief. She rushed to him and hugged him tightly. Then he felt her lips pressing hard on his cheek. "Oh Michael, thank God." Stepping back, she looked him over carefully. "Are you okay?"

"I'm fine," he said. Looking at her, he realized that he actually felt fine. For a moment, the last few months lifted like a fog, and he smiled.

They sat and she said, "Michael, I heard about what happened. I'm so sorry. It must have been terrible." She saw that he was uncomfortable and said, "I read the news reports and caught the ceremony. Michael, the things you did. I'm so proud of you."

The respect in her eyes was so profound that it lifted him for a moment and he forgot his shame. He wouldn't try to explain now. The last thing he wanted to do was bring her down. There would be plenty of time for explanations later.

"I just keep thinking about what might have happened if you had stayed with me," she said. "You really did something important out there. You did the right thing, joining Starfleet, and I'm sorry if I made it harder for you."

"You didn't do anything on your own. It took both of us," he said, smiling. She returned the smile, and Fuller felt himself lifted up once again. That smile, those eyes. He wanted to crawl inside them and stay there forever.

"I have some news for you, Michael, something I just want to get out of the way."

Now it was her turn to hesitate. He smiled at her, trying to make her more comfortable. "What is it?"

"It's silly. It's not even a big deal, but . . . Michael, I met someone."

Fuller was sure he could not have heard that right. "What?"

"I met someone. I'm with someone. He's a good man who has a business in San Francisco . . ." There were more details, but Fuller missed them. He tried to keep calm as he felt the blood drain out of his face and his stomach turn hollow.

". . . it happened so fast, but I really love him," she said, looking nervous and embarrassed.

"I'm glad for you," he said, nearly choking on the words.

"You were right about everything. Starfleet is what you wanted. It was what you were made for. And this is what I wanted. It all worked out for the best."

Fuller did not know what to say and he did not trust his voice.

"Oh, and there's something else that you need to know. The baby's going to be a boy."

"A boy?"

"You're going to have a son. So we can name him after your friend. We'll call him Sam."

Something tore loose inside of him and must have shown on his face. Alison's hand covered his, and Fuller closed his eyes and let her warmth flow into his body through that connection. When he opened his eyes, she was looking at him with concern.

"It's okay, I understand. I know you two were close," she said. They sat in silence as Fuller composed himself. "Your message said you wanted to talk about something."

"Just that I was sorry about the way things . . . about the way we said good-bye," he said. It sounded weak and ridiculous even to his ears.

Alison only nodded. "It's okay. Like I said, it all worked out for the best. And you really found your calling, Michael. You're just too much like your father."

She smiled. "I should have known what I was getting into."

They passed the rest of the lunch talking about the baby. Alison promised to keep him updated on everything and to send pictures whenever she could. Fuller said he would try to help as much as he could.

As soon as they said good-bye, Fuller headed back to Command and went straight to McCourt's office. He didn't have to wait. McCourt saw him right away.

"Mister Fuller, what can I do for you?"

"I think you were right, I think I might have been hasty in my decision," he said. "I'd like to stay."

McCourt looked at him with less surprise than he would have thought. McCourt held up the early departure form that Fuller had signed. "I never file these orders right away, I hold on to them for a few days just in case. I thought there was a girl and a baby coming."

"It didn't work out," Fuller said.

McCourt just nodded. "Are you sure this is what you want?"

"I realized that Starfleet is my calling. It's where I belong, sir."

"Have you thought about what kind of assignment you want?"

"No, but I would like to get back into space as soon as possible."

"If you wait just a few weeks I could get you onto the *Constitution*."

"That won't be necessary. I would like to go back on active duty as soon as possible."

"Okay, we can look at what I've got. In the meantime, you can do the honors," he said, handing Fuller the discharge orders. Fuller brought the stylus to the screen and touched it to the box marked CANCEL.

Then he and McCourt discussed his options. His notoriety was useful here, and McCourt assured him that he would be welcome on any vessel in the fleet.

He chose the one with the first available position, aboard the *U.S.S. Republic*.

First Epilogue

I.K.S. D'K TAHG
2267

WHEN DURAS HAD ENTERED the bridge for the second time, there was no posturing, no speeches. He had simply arrived silently and watched the forward screen. He did not even look at Karel.

"Time to the system?" Duras asked.

Koloth nodded to Karel, who said, "Two days."

"Hail them," Duras said.

A moment later the communications officer said, "They do not respond."

That did not surprise Karel. From what his brother had told him in his message, the Klingons there had very good reason to mistrust outworlders, even outworlders of their own blood—especially outworlders of their own blood.

"Tell them that Councillor Duras wishes to speak with them," Duras said.

A moment later the communications officer said, "I have the planet."

A chill ran down Karel's spine. There was something wrong going on here. Something dishonorable was at work. His blood screamed out its warning again.

Whatever happened, he was certain that this mission would not end well.

Second Epilogue

AMBASSADOR FOX was boiling inside, but worked to keep his face calm. It was possible that the message he had received from Ambassador Wolt was correct, that the dispatching of a Klingon warship to System 7348 was the result of a mistake or a miscommunication.

There was also the far more likely possibility that it was the work of a faction on the Klingon High Council that wanted war. Either way, Fox and his team might still be able to salvage the negotiations—provided they could meet with Wolt.

But for the last few days he'd received only text replies from the ambassador, who had finally agreed to another meeting on the Kraetian station. Yet, once again, he was making Fox and the others wait—and wait in the same room where Fronde had been killed.

As they waited, his staff looked at him with faith in their eyes. Before, that faith had given him confidence, now it seemed only to point up his failure. He had failed to reduce the tension driving both sides to war, and he had failed Fronde.

A voice inside him told Fox that he was wasting his time. That had never happened before, and Fox didn't like the fact that the voice sounded uncannily like Lieutenant West's at Starfleet Command. Fox shook off his doubts; they undermined his ability to do his job. If he didn't believe that a peaceful settlement was possible, then he could never convince the Klingons of that.

There was still hope, he was sure. Despite the tragedy of Fronde's death, he judged that Wolt was sincere and honorable in his own way. They had made progress. Perhaps they could get the negotiations back on track even after this setback.

Finally, the doors opened and his new chief of staff, a young woman named Helen Fitzpatrick, came rushing through them. "The Kraetians say the Klingons have docked and will be here shortly."

Fox and his people waited in tense silence, and less than five minutes later, the doors opened again and several Klingons entered.

Wolt was not among them.

"Where is Ambassador Wolt?" Fox said, realizing that his tone made the question a demand.

The lead Klingon was silent for a moment and considered him carefully. "Ambassador Wolt has been relieved. I am Ambassador Morg," the Klingon said.

"This is outrageous. I received messages from Wolt.

He agreed to meet with me here," Fox said, working to keep his voice even.

"Wolt overstepped his authority in his dealings with you," the Klingon said gruffly. "I am, however, authorized to revisit the points you discussed. Perhaps we can come to a new arrangement."

"A new arrangement?" Fox said, not bothering to try to hide his anger. "You want to go over trade routes and border disputes? You have a Klingon warship entering Federation space, even as we speak!"

The Klingon shrugged and said, "That is an unfortunate misunderstanding. The High Council sends its regrets on this issue, but the fact is that you did agree to allow a Klingon delegation—"

"Enough!" Fox said, and to his surprise, the Klingon became immediately silent. Fox took a moment to catch his breath, then said, "I'm afraid that I have to contact the Federation president. This changes things, and I have to make sure that *I* do not overstep my authority."

The new Klingon ambassador nodded and said reasonably, "Of course. Contact your superiors. We are prepared to resume negotiations whenever you are ready."

Fox gave the Klingon a clipped nod and turned to his people. "Come," he said as he headed for the door.

A few minutes later his group reached their temporary offices. When they were inside, Fitzpatrick asked, "Ambassador, what does this mean?"

Fox waved off the question for now. "I need a secure transmission to the Palais de la Concorde immediately."

His staff went to work and less than a minute later, Fitzpatrick said, "The line is open, Mister Ambassador."

Fox sat in front of the communications console and

hit the button to begin transmission of his heavily coded message. Like all codes, this one could theoretically be broken, but that would take years and this situation would be over long before then.

"Mister President, the Klingons have arrived for the negotiations, but Ambassador Wolt has been replaced. I believe that the Klingons are continuing talks in bad faith and that they are using them as a delaying tactic to cover their own preparations for war. I recommend that the Klingon battle cruiser headed for System 7348 be considered hostile. Fox out."

There was dead silence in the room for a long moment. Finally, someone behind him said, "Mister Ambassador . . . what do we do now?"

Fox turned and stood to face his people. The Klingons were playing a game of delay and misdirection. Well, he could play it as well. He mustered a grim smile and said, "We go talk to the Klingons. It's time to resume *negotiations*."

TO BE CONTINUED . . .

IN *ERRAND OF FURY* BOOK 2:
DEMANDS OF HONOR

About the Author

Kevin Ryan is the author of the bestselling trilogy *Star Trek: Errand of Vengeance* and the co-author (with Michael Jan Friedman) of *Star Trek: The Next Generation—Requiem*. He has also written the *USA Today* bestselling novelization of *Van Helsing*, as well as two books for the *Roswell* series. In addition, Ryan has published a number of comic books and written for television. He lives in New York with his wife and four children. He can be reached at Kryan1964@aol.com.

STAR TREK ®

Revisit the era of
The Original Series
from an entirely new corner of the
Star Trek universe

VANGUARD
A new *Star Trek* experience
beginning in August 2005 with

HARBINGER
by
David Mack

From Pocket Books
Available wherever books are sold
Also available as an eBook

OSV

It all began in the *New York Times* bestselling book *Ashes of Eden*.

James T. Kirk gave up his life and his wife for Starfleet, now he faces a threat that could bring down the entire Federation... his son.

STAR TREK·
CAPTAIN'S GLORY

William Shatner

with

Judith & Garfield Reeves-Stevens

This Summer from Pocket Books

STAR TREK
DEEP SPACE NINE

Our enemies, ourselves.

HOLLOW MEN

a novel by Una McCormack

The gripping follow-up to the
controversial episode
"In the Pale Moonlight"

From Pocket Books
Available wherever books are sold
Also available as an eBook

STHM

STAR TREK
VOYAGER®

Celebrating the tenth anniversary of
Voyager

Distant Shores

an all-new anthology of tales by

Christopher L. Bennett, Kirsten Beyer, Ilsa J. Bick, Keith R.A. DeCandido, Bob Greenberger, Heather Jarman, Robert T. Jeschonek, Terri Osborne, Kim Sheard, James Swallow, Geoffrey Thorne, Susan Wright

From Pocket Books
Available wherever books are sold
Also available as an eBook